FADE

AN URBAN FANTASY TRILOGY WITH TWISTS
AND TURNS

E. G. BATEMAN

CORNERDOWN PUBLISHING

ISBN: 9781999871413

Copy editing by A. Jack
Developmental editing by G. Withnail
Cover design by Cover Villain

Join my VIP reader list and grab THE FUGITIVE LEGACY.
The free prequel of Legacy of the Shadow's Blood.

https://dl.bookfunnel.com/olndiiuzje

For Mum

1

Someone is watching me, again.

I'm sitting on a bench in Somerset, at a castle ruin, or maybe it was an abbey (I haven't really been paying much attention). All that remains of the castle/abbey are a few walls jutting defiantly from the muddy ground. I know I should be more concerned about a random stranger watching me, but it's been happening for years, it's just a part of my life, and I can do nothing about it.

To be honest, I'm more bothered about the mud. Just to be clear about this, because, as a reader of my diary, you should picture this with sufficient horror, here are my brand new red Converse baseball boots and there is the river of mud seeking to destroy them. I've only had these boots for a week!

Anyway, yes, getting back to my other point, a woman is standing by a crumbling arch staring straight at me.

I can see her in my peripheral vision while I'm writing. She hasn't moved for at least three minutes, and, apart from my pen hand, neither have I. I knew someone was looking at me because the hairs on the back of my neck began to rise before I even noticed her.

Feeling her eyes probe my face, I know from experience, that if I move to look at her, she will appear to be staring at something near me. Her eyes will travel around casually before she wanders off somewhere. This time, I refuse to look up!

Okay, I looked. Silly me, of course, she's been staring at that fascinating piece of air, three inches from my head. She gazes around and then wanders off. Aarrgh! I've given up trying to convince people this is happening. I think Dad was on the verge of taking me to a shrink or having me carted off to the funny farm.

I SIGHED, closed my diary, buried it in my bag and jumped up from the bench. I looked around, but the woman was nowhere in sight. Dad said that people just randomly look at each other all the time and I shouldn't get so weird about it but, sometimes, it was different. I would feel a sort of tickle on the back of my neck, too hard to describe precisely, and I'd know.

Glancing at the sky, which was still cloudy, I could feel it warming up a little. That's promising, I thought.

It was the beginning of the summer holidays, if you could call it "summer" with the dismal weather we were having. I'd just finished the last of my exams at school, and my reward was this exercise in footwear destruction. It was time to go and find my best friend, Gill.

I'd usually find her shuffling along somewhere behind Dad. She'd been totally crushing on him, which was just so unbelievably gross there are no words. She was acting like he was Johnny Depp or something.

"Oh my God, Jenna! Your dad looks so much like Johnny Depp," said Gill later, as we sat at our table by the window of a Glastonbury café.

"He so, absolutely, does not," I replied. "Last year you said he looked like Brad Pitt and then six months later it was Matt Damon. You're ruining all the hot older guys for me."

"Have I mentioned he has eyes like Robert Pattins..."

"I swear to God, one more syllable and," I reached into the cutlery tray in the middle of the table and pulled out something plastic, "I'll stab you to death with this..."

I stared at the object in my hand. "What is this?"

"It's a spork," she said. "A cross between a spoon and a fork. How did you get to fifteen years and eleven months without knowing what a spork is?"

"Whatever! I'll stab you with this spork. Is that what you want everyone to read on your gravestone? "Here lies Gill Fielding, sporked to death because she couldn't keep her big mouth shut"."

"Okay," said Gill, "but you'll be known as The Sporker. That will be your serial killer nickname and all the other serial killers will laugh at you."

"Serial killer? Who else am I going to spork?"

Gill looked around. "Well, you might as well spork the kitchen staff in this place. They don't seem to be cooking anything."

I couldn't work that out. It was stupidly hot, but there didn't appear to be much cooking going on as far as I could tell. We French-plaited each other's hair as we sat at the table, although it was more of a necessity than a luxury for me. My fine light-brown hair had been looking possessed lately, so I'd taken to hiding it under a beanie.

"How much anti-frizz serum did you use this morning?" asked Gill. "Your hair is actually slippy. It looks like you haven't washed it in a month, and it's still frizzy."

Gill picked a wet wipe from her bag and wiped her hands with a look of disgust.

"It's not that bad," I said.

"It kinda is," she replied.

I plunged the beanie back on to my head and looked around the place. It was a vegetarian café, a cake shop, an art gallery and in the back room, a vinyl record shop. That's where my dad was. We could see him, looking at old Rolling Stones albums.

"Honestly, I don't think we've even got a record player," I said, "and I'm surprised they don't all just warp with the heat in here."

"Are you kidding? I'm bloody freezing today. Someone should sue July under the Trade Descriptions Act." Gill shuddered. "Maybe you're ill. You're all pink looking."

"Excuse me? I think you'll find that I'm Mediterranean Gold."

"Yeah, sorry, that wore off. You're pink now."

"Awesome!" I sighed.

I looked out on to the High Street. Glastonbury was weird, but I liked it. It seemed like every other shop sold crystals and pentacles, and the air was so thick with incense that you could cut it with a spork. Gill had just bought a pack of Merlin themed tarot cards, so we amused ourselves by attempting to read each other's fortunes while we waited for the food.

Gill turned over a card. "The Nine of Cups," she announced in a mysterious voice. "You will soon achieve your heart's desire."

That was good news. I might find out why complete strangers kept watching me in the street.

"And what does the Nine of Cups really mean?" I asked.

"I have nooo idea," in the same woo-woo voice. "I haven't read the instructions."

After that, the readings became more preposterous with each attempt. By the time the bean burgers finally arrived, I was going to marry a hunchbacked elf, and Gill was going to become the bearded lady in a travelling circus and give birth to a monkey.

Dad arrived about one and a half seconds behind the food as though it were tugging him along on an invisible ring through his nose.

"Move up, Little Duck," he said as he nudged me to shift across the bench so he could sit down. I would have died if he'd said that in front of anyone other than Gill. Luckily, I already knew her dad called her "Pudding" so my secret was safe.

"What's next?" I asked Dad.

"Well, I did notice a second-hand..."

"Bookshop," Gill and I chorused.

"Okay," said Gill, "weird meatless food first, then bookshop."

"Gill," said Dad, going into his teacher's voice, "a meal without meat is not weird."

"No, it's a side salad."

"Can I just point out that you're eating a burger the same size as your head? I don't think it could be called a side dish by any stretch of the imagination."

"Fair point!" Gill said. "So, bookshop. Anything in particular this time? Or are we in it for the long-haul and praying for padded armchairs?"

As Dad and Gill bantered, my neck prickled with the familiar feeling that told me someone was watching me again. I glanced quickly around. Sitting two tables away was a boy, maybe a year or so older than me, who was blatantly staring at me. He had a mop of wavy brown hair and a scruffy denim jacket over a grey t-shirt with a logo I couldn't identify. As I looked at him, the sun broke from behind the clouds and streamed in through the window behind me.

Intense green-hazel eyes were illuminated and directed straight at me.

I don't think I'd ever turned around and caught someone looking right at me. To be honest, I wasn't quite sure what came next. I could feel myself blush. His brow furrowed in apparent suspicion, or maybe confusion. He continued to stare for a few more seconds, and then he winked.

Talk about mixed messages. I was flustered, and I looked around to see if the boy was winking at someone else. No person other than Dad was near me, and I was fairly certain he wasn't winking at my dad. I turned my hot face quickly back to my food.

Dad was immediately on the alert.

"Jenna? Are you okay?" He sounded worried.

I tried for a casual tone. "Fine, just looking around."

Dad glanced around the café, not even pausing at the boy who was now demolishing a burger of his own. He didn't seem to notice anything unusual and turned back to me.

"Have you taken your pill today?"

"Of course! I never miss taking it." A little knot of muscle tightened in my shoulders.

"It's true, Mr Banks," said Gill, "you've turned her into a total junky. If she doesn't get her iron pill, she starts chewing the railings on the school gate."

"Gill, I think your food is getting cold," said Dad with an eyebrow raised.

"Mr Banks, have I ever told you how truly fantastic you are for letting me come on holiday with Jenna again? Seriously, I would be slaving in Dad's bakery for the whole six weeks if it weren't for you."

"So you're saying I've saved you from the inconvenience of developing a good work ethic?"

"Erm. Sort of." Gill pointed at her plate. "Oh look, my head burger *is* getting cold."

Dad shook his head, rolled his eyes and started on his food.

My shoulders relaxed. That had been a fantastic job of misdirection by Gill. Dad's totally over-the-top about my anaemia. He would have a fit if he knew the truth: I ran out of my iron pills after two days away; I never was the most organised at packing. I popped into a supermarket and bought some more straight away, refilling the bottle I usually used so Dad wouldn't worry. He's a bit weird about my pills always being the same brand.

I didn't dare look at the boy again for the remainder of the meal.

Dad finished his burger in two minutes flat. He had bought a book on the mythical history of King Arthur and read some interesting sections from it as we ate our food.

"...And so ended the night of Uther's deception," he said, putting the book away as we got up from the table.

"...And so ended the meal of the Spork," I added to Gill's giggles as we walked to the door and I held the spork aloft like it was Excalibur. Embarrassed, I remembered the boy and shoved my hand into my pocket. I glanced around towards his table and was surprised to discover that he was gone. I hadn't even noticed him leave.

We walked into the bookshop, which was even warmer than the café had been. Gill and I had a great system for surviving Dad's book worshipping trips. Dad would announce that he was going to look for science books and head straight for the Sports section, then Gill and I would mutter something about teen fiction and hunt for some raunchy adult book we shouldn't be reading.

We hid our raunchy book this time inside a *Harry Potter*

and took turns to read a few pages while the other stood on lookout. I would have preferred to read the teen fiction, but I enjoyed the whole cloak-and-dagger exercise too much to admit that to Gill. She didn't seem to notice that I'd only been turning the pages of the *Potter*.

I stood in the corner with the book, well beyond Dad's field of vision. It was getting difficult to read because the light above me had started to flicker, so I was holding it close to my face.

"Are you sure you should be reading that?" an accented voice drawled from behind me.

I almost jumped out of my skin and just managed to swallow a shriek. I whirled around to see the boy from the café. How the hell had he got behind me without me seeing him? I had virtually rammed myself into the corner.

"I...well..." I was almost speechless with embarrassment. I closed the books and looked intensely at the bookshelves, wishing that Gill would come back.

"Tell me the truth," he said. I could tell his accent was American and it had a slightly mocking tone. "You're reading the outside book, aren't you?"

"Yes, obviously," was all I could say as I scanned the shelves and resolutely refused to make eye contact. Obviously? Why did I say that?

"Well that's...complex." He chuckled, seemingly more to himself than to me. I turned around and looked him dead in the face, unamused.

He smiled uncertainly. Being this close to him, I had the full impact of his green-hazel eyes. He had a scar above his lip which did nothing to dampen his looks. I could feel my face flaming up again. He looked suddenly alarmed and promptly backed off. As he moved away, I could see that the faded logo on his t-shirt was from some American sports team. He turned around and marched away, leaving me alone with hot cheeks and a dropped jaw.

Almost on cue, Gill popped her head around the corner to demand her five minutes with "the book of sin."

"Holy smoke! You're red up to your ears. You must have found a good part," she said as I handed the books to her.

I don't know why I didn't tell her about the boy. I just took my turn around the corner at the lookout post. The light above me here was also flickering, even more than the other one, and the heat in the shop was getting quite uncomfortable. My cheeks were warm, but I couldn't tell if it was from the residual embarrassment.

Within a few minutes, I began to hear a buzzing in my ears. I shook my head as though that would dislodge something, but, of course, it didn't stop. Sweat prickled on my scalp, and my back and arms were unpleasantly damp. I could see another entrance at the back of the shop and thought that if I could just get a few seconds of fresh air, I'd be okay and back at my post before Gill noticed I'd gone.

I stumbled through the door into an enclosed courtyard, empty except for a couple of tables and benches. My vision was blurry. I rubbed at my face, feeling the pressure of what I imagined was a fist-sized lump trying to push its way out through my skull. Something was not right. I clung to the wall and wondered if I might be able to make it to one of the benches before passing out, which is pretty much what I thought was happening.

My knees began to buckle, but someone caught me before I could fall. I looked up and saw it was the boy again. His arm was around my waist while his other hand held on to my upper arm. I was feeling faint, but was still aware that he seemed to have come from nowhere again. I also felt stupid. This guy was witnessing me being such a wimp. It's strange how you can feel like you are dying, but still be embarrassed that you might look bad doing it.

I leaned on him, thinking that he was trying to lead me to a bench. Instead, he attempted to steer me towards the back fence.

"What the hell?" I demanded, although the words wouldn't come out right. I was starting to panic, thinking that this boy must have somehow drugged me. I toppled off balance, which caused him to lose his grip. The strength left me, and I crumpled to the ground. I couldn't move my arms and legs, and I could feel my eyes rolling back.

Suddenly, my brain seemed to burst. I felt pressure on my face, as though I were near a blast, and there was a loud bang. I couldn't make sense of what was going on around me. The sound of electronic wails pierced the air, and the wind must have picked up because all the benches and tables had toppled down. My eyes were stinging, and I couldn't see properly. It looked like all of the colours had leaked out of the world.

I heard running feet coming from inside the bookshop. The boy must have heard them too.

"Next time, Jenna," he said, and then he just dissolved into a yellow mist, right in front of me. It looked like a can of spray paint had burst in the air. I tried to look at him, but all I could see was a strange bright yellow blob. It was the only colour in the world. Everything else seemed to be varying shades of grey.

The yellow cloud moved backwards and seemed to melt through the fence.

I sat staring at the fence, transfixed, trying to make sense of what I'd seen. I was almost unaware that my dad was leaning over me, calling my name. Strangers stood around gawking. A few attempted to take pictures of me on their phones, pressing the buttons in frustration. The boy wasn't among them, but the girl from the castle that morning was there. I was sure there was a moment when she and Dad exchanged the briefest of glances.

Gill was also there with a worried look on her face and *Lady Chatterley's Lover* gripped to her chest, forgotten.

"Dad, what happened? There was this boy and..."

"You're okay, sweetheart. It was a strong gust of wind. It seems to have knocked you sideways. Can you get up?"

I stumbled as I got to my feet, but Dad held me steady. I realised that the colour had returned to my vision.

"But, Dad, there was this boy from the café, and he grabbed..."

Dad looked around the courtyard. "Just concentrate on walking. Let's get you back to the hotel. We can talk there."

As we walked back towards the bookshop, Dad glanced up. "Gill, dear, you might want to return that "teen fiction" book."

AT THE HOTEL, dad saw us back to our room, but when I tried to follow Gill inside, he held on to me.

"Not you, young lady. This way."

We carried on to Dad's room. He pointed to the chair, and I sat. I told him about the boy in the café.

"The brown haired lad in the denim jacket?" he asked.

I was surprised he had noticed the boy enough to remember any details about him; he hadn't seemed to at the time. Dad's face was troubled.

"When did you stop taking your pills?" he asked.

"I didn't. I mean..."

I sighed and told him about the replacements I'd bought.

"We need to get home. Go start packing."

"Dad, I'm sorry."

"It's not a punishment. You need to get back to your pills."

An hour later, as Dad started the car and we pulled away from the hotel, I had the feeling that someone was watching, but I didn't even look up.

2

———

I wasn't sure that Dad should even be driving. He looked stricken. Gill and I sat silently in the back, and he spent more time looking into the rear-view mirror than at the road ahead. I couldn't tell whether he was watching the road behind us or trying to give me reproachful looks. I scooted across the back seat, moving out of sight just in case.

When I'd gone to pack, I had told Gill that Dad thought I'd fainted because I was on the wrong strength of pills. I explained that we had to get back home. She hadn't said anything about it then, but now she was attempting to improve the mood in the car.

"Did you hear all those alarms going off? And that cyclone coming out of nowhere? I thought the bookshop was going to fly apart. The windows were rattling so much. I've never seen that kind of weather..."

She stuttered to a halt mid-sentence as the back of Dad's neck and ears were going dark red. He looked like he was going to have a heart attack.

I thought about it all the way home. Was that strange

wind something to do with what had happened to me? Common sense told me it couldn't have been, but the timing was so much of a coincidence.

We dropped Gill at her parents" house and carried on silently home. I went straight upstairs and took my pill. In the shower, I touched the bruises forming on my arm from where the boy's fingers had gripped me. Whatever other weird hallucinations I'd experienced, I knew I hadn't imagined him. I rested my cheek against the cold tiles and cried.

After a couple of hours in my room, I quietly stepped out. Sitting on the top step of the staircase, I could see down into the living room. I felt a warm nudge at my side and looked down to see my cat, Felix, snuggling up to me. Our next door neighbour, Mrs Cowen, the local cat lady, had been looking after him while we were away.

Dad was sitting motionless in the sitting room with the phone in his hand, a distant look on his face. Finally, he sighed and dialled a number, holding the phone to his ear and his head down.

"Hello, I'm not sure...I was told to call this number if... My daughter..."

He stopped for a few seconds, drew in a breath and began again.

"This is Neil Banks. It's happened. Please advise how best to proceed."

He disconnected and continued to stare into space.

I returned to my room with Felix padding along beside me and closed the door quietly. Dad's face had been pale and sweaty. I assumed he had been speaking to our doctor or perhaps the specialist who had prescribed my pills. That had been so long ago, I didn't even remember it. Although the message he'd left was strange – it's happened. What's happened?

I was just too exhausted to think about it. I climbed into my bed and pulled the sheets over my head. Felix jumped up and settled at the bottom of the bed as I went to sleep.

I WOKE the next morning with Felix stretched across my face. He knew how to get my attention when he wanted to be let out.

I sat up and played yesterday's hallucinations over in my mind. The boy just disappearing through the fence. It couldn't have been real. I was still convinced I'd been drugged.

I checked my phone for messages, but it seemed to have lost its charge. As I walked downstairs to see Dad, I expected to be grounded for the day. Actually, I expected to be grounded for ever, so I was surprised when Dad told me that Mr Fielding, Gill's dad, would be picking me up and I'd be spending the day with her.

Dad looked like he hadn't slept.

"I'm so sorry for messing up the holiday," I said. "I was stupid to keep the truth about the pills from you. I thought I was doing the right thing. But Dad, some strange things happened yesterday."

Dad sighed. "We can talk about that later. Don't worry. I do know what you're talking about, but it's a much longer conversation than we have time for right now. You do need to know that many years ago, I made a promise to your mum. It was about trying to keep you safe and giving you the childhood you deserved. What happened yesterday, it isn't something you can talk about with Gill. You have to trust me on this. It's of vital importance. Can you do that?"

"Yes, I promise."

I was bewildered by what Dad was saying, but he looked so serious.

"Now," he continued, "I have a meeting today, and I need to prepare some paperwork for it."

I remembered the phone call from the night before. I badly wanted to ask him about it, but I didn't want to push it. I just said, "Oh God! You're finally going to have me committed, aren't you!"

I was only half joking.

He smiled. "It's work related. But don't think I haven't considered that option."

I hugged my dad. I wasn't the "Daddy's little girl" type, but we didn't talk about Mum often. When we did, it made me remember I only had one parent left, and suddenly, for a few moments, he wasn't so annoying. I thought about apologising again, but things seemed as okay as they were going to be for now.

Twenty minutes later, a horn beeped outside and I grabbed my bag, ready to run out of the door.

"Jenna?" Dad called from the kitchen. "Stay at Gill's today. Don't go out, just in case you haven't fully recovered. Call me if you start to feel unwell."

"I think my charger's broken." I said. "I'll charge my phone at Gill's."

Dad just stared at me. He looked lost.

"I don't have to go at all. I can stay here in bed, all day if you want." The truth was, I was embarrassed about the previous day's weirdness, and I didn't want Gill asking questions. I loved Gill, but the whole thing was probably already on Facebook. I hadn't had the nerve to look yet.

"No, that's okay. You're still on holiday. You might as well enjoy the company of your crazy friend."

"Dad, you're not throwing me out to have some floozie round here, are you?"

He smiled. "You got me. Mrs Cowen's coming round with her tartan shopping trolley of delights."

"Eww, Dad! She's like ninety! Gill says she smells of wee."

"That, as you girls might say, is gross. Off you go. Love you, Little Duck."

"Love you, Dad."

As I ran down the path to Mr Fielding's car, I felt the prickle of someone watching me. I stopped and looked around, half expecting to see the hazel-eyed kidnapper, but the road was empty. I suddenly felt nervous about leaving Dad alone, but what could I say? Mr Fielding was giving me the "hurry up" look, so I climbed into his car.

I tried to look around as we drove away, but Gill's dad was talking to me.

"I hear you had a bit of a turn yesterday. How are you feeling today, Jenna?"

"Oh, I'm fine now. How come you're not at the bakery today?"

"We've got a day off. Dan's got the shop today. He's been wanting more responsibility, so today's the big day."

"Are you nervous about it?" I asked.

"No. Dan's been a great apprentice and employee. I'm sure he'll do great."

After a couple of minutes, he said, "Actually, there would be no harm if we just drove past the shop, would there?"

3

Neil Banks wandered through the house, repositioning pictures and chairs before putting them back as they were. He hovered by the window, then did another circuit of the pictures. He had promised to call the number, and that's what he had done, but he didn't know if anyone would have listened to the message or be coming to see him. He had been surprised that the phone number his wife had given to him so many years ago had connected at all.

He decided he'd give it a day, and if no one came, he'd have to forget about it. He knew he would need to take Jenna to the Academy. Part of him was a little excited about that. He'd never been able to share his important work with Jenna before, and now he could.

Finally, the doorbell chimed. He opened the door and sighed with relief.

So, that's who was at the other end of the phone, he thought.

"May I come in?" asked General Cavendish.

"Sorry, of course, come in. I just...Thanks for coming,"

Neil stuttered as he stood back to allow the General to enter. Cavendish was the top man at Hilltop Military Base where Neil worked. Neil knew him to be a decent man, but the fact that the General was top brass and standing in his living room was making him fidget like a schoolboy.

"To be honest, I didn't know what to expect, but Tessa gave me that number and made me swear to call it if Jenna awakened. If I hadn't given her my word, I wouldn't have done it. I was worried about what I might be getting myself into." Neil knew he was chattering on and forced himself to shut his mouth. He remembered that he, himself, had been the one to make the call which had brought the General to his home. This must be a good thing. At least the General was a familiar face.

He began to regain his composure.

"Please, sit down, sir. Can I get you anything?"

"No, thank you," Cavendish said, turning to face Neil. "You did the right thing, Neil. It sounds like the possibility of this happening has been a worry to you. I didn't even know Tessa had given you that number. If I'd realised, we'd have briefed you years ago. Actually, I think I would like a drink. Coffee if you've got it."

"I've got some filter coffee on."

Neil walked into the kitchen. He could tell that General Cavendish was about to tell him something important. Lifting out a tray, he arranged sugar, milk, and filled two cups with coffee. He stopped for a second, considering whether he should take biscuits in, too.

Sod the biscuits, he thought, and took the tray in.

The General was looking at a school picture of Jenna. He took a cup, waved away the milk and sugar, and sat. Taking a sip of coffee, he appeared to be considering before speaking.

"You'll remember that I was a young officer back then. I

knew a little of what I'm going to tell you, and the rest I've gleaned from old files. I don't have the full story, but I'll tell you what I can.

"The fact is, there were grave concerns that the project had been infiltrated. Tessa, you'll recall, was one of our brightest Trackers. She had been approached by a Fader who tried to talk her into working for them. They said she wouldn't be the only one. She told them she'd think about it, but of course, she reported it immediately. She wouldn't speak to anyone other than the commanding officer. She was terrified of inadvertently going to the mole. She was given that number as a direct contact to the base Commander.

"It was at the same time that she began to exhibit signs of paranoia. Because there really could have been a mole, no one looked for another cause until the paranoia became extreme. Eventually, the tumour was discovered too late."

"Was there a mole?" asked Neil.

"No. The search was extensive. No one else had been approached and we never found the Fader who contacted her.

"And on to today. I gather we have a situation. Your daughter – Jennifer, isn't it? – awakened at 14.08 hours yesterday in Glastonbury, Somerset."

"Yes, that's correct, sir." Neil knew that as a civilian, he wasn't expected to call the General "sir", but he couldn't help himself.

"What is her age? Sixteen?"

"Fifteen, sir," said Neil casually, as though fifteen didn't sound so bad. Fifteen was unbelievable, and they both knew it.

"Quite, almost sixteen," said Cavendish. "We've never

had an Awakening this late before. Any idea how this could have happened?"

Neil knew exactly how it had happened, and something in the General's eyes told him Cavendish realised this. If he admitted it, though, the General would be forced to discipline him.

"None, sir. We have had a few late bloomers in the past," said Neil, trying to breeze over the fact that the latest ever known had been two days short of their fourteenth birthday.

"Where is Jennifer now?" asked Cavendish.

"She's spending the day with a school friend. It seemed best to..."

"That's right. Gill Fielding. The local baker's girl."

Neil knew he had well and truly lost the upper hand in this conversation.

Cavendish stood and continued his walk around the room, looking at family pictures. He picked up a photo of Jenna as a toddler with her mother. His face softened.

"Her mother was one of our best, and beautiful. I still remember the two of you sneaking off to get married. The top brass hit the roof." He chuckled and returned the photograph. "Does she know anything about the Faders?"

"No, sir. She's never shown any sign of Awakening. That made her a civilian."

"Quite right," said Cavendish. "Has anyone been paying unusual interest in her? Any activity?"

"Not as far as I'm aware. Not before yesterday, anyway. The Trackers are around the area frequently. There have never been any sightings anywhere near us."

"Not before yesterday?"

"There was a boy in the vicinity when it happened. She thinks he was trying to abduct her, although she was in quite a state at the time." Neil described the boy to the General. "He may have faded or just walked away in all the confusion. I saw Marguerite there within a few minutes; she'd know if there had been a Fader."

"Marguerite did confirm Fader activity in the vicinity. She reported it immediately, but it was too late to follow the trail. I brought a Tracker team with me. They're doing the rounds now."

The words were barely out of the General's mouth when a man of military bearing in civilian clothes entered the room with a teenage boy, who looked surprised to see Neil.

"Hello, sir," said the boy with the awkward shyness of one realising he was standing in his teacher's house. He was one of Neil's Year Twelve pupils at the Academy.

"Good morning, Martin," replied Neil.

Martin sat next to the cat on the sofa and attempted to play with him. Felix looked at the boy with indignation and moved away.

"Adams?" the General said to the man.

"Sir, we picked up a trace just before it dissipated. They appear to have driven away in a car about ten minutes ago."

"Jenna!" Neil leaped up, his face a picture of panic.

"It's okay. We've got someone following her. She'll have to come to the Academy; you realise that."

"Yes, of course," said Neil. "I'm not going to risk my daughter's safety. The Academy is now the safest place for her, and she has responsibilities."

"Indeed," said the General. "You'll need to get packed up immediately. We'll send someone with boxes within the hour so you can take the essentials, and a removal van will be along in the morning for the rest. The Trackers will sweep the neighbourhood until you and your daughter are out."

"Thank you, sir."

And he was alone again.

The first thing Neil did was to flush Jenna's pills down the toilet. It was obviously too late for them; now they were just evidence that could incriminate him. He then started packing the essentials into a suitcase, wondering how he was going to explain all this to Jenna. He'd tried so hard to keep her out of the Academy, even though it hadn't been his choice. He had always believed in the vital work being carried out by the gifted kids at the Academy, but Tessa, his wife, had been adamant that they would do everything possible to keep Jenna out of it. After losing his wife, Neil had felt like it was an easy promise to keep as he had been in the right place to do so.

He'd told Jenna he was a teacher at the Academy, and two days a week, he really did teach Chemistry to the kids. That much was true, but the rest of the week he worked in the Chemistry Lab at Hilltop Military Base. Neil had been stealing the little dark red BLOKX13 tablets from the lab. It was easy enough to record that he was testing the pills on mice or rats, but instead Neil had been giving them to Jenna since she was five years old, attempting to stop what those in the Academy called the Awakening. He knew the Agency would eventually put two and two together and guess what he'd been doing.

He had done a good enough job of covering his tracks over the years. He had never written down the subtly-changed formula he had been using and decided he would just bluff it out now. If the Agency couldn't prove he'd been taking the pills out of the lab, they probably wouldn't go as far as firing him. Strangely, he didn't regret it. Tessa had been a Tracker. Her ability to track the monsters had awoken when she was twelve years old. She had started out

in an Academy in upstate New York, but was transferred to
the Oxfordshire facility along with her adoptive parents.

Faders had killed both of Tessa's parents.

How was Neil going to explain to Jenna that she lived in
a world of monsters?

OUTSIDE, the Tracker team passed the house. Martin looked
around and bounced a ball as he and Adams chatted and
walked, looking like a man with his teenage son. As they
drifted out of sight around the curve of the crescent, a boy
with a mop of brown hair and hazel eyes slipped out from
behind a house across the road and walked up the side of
the garage to the back of Neil's house.

A few minutes later, the chime of the doorbell brought
Neil out of his reverie. He opened the door to a whistling
man with his arms full of flat-packed moving boxes. He staggered past Neil in through the door.

"There's another pile in the car, mate," the man said as
he headed towards the living room with his load.

The hazel-eyed boy was at the back of the house now,
waiting for his moment and watching through the window
as the man deposited the boxes on the floor and retrieved
packing tape and pens from his pockets. As he watched the
man, the hazel-eyed boy began to fade. He became translu-
cent and then invisible. Moving forward, he passed through
the wall into the house.

The man inside went about his business, oblivious to the
stranger now standing inches away.

Neil collected another pile of flat packing boxes from the
van and carried them back up the driveway, into the house.

"A car will come for you at 8pm," said the man on his
way out. "Leave your key with security when you get to the

base. A truck will be here at 10am tomorrow to take the rest of your stuff and bring it to you. You're heading for one of the family houses at the base tonight. Security will tell you where to go when you get there."

It all seemed to be moving too fast for Neil. He would have to explain things to Jenna when she returned home. He couldn't imagine how to begin this conversation.

He closed the front door and stood, watching the man drive away. His shoulders sagged as he wondered where he should start with the packing. He picked up the cat, wondering if pets were even allowed on the base. Turning to put the cat outside, he heard a sound behind him. He stopped still, listening, trying to hear over the hammering of his heart.

Walking into the kitchen, he stood uncomprehending, watching something turning around inside the microwave that most certainly didn't look like food.

As MARTIN, still bouncing his ball, turned the corner back on to Neil's road, something drew his attention. He turned to alert Adams as an explosion shattered the silence and blew the two of them off their feet.

The home that Neil and Jenna had shared was vaporised. The hazel-eyed boy looked out from his hiding place and smirked.

"One down, one to go."

4

_____

We were having a pretty good day. Gill, mercifully, hadn't known much of anything. Her Facebook update had been "Home early. A big breeze knocked Jenna off her feet. #What-A-Daisy".

Gill's iPod was in its speaker dock, spilling out the contents of her playlist at a volume that would have had my dad hammering on the door. Gill had a spare bed in her room, which was basically my bed. I stayed there when Dad had to travel for educational conferences. He went to more of those events than any of the teachers at my school. I'd stayed at Gill's for three nights a few weeks before when Dad had gone to a TED conference in San Francisco.

We lounged on the beds on our laptops doing one silly online quiz after another.

"Okay," I said, "how about this one? "What *Game of Thrones* character are you?""

Gill was lying on her back, across her single bed with her legs up the wall and her head hanging over the edge, looking at me upside-down.

"No point," she said. "Dad won't let me watch it."

"Yeah, me neither," I said, continuing to scroll.

"Helloooo!" said Gill.

I looked up and saw that from her strange position, Gill had seen something of interest under my bed. I put down the laptop and dropped my head down to see what was under there.

"Helloooo!" I said, staring at a stash of M&Ms. They were my last-minute overpriced airport gift from San Francisco.

We split the sweeties into a pile each and started aiming them towards each other's mouths across the room, giggling and squealing like idiots. Neither of us had heard the front door.

Gill's bedroom door opened and her dad walked in with a face as white as ash. Gill took one look at him and turned the music off.

"Jenna, love," he said, "can you pop downstairs? Someone needs to speak with you."

I climbed off the bed and looked out through Gill's door. Her bedroom was at the top of the stairs, and the front door was at the bottom. I could see the figure of someone large standing right outside the obscured glass door.

Gill moved to follow me, but her dad stopped her. I think maybe I knew then, but I wouldn't let myself consider it. I put my shoes on and my laptop into my bag, somehow knowing I wouldn't be coming back upstairs for them. From the landing, I could hear Gill's mum crying, and my eyes started leaking too, as though in sympathy. I wasn't wailing or crying, but the tears wouldn't stop running silently down my face.

As I reached the bottom of the stairs, I heard Gill cry, "No!" and turned in time to see her bedroom door click shut.

I walked into the living room. Mrs Fielding's face was bright red, in contrast to the white of her husband's. She was wringing a tea towel in her hands. It was the one Gill had bought when Dad and I had taken her to Edinburgh in May with a recipe for shortbread printed on it. I noticed this because there were two uniformed men in the room and I didn't want to look at them. I focused on that tea towel as if my life depended on it.

Eventually, one of the men spoke. "Jennifer, there has been an accident at your house, a gas explosion. Your father...I'm sorry."

Finally, I looked at him. I'd been expecting him to be a policeman, but this was a military officer. He was still speaking, his lips were moving, but I couldn't hear him. The TV on the wall beside him had started to hiss and flicker. I looked at it and saw something in black and white.

The hissing of the TV got progressively louder, and the picture turned into a series of rolling lines. I looked back at the officer, but he looked different; he was black and white too and had stopped speaking. He glanced up at the flickering light bulbs and then stared at me. I gazed around the black and white room and looked at the black and white Mrs Fielding.

"Is this an old movie?" I asked. I don't know why I said that. One of the officers muttered something to Mrs Fielding. She nodded and scurried to the kitchen. The other officer took out a hypodermic needle from a briefcase. I looked at it and thought, He's going to stick me with that. Before he had taken a step, Gill's mum had come back in and wrapped her arms around me. When I looked around, all the strange flickering had stopped, and the man had hidden the needle away. I just felt numb.

Mrs Fielding walked me over to the sofa. Gill came in, sat next to me and stroked my hair, crying. Her mum was hovering over me with a glass of water. Mr Fielding was asking why I couldn't stay with them and one of the officers was muttering a response I couldn't hear – something about an investigation. Gill's mum kept glancing worriedly out of the window behind me, and I realised I could hear alarms going off in the street.

Someone said it was time to go and I got unsteadily up and walked towards the door. Gill hugged me and put my bag over my shoulder. She pressed my duffle coat into my hands.

"She's in shock. We'll look after her," said an unfamiliar voice.

I climbed into the waiting car and looked out as Gill's house was left behind. As we slowed at the end of the road, I stared at a boy of about fourteen, who was almost not looking at me.

The men in the car muttered to each other.

"What do you think that..."

"Not a clue," interrupted the second voice.

"Well, just in case," said the first voice.

I felt a jab in my arm and remembered the needle. I didn't look until after the needle had been removed. Then I stared at the little red dot on my skin until my eyes closed moments later.

5

I woke up in what seemed to be a hospital bed. At first, I couldn't remember why I was there. I called out for my dad, but then, an instant later, I remembered, and the breath was knocked out of me.

A nurse came in and told me I was in the medical block at Dad's Academy. I had a vague memory of a nightmare; lights flickering and popping; an alarm going off somewhere. I wondered if I'd been dreaming about Glastonbury.

I was still wearing the previous day's clothes. The nurse led me to the shower. Afterwards, putting the same clothes back on again felt disgusting. I wondered if I had any belongings left or if they'd all just disintegrated. My brain started to wonder what and who else had been burned away. The thought of Dad almost got through, but I stopped it. Instead, a vision of my little black and white cat popped into my head and I cried anyway.

After a few minutes of sitting on the floor, I stared at the little bruise on my arm, the tiny needle spot in the middle of it, and forced the thoughts away. I left the bathroom to find that the nurse had made me a cup of tea and was giving me sorrowful looks. When she left the room, I attempted to check my phone for messages, but it was still dead. I wanted a text from Dad, explaining that it had all been a huge mistake.

I didn't want to see the nurse's sad eyes again, so I gathered my things, avoided her little office, and walked out of the hospital room, towards the main doors of the building. A man in uniform was waiting for me.

"Miss Banks, I've been asked to take you over to the Principal's office."

We got into his Jeep for a journey that lasted less than a minute. The soldier escorted me into the building and spoke briefly to the receptionist, who gave me the sad eyes and took me up to the first floor to another woman. This woman looked like she had been crying. I didn't know how I should feel about that. For some reason, I felt offended by their grief. It made me angry. How dare they parade their pain in front of me? I thought. I'm the one who has the right to grieve. I don't even know who these people are.

It was childish, and I knew it. The problem was, I couldn't face the grief for my dad. After waking that morning, I had reached within myself and tentatively searched for it, half afraid of finding and then having to face it. Then when it threatened to surface, I'd squashed it down as best I could. All I could find now was anger and the awful feeling that I had been abandoned, again!

I knew I was being unfair to these people. Some of them might have known my dad longer than I had. He'd been teaching here since before I was born.

While I sat, shrunken into the chair outside the Principal's office, two men walked towards the door.

One of the men, in a crumpled brown suit, said, "He

can't just have vanished without a trace, we need to find him. No one is safe while that..."

He saw me and abruptly stopped.

"It's being handled. If he's still in the area," said the other man, glancing at me, "we'll address the issue." With that, he walked away.

The man in the brown suit said, "Jennifer, I'm Professor Abbott. I'm Principal at this Academy. I knew your father well, he worked for me for many years. He was..." he faltered, apparently unsure how to continue, "...a good man."

He opened the door to his office and said, "Please come in."

I walked into an old fashioned office with its large dark wooden desk and chairs in the middle of the room and a fireplace off to the right with two leather sofas facing each other across a coffee table. The Professor started to direct me to one of the chairs at the desk, but seemed to think better of it and moved towards the sofas.

"Can I get you anything? Some water?"

I attempted to say, "No, thanks," but found that my mouth was parched, so I nodded.

The secretary brought in a glass of water, and I refused to meet the woman's eyes. "Thanks," I said, staring directly at the glass.

Professor Abbott seated himself on the other sofa and said, "Jennifer, I can't imagine how you must be feeling right now. You obviously have a lot to deal with."

"Why am I here?" I asked. I just wanted this over.

"As I was saying," continued the Professor, "I know this is a difficult time, and if there were any way of putting off this conversation until we might better prepare you for it, believe me, I would, but we are in a serious situation."

I heard my hollow voice respond, "My dad died in a horrible accident yesterday. I can't say the seriousness of this "situation" has escaped me."

"I'm sorry, Jennifer, it wasn't an accident. Your father was murdered."

I stared at him. Before I knew what I was doing, I'd launched myself off the sofa. My body didn't know what to do. I turned to the door and then back to him, but my feet wouldn't move in either direction.

"He...I don't..."

I blinked. To my horror, everything was monochrome again – the Professor, the desk with its flickering lamp. It was the same as had happened in Gill's house. A persistent buzzing noise invaded my ears.

"Come on, sit down." The Professor was probably trying to guide me back to the sofa, but for a moment, in my mind, it was the boy forcing me towards the back fence of the courtyard. I panicked and wrenched away, looking around and feeling confused. I dug my palms into my eyes, and just as quickly as it had changed, everything was back to normal. The buzzing had stopped, and the man was staring at me with concern.

"Was it the American boy from Glastonbury?" I asked as I dropped back on to the sofa.

Professor Abbott scribbled a note on a pad sitting next to him.

"Someone who was matching that description was spotted yesterday. We've got a lot of people out there looking for him. Can you tell me what happened?"

Wondering who had given the Professor the description, I told him about the boy and that I thought he might have drugged me. I described the monochrome and yellow haze hallucinations that I hadn't even had the opportunity to tell

my dad about. I even explained to him about how I thought
people were watching me sometimes. It was all very relevant
now.

The Professor seemed deeply concerned to hear that I
thought strangers were following me.

"Had you ever hallucinated like that before, or since?"

"Well, just now."

He appeared startled. "You saw a yellow haze in here,
just now?"

"No. Everything went black and white. What is it?"

The Professor audibly blew out air and walked to the
window. "This is happening because you have an ability.
Your mother had it too. It usually presents itself earlier,
around age eleven or twelve. Your talent has awakened quite
late. We don't know why."

"So what is this talent and what does it have to do with
my dad's...my dad?" I couldn't bring myself to use the word
"murder". I had thought yesterday that at least a gas explosion was quick, but now, all I could think was did he suffer?
Was he scared?

"It's very likely that the young man who tried to abduct
you in Glastonbury followed you home and is responsible
for the explosion at your house. The gentleman you saw me
talking to earlier is General Cavendish. His team is responsible for tracking this individual down, and I can assure you,
they are excellent at their job. The information you and
your father have provided will be beneficial."

"You spoke to Dad?" I asked.

"Not personally, but he explained some of what
happened to General Cavendish. What I'm about to tell you
will seem downright unbelievable, but there is plenty of
evidence here to support it. While it may be far-fetched to
you, it is a truth that we at the Academy have learned, and

ultimately, it is the core of this place and the duties of the people here."

"I thought this was a school for military kids."

"It is, Miss Banks. In the 1950s, following a series of unexplained crimes, including assassinations and the thefts of sensitive state documents, it was discovered that there are, let's say, "creatures" living among us who are not exactly what they appear to be. To most of us, they look like normal, regular people, but in their natural state, they are not human."

The Professor paused, apparently giving me a few moments to absorb this.

"They can alter their physical state and walk freely through the walls of banks, prisons, palaces – anywhere."

I thought about the boy disappearing through the fence, and shuddered as the Professor continued.

"We believe they must have been with us for a very long time because, eventually, some humans developed an ability to perceive them. These talented people are called Trackers. They can engage this special sight – we call it "blinking in" – which allows them to see the creatures. The ability comes from an extra gland at the base of the skull, which allows the Tracker to perceive and track these creatures, which we call Faders. The ability to see them does not last for long, usually until the mid-twenties, then it becomes unreliable and unstable."

As he spoke, I couldn't get the picture of the boy fading into a yellow mist out of my mind. It was real, all of it.

"Wait, my dad knew about this? That my mum could do it? That I might be able to do it, and he didn't tell me? Why would he do that?"

Finding out that Dad would lie to me about something so important was almost intolerable, especially now.

"Your father wouldn't have kept this from you lightly. We are part of a military operation. He signed the Official Secrets Act. If he had told you about this, he could have gone to prison. He was protecting you, and us."

"And what if this had happened to me sooner?"

"There are protocols, irrespective of your age. Your safety is important to us, and was essential to your father. Yesterday morning, he met with our Security people. He was preparing to move you both to this base by the end of the day. He would have been the one explaining all of this to you now.

"We believe the Faders were watching you for signs that your talent was awakening, and obviously, they know that now it has. Nearly half of Somerset discovered it. Most curious.

"I know this has been a lot to absorb, but you are, by no means, out of danger, and this is the safest place in the country for you right now. The Academy Counsellor is going to spend some time with you and make sure you get something to eat and some rest if you need it. Then, if you like, you can visit your father's students. Some of them are the same age as you, and you might find it easier to ask them about the Faders and what we do here.

"We will talk again."

Professor Abbott stuck his head out of the office and asked his Secretary to take me over to the Counsellor's office. He held the door open for me, and on my way through, I turned back to him.

"Professor Abbott, I want to make them pay for what they did to my dad."

"Miss Banks, if that is your wish, you are absolutely in the right place."

6

My meeting with Helen, the Counsellor, was brief. It was pretty clear that as my dad had been dead fewer than twenty-four hours and my whole understanding of the world had turned upside-down, I was confused about everything, especially myself. Helen had been kind enough, but she agreed that I needed time to process things on my own and I made an appointment to see her the next day. I was grateful for that; more than anything, I just needed time to think. These Faders, these monsters which were now a part of my world, were at least something on which I could focus.

At the end of the meeting, I opened the door and walked into the corridor. A boy who looked about my age was waiting outside the office, looking bored. He was playing with a lock of his sandy blond hair, repeatedly pulling it down the centre of his forehead and watching it spring back up to dangle there. I could tell he knew I was there, but he didn't seem to be in much of a hurry to acknowledge me.

Helen came out behind me.

"Marcus," she said, "I asked Orla to meet us."

"Orla got a detention, so I came."

Helen raised her eyebrow. "Orla's not in classes, Marcus. No one is. Why isn't she here?"

Marcus stood up. I was struck by how tall he was; easily six foot four, he towered over both of us. He smiled sheepishly at the Counsellor, showing two deep dimples in his cheeks. "I told her to meet you at the medical block. Sorry." Glancing briefly at me, he said, "I heard she set off every car and house alarm in a two-mile radius." Then he spoke directly to me. "That was quite something. Apparently, it showed up on satellites."

I didn't understand what he was talking about.

"Marcus, this isn't the time," warned Helen.

Marcus's face fell. "I'm so sorry about your dad. He was one of my favourite teachers. I don't know what to say."

A nod was all I could manage.

"Well," said Helen, "since you're here, take Jenna to the canteen, introduce her to the gang and get her something to eat."

As we began to walk away, Helen called after us, "And make sure Orla knows we're not meeting. If she kicks your butt, I'm turning a blind-eye."

"Listen," said Marcus as we walked out of the building, "there was an announcement this morning about your dad, so the students who are here already know. If you'd rather just pick up a sandwich and go somewhere quiet, we can do that. Just give me a signal. Try screaming, "Marcus, get me the hell out of here." I'm good at picking up social clues like that."

"Thanks," I said, and I meant it.

"I can't imagine how weird all this must be for you. At least I grew up with it."

We walked through the campus and into the loud buzz

of the canteen, which instantly softened into whispered conversations as we entered. I was horrified at the intensity of all those eyes on me. Those years I'd spent being watched could have prepared me for it, but apparently not.

As if the whispers weren't enough, I could hear a few sobs around the room. I began to feel the anger rising again at being forced to face other people's grief. Whipping my head towards the sound, I met the startled eyes of a little girl who couldn't have been more than ten. Instantly, I felt ashamed. I felt my face soften and managed a tiny smile for the girl, whose face just crumpled into more tears. I wanted to go to her, but I didn't know what to do with my own feelings, much less someone else's.

Marcus and I picked up a tray each, and I gazed unenthusiastically at the food. It looked good, and I thought I might be hungry, but it seemed that eating food was something you should do if your dad was alive and everything was okay. The thought of enjoying food felt somehow disloyal.

Marcus looked at me, and by the softness of his eyes, I knew he could tell what was going on in my head. "Do you usually like tuna sandwiches?" he asked, phrasing the question strangely, but the way he said it was so appropriate. If this was a regular day and my world hadn't just fallen apart, then yes, I would like tuna sandwiches. His perception touched me.

"Yes," I said.

I smiled at him gratefully as he got me through the rest of the options with questions like "It's Tuesday today, would you ever eat a banana on a Tuesday?" and "Would you regularly drink orange juice in the summer?" Finally, he threw brownies on to his tray and mine and led us to a table with four empty chairs.

I looked around as I sat down. Most eyes were on me, but one particular face jumped out. A gaunt girl seemed a little familiar. The skin beneath her eyes was dark and hollow, and her lips were pale. What had startled me was the way she looked at me. She was giving me a stare of pure malevolence.

"What's her problem?" I asked. "The one staring daggers at me."

"She's a bit weird, just ignore it," said Marcus, a little too quickly.

I turned away, opened my sandwich and began to nibble at it. My body's need for sustenance took over and soon I had finished the sandwich, the banana and the bottle of orange juice.

Throughout the meal, Marcus rattled on about how many times he'd been to the Medical Centre, how many stitches he'd had and where he'd had them. He left spaces for me to comment that I chose not to fill. I was, however, very grateful to him for seeming to know exactly how to get me through this.

Marcus made his brownie disappear at a speed that left my head spinning. I looked at mine and said, "I don't think I can eat that."

He smiled, and his dimples reappeared. "That's okay. I figured you wouldn't, but I wanted two."

His hand snaked out, and my brownie was gone. I stared at the empty tray.

"What?" he said. "I'm a growing boy."

"You'll be growing out-the-way instead of up-the-way if you're not careful," said a tall girl with an Irish lilt. Her long ginger hair was a stunning mass of frizzy curls which all seemed to have different ideas about what direction they should be going in. "You won't be doing much tracking if you're panting and wheezing over a big, bouncy gut."

"Oh! Hi, Orla," said Marcus.

"Don't you "Oh, hi" me, Marcus Headley. What are you up to, giving me the runaround?" Orla put her tray on our table and sat down. "And I hope you weren't behind the shenanigans at the Science Block last night. I heard the power and the backup generator both failed."

"How could you think I'd be behind that? I'm not that daft."

"Daft?" Then to me, she said, "Last year, he and his loony friend, Nathan, planted daffodils so they'd burst through in the spring spelling "Bugger Off". It was so big, a police helicopter pilot reported it." To Marcus, she added, "I have no idea how to measure the daftness of you."

She didn't wait for an answer, but turned her attention back to me. "Hi, you must be Jennifer. I'm Orla. We're going to be in the same dorm room."

"We are?" I was shocked. "I live here now? It was nice of them to tell me."

Orla froze, looking horrified that she'd put her foot in it.

"Well, this is awkward," said Marcus.

Orla looked around at the staring faces. "Marcus, your ex is looking...well...stabby. Has she lost more weight? She looks awful."

I glanced over at the girl. It was the one who looked strangely familiar.

"So that's your ex?" I asked Marcus.

"Sort of," said Marcus. "Well, yes."

"Listen, we don't have a lot of privacy here," said Orla, "and I'm sure you must have a lot of questions. How about if we go to the dorm and chat there?"

"Good idea, we'll do that," said Marcus.

"Yes, let's go to the *girls*" dorm and chat. This reprobate can pine at the entrance for you." Orla became all business. "I understand we'll need to take an inventory of the things you'll need."

Heaviness sat on my chest as I remembered that everything, including my father, had disappeared in the explosion. Orla instantly realised what she'd said.

"I'm sorry, Jennifer. I'm an eejit of the worst kind."

"It's Jenna," I replied.

After saying goodbye to Marcus at the canteen, I walked with Orla across the campus to two buildings with six floors.

"The girls" block is on the left," said Orla. "We're on the third floor in room 3b." Orla gave me the code to enter. "Don't, for the love of God, tell Marcus. We'll never see the back of him."

Orla moved aside to let me enter the code. I pressed the buttons, the door buzzed and I pulled it open.

We walked up the stairs, and Orla pulled a key card from her pocket and used it on the door to 3b. The room wasn't a bad size. It was orderly, with two single beds, desks, chairs, cupboards, drawers and shelves. A small refrigerator sat under a shelf, and a shower room lay off to the left.

Orla began, "Well, they've told me you know absolutely nothing, so that's how I'll continue. If I start going over something you already know, just tell me to move on. I'll ease you in with the boring stuff. First, this building: the first floor has Years Seven and Eight. There are six large dorms with six beds and a side room off each for the monitor who looks after them. There's also a shower block. They make a hell of a lot of noise in the mornings. The second floor is for Years Nine and Ten. They get smaller dorms with four beds and fewer monitors. If you ask me, they should be monitored more instead of less; they're a bunch of little sociopaths. The third and fourth floors are for us, Year Elevens, two to a dorm with a shower per room. We have a monitor in the end room on each floor.

"The fifth and sixth floors are for sixth formers. That's the holy grail of accommodation for people who want to stay on at this Academy. No monitors, mainly because it's the sixth formers who do most of the monitoring. We call it the penthouse. A room to themselves, a private kitchenette and bathroom with a real honest-to-God bath, not just a shower like we get.

"It's not so bad. Some of the sixth form girls will let the Year Elevens have an hour to get foamy and wrinkly in their bathtub if they take one of their monitor shifts. I've done it a couple of times, but it's hard to sleep with all that farting and giggling – and remember, these are girls we're talking about.

"There are other Academies around the world. I'm transferring to the one in upstate New York for my final two years, so I'll be leaving in a few weeks. That's why I'm still down here. It's not worth my moving upstairs then moving again six weeks later. Zoe, the girl I shared with, she's staying on in the sixth form here, so she's moved up to the penthouse already."

A girl's head with short black and spiky purple hair popped around the door. "My ears are burning. I hope you're saying nice things." She was about five feet tall and slight, with ripped leggings and a baggy long-sleeved t-shirt. Following her was a tall, gangly boy with bright blue eyes and caramel coloured skin, wearing tracksuit bottoms and t-shirt.

"Jenna, this is Zoe. And the boy you can't see behind her, because boys aren't allowed in this building, is Nathan."

"Hi," said Zoe and Nathan at the same time. To Orla, Zoe

said, "Nate's just helping me move some stuff around." She turned to me and said, "I brought you a few things, I hope you don't mind. I heard...well. I'm sorry about Mr Banks; I really liked him. I mean, I was rubbish at Science, but he was a nice teacher. Anyway, here are some bits and pieces. I had some clothes to give you, but I saw you in the canteen. You're about six inches taller than me, so I left them. Here are some bathroom supplies, a toothbrush, some tooth-paste, and shower gel. Orla has a fit if you borrow her stuff."

"I have a fit at you when my stuff vanishes, all the time," Orla corrected her.

Nathan said, "Anyway, I hear you, like, blew all the street lights in a five-mile radius when you awakened. How does that even happen?"

A heavily-breathing voice came from the window. "The force is strong in this one."

"Marcus," sighed Orla, "I'm getting the monitor."

"Fine, but can you let me in first? I'm losing my grip."

As Nathan and Zoe pulled him in, I looked out of the window and down at what looked like a sheer drop. "How did you get up here?"

"It was a heroic effort. I faced perils and stuff," Marcus replied with a dimply grin.

"I'm still getting a monitor," said Orla through gritted teeth.

"There's already one here," Marcus said.

Zoe and Nathan both jumped and looked at the door. "Where?"

"You, you Muppet!"

"Oh right, I suppose I am," said Zoe. "Right, you," she shook a finger sternly at Marcus, "don't do it again."

"Oh jeez!" said Orla. "Please don't tell me that's your A-game."

"So, Jenna," asked Marcus, bluntly changing the subject, "do you have any questions?"

"Will I be able to kill the monster who murdered my dad?" I asked.

The room went quiet, the tentative joviality evaporating. Zoe's eyebrows shot into the air. They probably hadn't been expecting that to be my first question, but it had been burning at the back of my mind since my meeting with the Principal.

"It might be best if we explain exactly how it works around here," said Orla as she sat in her desk chair. "Manage your expectations, as it were."

Zoe closed the door, crossed to Orla's bed and sat on it, while Nathan sat on the floor beside her and flipped one of Zoe's hanging legs across his shoulder and chest. Marcus eyed what was meant to be my bed, but sat at my desk instead. There was a loud creak as he sat down.

"Careful!" Zoe and Orla shouted. "That chair's on its way out," added Orla. Marcus stayed gingerly still.

I sat on the end of my bed and signalled Orla to continue.

"We all awakened between the ages of eleven and thirteen. We're invited to attend the Academy, and we do all of the regular lessons like you'd do in any other school, but we also learn to use our ability to find Faders and their nests.

"We take part in two main activities here: spotting and tracking. Up to age eighteen, all we do is spotting. We sit in high traffic areas like shopping malls and report anything we see. When we find a nest or an area with high Fader activity, we don't go near it. The idea is for us to simply look out for them and report when we see them. We are taught self-defence as a precaution from the first day we arrive, but we never engage the Faders directly. If we're doing our job right, they shouldn't even be aware of us. We're removed from the scene before the Trackers go in. They never put us in harm's way."

"We're the talent," added Marcus.

Orla rolled her eyes.

"At eighteen, we become Trackers. That means when a Spotter reports a sighting, the Trackers follow the trail with the intention of locating the Fader's nest. The training can get quite intense. It's the same training people in espionage receive."

"But what actually happens?" I asked.

"When they fade, they are invisible, but we can see them with the Sight as a bright yellow mist," said Orla.

I shuddered, remembering.

"Also, they occasionally emit that yellow mist while they're in human form so you'll see a human looking person suddenly surrounded by a yellow cloud. We call that "emitting"."

"We call it "farting"," said Nathan and Marcus together, with a laugh.

Zoe slapped the back of Nathan's head.

"He said it too," said Nathan, rubbing his head and pointing at Marcus.

"The Agency guys work with the Trackers. Once the Fader has been identified by the Trackers, they are there tranquillised before they get the chance to fade."

"How do they know if they've got them all?" I asked. "I mean, how do they know there isn't another dozen of them floating around?" I shuddered at the thought of it.

"We can see them when they're faded, but something weird happens to their clothes. When they fade back, they're naked," said Zoe.

"But they kill them, right?" I asked.

"Honestly, I'm not so curious about that part," said Orla.

"What do these Faders do? Why did they kill my dad?"

"It's likely they were after you," said Zoe.

The others just looked at her.

"It's best that she knows," said Zoe defensively. "What about Washington State?"

Before I could ask what that meant, Zoe continued.

"We can see them. We're a danger to them, and we're easier targets if they can get us while we're young or if we're unprotected."

"Well, what's to stop them from coming here?" I asked.

"The soldiers guarding this place are a unit of Trackers," said Marcus. "They keep the Sight switched on all the time they're on duty. It's tiring; I've tried to do it. It gave me a migraine."

"Wuss," said Nathan.

"So if they fade, they can't be caught?" I asked.

"I think they have to eat when they're in human form, so they have to fade back sometime," explained Marcus. "If we can follow them closely enough, eventually we'll catch them, hungry and bare-assed. The problem is, if they start fading through walls and we haven't got enough people surrounding a building, they can get away. They leave a sort of trail, though: a yellow mist that we can see and follow if we're within a few minutes of them. It dissipates after that."

"What if it's dark?"

"It's not actually seeing," said Orla. "The yellow isn't really there. It's more like perceiving and your eyes pick up the signal. So yes, you can still see it in the dark."

"It's like smelling. You can smell in the dark," added Nathan.

"You're confusing things, dear," said Zoe.

"Are they expecting me to be a Spotter?" I asked.

"I wondered about that," said Marcus. "I don't know where they'd put you. you'd have a lot to learn, and it's pretty late in the game. It's obvious the Faders have been watching you so I can't see you being much use as a Spotter if they already know what you look like. We're all due to stop tracking in our twenties anyway. The Sight becomes unreliable and Trackers can start giving false positives. No one wants to get that wrong."

"What happens then?"

"They fix it," he replied.

Who fixes what? I wondered.

Marcus continued, "But for those few years, once you're able to use the Sight, there are opportunities in all walks of life. If you're not very academic, you could end up serving tea and biscuits to the Queen until you stop tracking."

"My auntie was a typist at 10 Downing Street until she lost the Sight," said Zoe. "She runs a recruitment agency in London now."

"Does this gene always go in families?" I asked.

"Most of us are born to two Tracker parents. To be honest, I think they encourage Trackers to get together. I suppose it's a difficult life to explain to someone who doesn't know and could never know," said Zoe. "As I understand it, it's a sure thing that if both parents are Trackers, their children will be too. It's not so definite if only one parent is a Tracker.

"Some Trackers move to the military unit. They are the ones who go into nests after we've identified them. Some Trackers get selected for special duties and whisked away by the Agency. That's top secret stuff. You can't apply; you have to be chosen."

"The Agency?"

"You'll see them around. They're not in regular uniforms. They wear all black and don't smile much."

"They're like goths," said Marcus.

"They are nothing like goths," said Orla. "My older brother, Sean, was sort of friends with one of them very briefly, but the guy got reassigned just for chatting with him."

"Why aren't they allowed to be friendly?" I asked.

"Years ago, an Agency guy was being attacked by a Fader and one of the kids jumped in to save him. The kid got killed," said Orla. "Since then, there's no fraternisation with the Agency. They can't risking a dope like Marcus getting himself killed by trying to be a hero."

"That's right, ladies, I'm dope," said Marcus.

"No, you're *a* dope. Anyway, we keep our distance, out of respect for the difficult job they've got. If you want to go down the military route, you go over to the training facility at seventeen and start off in a role that utilises your Sight until you have the GTrack removed. Then you can join a clean-up squad if you want or go off and join the regular military."

I wondered what a GTrack was, but I was becoming overwhelmed.

"Nests, clean-up squads and the Queen. This is all...well, I don't know what this is," I said.

"Sorry, we're blowing your mind a bit, aren't we. So how about when you awakened? That must have been scary," said Zoe.

"I know, seeing all that black and white for the first time – it's freakish, even if you know to expect it," added Nathan.

"It was weird," I replied. "And all that yellow. It was like a tin of paint had exploded."

"Yellow? You saw yellow when you awakened? There was a Fader?" Zoe's jaw had dropped.

"Yes, he...he was trying to kidnap me." I shuddered at the memory.

"Holy crap! Really?" asked Marcus "That's intense."

"Dad came and the guy just melted away. I thought I was hallucinating."

"Well, that's why they're called Faders," said Zoe, not immediately realising that the mood had become sombre again at the mention of my dad.

"Okay, well I'm going to sneak out before I'm busted," said Marcus.

"Ditto," added Nathan.

"Yes, perverts!" said Zoe. "Out you go before I get someone to tranquillise you. Come on, I'll put you out."

And the three of them left.

After they had gone, Orla said, "If you like, I can lend you my panic alarm. If you set it off every time Marcus comes near you, he'll get the message."

"That's okay." I smiled. "He's been great. He seems to know just what to say and when to shut up – an extraordinary talent in a boy."

"Ahh! Well, something similar happened to him. Just after he awakened, both of his parents died in a car crash."

I didn't know what to say to that. Orla looked awkward as though she realised she'd been indiscreet.

"Do you think there's any chance I'd be able to take the military route?" I asked.

"Honestly, Jenna, I don't know. You're miles behind on the most basic training. You haven't started learning to control your ability. It can take months to control the Sight. But...well, there's more you have to consider."

"Like what?"

"Would your dad have approved?"

I couldn't think of a response to that. In fact, I'd been trying pretty hard not to think about Dad at all.

Orla continued carefully, "You should know there's a rumour been going around. People think that because your dad was a scientist here, he did something to you to stop you from awakening."

"That's ridiculous!" I said, although I had already realised that when my dad said he had been keeping a promise to my mum, he must have meant the pills. Dad worked with these kids every day, but at the same time, he was trying to stop me from turning into one of them. Would they think he was disloyal, that he believed I was too good for this life? Anyway, I wasn't going to share that with anyone.

7

I woke up with Dad standing over me. We were in the
courtyard of the bookshop in Glastonbury. He tried to help
me up, but all the people around started moving in towards
him. They were yellow; their faces were monstrous. Dad reached
for me, but they swarmed over him. Standing and sneering with
bright yellow eyes was the Fader boy. I screamed for Dad, but I
couldn't reach him.

"Jenna! Jenna! Wake up." Orla was tapping my cheek.

"I'm sorry, I was dreaming," I slurred, still half asleep. "Is
it morning?" I asked, looking at the alarm clock which was
beeping away loudly.

Orla hit the top of the clock, and it fell silent. "No, it's
about 3 am, I think. The alarm clock was having a fit. Don't
worry about it."

I meant to say something more, but I fell instantly back
to sleep.

Orla had already left the room when I woke up the next
day. I disconnected my phone from her charger and tried to
switch it on. It was still dead. I guessed it must have been the
phone that was broken; this was the third charger I'd tried.

I was still exhausted and considered going back to sleep. Instead, I padded to the bathroom and brushed my teeth. Orla had left some jeans and a t-shirt on my chair. I pushed my feet into my ballet pumps, the only shoes I still had, and tied back my hair.

Zoe had left her old room key card with me. I slipped it into my back pocket. I still couldn't get any life from my phone, so I put it in a drawer and left the room. Halfway down the corridor, I considered that I might find someone who could have a go at fixing my phone, so I went back to retrieve it. I tried the key card on the door a few times, but it wouldn't work.

I walked past the lift with an Out-Of-Order sign on the door and descended the stairs. Outside, there were groups of kids lounging about here and there. A few kids were hanging out near the steps to one of the campus buildings. I stopped to ask for directions to the Counsellor's office, but something struck me as unusual about their behaviour. It wasn't so much that they were hanging out, it looked more like they were staking out.

I looked around and asked, "What's happening?"

One of the boys replied, "Nothing, why?"

"I don't know. It just looks like you're waiting for something."

"Ha! Busted!" laughed Marcus, coming down the steps with Nathan and Zoe trailing him.

"Sorry?" I was confused.

"They're practicing spotting. This is where we learn to look like a bunch of bored kids with nothing better to do, when the Agency guys take us to shopping centres and other populated areas. We occasionally practise in the local town, too. As well as using it to look for Faders we also check on kids who might awaken, except we're looking for different things there: change in face colouring, red as a beetroot, and excessive static hair frizz."

"Very cunning," I said as it all fell into place, the people watching me. Well, that answered my question. The Nine of Cups had been right after all. "I'm sure the people you watch have absolutely no clue of what's going on. How do you know you're doing it right?"

"We're tested on it. We have to be able to identify things we have seen in our peripheral vision while we were looking in another direction."

As I looked around, I saw Marcus's ex walking towards me. Up close, she looked older than me, about eighteen maybe. She stood there with her arms folded.

"So how did he stop you from awakening? He must have done something."

I'd only been shown kindness up to now, and I was shocked.

"I don't...I..."

"For God's sake, Tiffany!" said Marcus. "She's just lost her dad, what's wrong with you?"

"None of us got the chance for a normal life. Why did she?"

As I looked at her, I realised why I recognised her. "The charity shop in the High Street."

"What?" asked Marcus.

"I was looking at a Michael Kors handbag in the window, and you were behind me, watching my reflection. When I turned around, you were just looking in the window, but you'd been staring at me. I know you were."

Tiffany went red-faced. Even her friends had started to giggle. She spun around, pushing violently through her friends as she stormed off.

"Bloody hell, Marcus," said Zoe, "what did you do to Tiffany? You totally broke her brain."

A flash of anger crossed Marcus's face.

"You had one parent with the Sight and one without," Nathan said to me, "so they would have watched you closely when you were younger for signs that you were going to awaken, but less often the older you got. I'm surprised they hadn't already given up. Did you catch people watching you often?"

"I guess so. It wasn't anything I could put my finger on. It just didn't look right. Dad used to tell me it was all in my imagination."

I looked around the campus green and could see now that everyone was spotting. Some were doing better than others, but now that I was looking, it was clear that they were all a little more alert than they appeared to be. This made me realise something.

I turned to Marcus. "You were practising yesterday, outside Helen's office when you were playing with your hair."

"Now that is truly embarrassing," said Nathan, laughing. "Marcus is supposed to be one of the best. Mind you, so is Tiffany."

Marcus blushed, and I felt mean for calling him out.

"I'm looking for Helen's office now, but a lot of these buildings look alike to me," I said.

"Then allow me to escort you," he said, offering me his arm. I just looked at it. He didn't seriously expect me to take his arm, did he?

"You're not going to leave me hanging, are you?" he asked as he stood motionless.

"Damn right I am," I said. Marcus smiled and withdrew his arm as Nathan picked up a basketball and bounced it off the back of his head. It was like walking along with a couple of five-year-olds as they tried to trip each other up and give each other dead arms.

As we reached the edge of the green, Nathan said, "I'll wait for you here, Marky."

"Sure, Nate."

They did some convoluted handshake, and then Nathan turned back. Marcus and I walked across the compound.

"I hope I'm not late. I can't get my phone to charge," I said.

"I hear you blew the electrics in the girls" block last night. The lifts are out and everything."

"That was me? I don't understand what's happening to me."

"They'll figure it out, don't worry."

We stopped talking, and the silence felt awkward. Finally, he broke it.

"Orla told me that she'd bored you with the tale of my parents" least successful car journey." The words came out sarcastic and bitter.

"I'm sorry. We don't need to talk about it if you don't want," I said.

"That's okay. There's not much to tell. It was just after I had awakened. I was due to come to the Academy, but Mum and Dad decided we were going to have a holiday first. I was supposed to be staying with my grandparents the night before the holiday. My parents drove me there, but I was a spoiled brat and insisted I wanted to go back home with them. Otherwise, I wouldn't even have been in the car.

"I was playing Pokémon on my Gameboy in the back of the car. We'd only been on the motorway a few minutes when Dad yelled that the brakes weren't working. I remember the car skidding and rolling, and I don't remember anything after that.

"By the time I woke up, a week later, they were already buried. They had both died instantly. When I left the hospital, I came straight to the Academy. And that's all, folks!"

He attempted a smile, but the edges of his lips refused to make the upward curve. I hugged him impulsively, but when I tried to step back, he was clinging on to me tightly.

"I think I'm going to need my ribs," I said, and he let go.

When I looked at him, his face was showing surprise, maybe even shock. "I'm sorry," he said, awkwardly. "I just haven't spoken about that for a long time, but I shouldn't pile my crap on top of your already impressive pile of crap. And I don't want to ruin a summer's day."

I looked around. I hadn't even noticed it was sunny.

"What are you going to do? Career, I mean," I asked. "Do you know?"

"I've only ever wanted to do one thing. I'm going to be a Physiotherapist, here or at another base."

"Why that?"

"That's what my dad did, and I like to help people."

"Fair enough." I envied his determination. "Can I ask, what's up with your ex? You looked angry about what Zoe said."

"I'm not angry at Zoe, just at myself. I do feel responsible for what happened to Tiffany. I don't know how she ended up like that, but I feel like it's somehow my fault.

"I went out with Tiff for a couple of months last year. She seemed okay at first, but then she started getting clingy. I hadn't had a girlfriend before and I didn't know how to handle it. When I ended it with her, she lost it, screaming and shouting words that didn't even make sense at me. She had a fit right there and then. Full on foaming at the mouth.

I was terrified. I thought she was going to die. I don't think she's been right since. She was in the med-block for a couple of weeks and then she came back to the Academy.

"At first, she seemed okay, but she kept following me around. Then it became apparent that she wasn't eating. They moved her back into the med-block again for about a month. When she came out, she just kept to a few friends and hasn't spoken to me once. Today is the closest I've been to her. She still looks ill."

"Do they know what's wrong with her?"

"Not a clue. I try not to get involved." He shrugged. "I don't mean to sound harsh, but I tried to help. Being around me just made it worse for her, I think. I stay away from her now. She's still got her mates looking out for her."

"That's another thing – why are there still so many kids around?" I asked. "We're in the summer holidays. Don't they go home?"

"We don't have a proper summer holiday," he explained. "Most of the youngest kids are off for six weeks. Some of them live in family accommodation on the base with their parents and haven't gone away anywhere, so they're still hanging around. The Academy puts on activities for them. Others have gone away with their families. Some are on duty and will be starting their holidays in a couple of weeks when the first lot get back.

"And this is the medical block." He gestured to the door we had reached and, for some reason, patted my shoulder.

"Thanks," I said. I turned away quickly, feeling awkward again.

In Helen's office, she and I sat in armchairs and I looked around the room.

"How are you getting on with the others?" Helen asked.

"Okay. They're surprisingly normal, you know, for vampire slayers or whatever."

Helen looked concerned. "You have been speaking to people other than Marcus, haven't you?"

"Yes, I'm just kidding."

"I'm relieved. Marcus has a strange sense of humour so I wouldn't be surprised if he told you he slays vampires."

"Orla, Zoe, and Nathan have been explaining the Faders to me." I gazed around the room at the academic degrees and photos on her wall as I spoke. "I'm still confused about what my place will..."

My eyes had rested on a picture and my dad's face smiled out at me. It stopped me in my tracks. The next shock was that my mum was in the picture too, and Helen. It was a group shot, taken in a restaurant.

I stood up and walked over to the picture. "They look so young and happy," I said.

There was a candle on the table and it lit up my mum's face. She was smiling, and Dad was sitting behind her with his chin on her shoulder and a goofy grin.

"You're in that picture too," said Helen.

I searched the picture for my face, and after a few seconds, I found my dad's hand wrapped around mum and resting on her pregnant belly.

"They should have had their whole lives together. I should have had them both. I barely remember my mother. A few flashes of memory, that's all. I was three when she died."

"I know. I was at the funeral," Helen said. "Tessa was my best friend at the Academy. We grew apart when I left for university. This picture was taken not long after I finished my degree and came back to work here. I'd missed the wedding by a year and returned to that big swollen belly. But it was like the years between had disappeared and she was my best friend again. I bought you a giant stuffed Pooh Bear when you were born."

"I still have...had that."

I looked at Helen. She was as lost in the picture as I was. "Why don't I remember you?"

"Your dad took a leave of absence after she died. He was angry at the Agency, the Academy, all of it. He didn't want us to come near you. He came back a year later, by which time I was married and had my own life going on. I thought he might invite me over to see you, but he never did, and I never asked."

"Why would he be angry with you? She died of a brain tumour."

The second it was out of my mouth, I knew there was more to it. I didn't even have to look at Helen.

"Mum didn't die of a brain tumour, did she?"

"Yes...well, sort of." She sighed. "It was the Tracker Gland. Like any part of the body, they can become malignant."

I walked back to the armchair and dropped myself into it.

"Helen, what am I doing here? I mean, I get that you're all trying to keep me safe, but I'm supposed to be starting sixth form in a few weeks."

"You'll be able to study at the Academy. You're interested in Design, right? There are..."

"I don't want an A Level in Staring at Goats or whatever the hell it is you people do. If I can't learn how to blow the brains out of the evil monster that killed my dad, I just don't see the point."

I drew to an abrupt halt as I realised the subdued

lighting in the room was now dazzling, and the room was flashing from colour to monochrome. Noise from across the room drew my attention. A games console in the corner was all flashing lights, and the disc tray was repeatedly going in and out. I dug the heel of my hands into my eyes and took a few breaths. When I lifted my face, the room was back to normal.

I sighed. "And then there's all this. How am I supposed to control it? Nathan says this doesn't usually happen, so what's wrong with me?"

"Usually, when the talent awakens there's a release of static electricity. The child may experience unusual activity for a while before and after the awakening: static shocks, hair-raising, that kind of thing."

I remembered my hair frizzing up and flying away earlier that week.

"It's best not to wear nylon, and knitwear can look, well, weird," Helen continued. "This usually calms down fairly quickly, and if it doesn't, it stops when we get the implant."

"Excuse me?" Now both of my eyebrows were at my hairline.

"We have an implant called a GTrack injected near the site of the gland which controls the tracking ability. It's a slow release hormone capsule which lasts for five years and stops the haywire reactions. We used to have little dark red pills, but they sometimes affected our ability to track."

I tried to move on smoothly without reacting to the "red pills" comment.

"I think I heard the term yesterday, but it didn't sink in. So why haven't I been offered that yet?"

"You've been causing a bit more than static shocks. We're just not sure what the best course of action is for helping you at the moment. If they're not going to offer you the implant immediately, you need to start learning how to control the Sight. It may help you to control whatever is happening to you.

"I think it will also be useful if you get into a routine as soon as possible. And you don't have to "stare at goats" if you don't want to. I'm pretty sure we don't have goats. Anything you wanted to study at your old school, you can study here. We'll see to that. But if you're in danger, so are your friends at school. I'm sure you don't want that."

I SAW Helen every day for my first week at the Academy. I cried; I asked questions; sometimes I got angry or frustrated and made bulbs pop. She taught me relaxation exercises, but every time I went to her office, there was less stuff in it. The computer was gone; the TV and Xbox had disappeared.

On my seventh visit, Helen asked, "How do you feel, Jenna?"

"I read that leaflet you gave me," I said. "I think I'm going through all the stages of grief at once. I still can't believe it. In my head, our house is still there. I can walk through the house in my mind, and I know where everything is. I know what's in the fridge. There's a mug in the sink with a teaspoon in it, and Dad's standing in the kitchen. I want to reverse it all, like a DVD.

"At the same time, everything in my life is moving on, carrying me further away from him. Things happen, and I want to tell him about them, but I remember I can't. It's annoying. I feel angry that other people here knew him longer than I did. I can't let myself think about the boy, the monster. I want to kill him."

The lights began to flicker.

"Jenna, start your breathing exercises."

I closed my eyes, pictured a field and breathed deeply.

"Well done. You're making real progress."

I sat quietly for a few minutes, but I had something to ask Helen. I was frightened of the answer, but I asked anyway.

"Helen?"

"Yes, Jenna?"

"Is there going to be a funeral? I mean, is there...was there...?"

I couldn't continue.

Helen sighed and began to speak with what I guess would be called "professional detachment".

"Yes, there was a body. No, you won't be allowed to see it. There is currently an investigation, but I understand the authorities will be releasing your father's body for cremation within a couple of weeks."

"Cremation?" I asked.

"According to his files, that was his preference, but I already knew that. He said when he lost Tessa, he wanted his ashes to be scattered with hers. That was in the Garden of Remembrance outside the Chapel on the base.

"I'm sorry you've lost so much, Jenna. Your mum was only one year old when she lost her mother, and her father had died before she was even born."

"What happened to my grandparents?"

I couldn't believe the question had never come up with my dad. Was I that self-absorbed?

"Tom and Vanessa Harvey lived near the Academy in upstate New York. Your grandfather, Tom, died in the worst Fader attack we've ever had, in 1978. When your grandmother was seven months pregnant, Tom went to the Academy in Washington State to attend a conference. One night, the Faders attacked. They killed everyone. They murdered the kids, some as young as ten years old. All the staff, the soldiers, everyone, just gone. It was horrific.

"Your grandmother, Vanessa, went missing in 1979. She went shopping to New York City, to buy some gifts for your mum's first birthday. Then she was supposed to meet up with friends, but she never showed up. She was never seen again."

8

VANESSA – NEW YORK – 1979

"Jerk!" muttered Vanessa Harvey at the back of the man who had barged into her on the sidewalk outside Macy's.

The crowds on Broadway were packed like sardines, blocking the sidewalk as they waited to cross the street. The oaf hadn't even made five more steps before the crowd penned him in.

Ha! Karma, she thought.

She bent to retrieve her fallen shopping bags, stepped aside of the busy store entrance, and briefly closed her eyes. She was trained to scope out every new environment she entered. Opening her eyes, she scanned from left to right.

The colour of the busy street around her had leached away, leaving a monochrome world filled with monochrome people, except the buffoon who had crashed into her. He had vanished and there was a bright yellow trail leading away.

Her jaw dropped from the shock of it. She had made

physical contact with one of the monsters called Faders. She felt sick.

At twenty-five years old, Vanessa had seen with the unique Sight for half of her life, so she knew that what she saw on the street was no human. An intense yellow light in the shape of the man moved away through the crowd, leaving yellow footprints on the sidewalk and a yellow mist trailing after him in the air.

She was off-duty, and there were protocols for off-duty sightings: make a note of the location, date and time and any details she could remember about the creature, including the direction he was going. It had all happened so fast, she hadn't even noted his disguise: his "human" features and clothes. Not that the clothes mattered; they would have disappeared now.

He had seemed unaware of her, so instead of continuing her journey to Times Square, she followed the yellow haze in the opposite direction. It would have been better if she hadn't been so laden with bags full of gifts for her daughter's first birthday, but the crowds had slowed him a little, so keeping up with the trail wasn't a problem.

Finally, she pursued the yellow trail into an alley and watched as the particles coalesced on a wall to her left. He'd walked through the wall.

She had all the details she needed, but as she turned to retrace her steps, a yellow streak reached back out through the wall. An arm took shape and grabbed her hair, pulling her head roughly back towards the wall. It was so fast, she didn't even have time to comprehend what was happening.

While the Faders could move about freely through solid brick, she could not. Her head slammed hard against the wall, and she slid to the ground as she lost consciousness.

.   .   .

VANESSA AWOKE in an unfamiliar white-tiled room and groaned at the pain and her stupidity. She knew why she had done it. Having lost her husband to a brutal Fader attack the previous year – he hadn't even lived to see the birth of his daughter – Vanessa had been too full of hate, too eager for revenge.

When she tried to move and realised she couldn't, her eyes darted down to see straps across her body, pinning her to a gurney. She immediately panicked and felt pinpricks of sweat on her face.

She tried to calm herself. The Academy would know she was missing by now. She'd been supposed to meet up with friends in Times Square.

As she struggled with the bindings, she blinked in, engaging the Sight, and froze. Her surroundings should have been monochrome, but they were awash with bright yellow trails slowly dissipating in the air. The monsters had clearly been in the room within the last few minutes. The yellow mist was across everything, including herself.

The sight of the yellow stains on her skin made her feel nauseous. She blinked out, so the yellow stains were no longer visible. Vanessa's body was gripped with fear as she faced reality: the monsters had taken her.

A thought came unbidden into her mind. Who will look after my Theresa? My stupidity has made my baby an orphan.

She couldn't think of that. Her training kicked in. She knew what to do in this circumstance: she was supposed to take her little white pill. Her daughter's face appeared before her, but she began her breathing techniques.

I've done it now. Focus, focus, she silently told herself. The first rule: if you get caught, take the pill.

Being tied down, Vanessa wasn't sure she'd be able to

reach it. She had heard stories about the things these monsters did to Trackers, which were motivation enough to make her try harder. Would it still be there, hidden in the waistband of her jeans? She struggled and twisted until able to reach the small, hidden pocket with the edge of her fingers. As she teased apart the opening, the little pill dropped into her hand.

She sighed with relief. Now she had to find a way to get her hand closer to her face. The monsters had strapped her to the gurney by the wrist and elbow, but she was able to lever herself up and move her face towards her hand. It was a stretch with the other elbow also gripped to the gurney.

As she moved her head closer to her palm, the floor of the room became visible, and there, in the corner, were the shopping bags containing her daughter's birthday gifts. She thought of her Theresa's face and for a moment lost her resolve. The realisation that she would never see her child grow up hit with such ferocity, she keened.

The pill was within reach now. She opened her mouth, moving her head towards it, but her palm began to disappear as a rough-skinned hand materialised over her own. Along with the hand came a body, and standing beside her was the man she had followed from Macy's. She could see his naked torso from the waist up. He must have been there, faded right behind her.

"I don't think we can let you do that," he said. "We have our ways of dealing with Trackers and it doesn't involve you slipping quickly and quietly into the arms of the angels."

He knocked the pill out of her hand on to the floor and faded again. When he returned to the room, he was wearing a pair of jeans and a Debbie Harry t-shirt.

"What are you going to do to me?" she asked, trying, unsuccessfully, to keep her voice from shaking.

The man picked up a syringe and stepped towards her. "Put it this way, Tracker, you won't be following us again," he said, and plunged the needle into Vanessa's neck. A fire-like pain spread outward from the site.

"Theresa," she sobbed. Then Vanessa screamed once, and no more.

9

"A couple in the programme who had just had a baby of their own adopted your mother. Eventually, they moved over to England and lived on the base here. Tessa and I met when I arrived on my first day at the Academy."

Helen stopped speaking for a few moments but then shook herself.

"Let's take a walk down to the lab. It's on the ground floor at the back of this building. Dr Narayan has asked to speak with you. Your dad's office is in the Science Division. Maybe they'll let you take a look."

We walked down the stairs to the ground floor and turned down a corridor with Science Division on a sign at the entrance. I could see armed guards standing outside the door at the far end. We were at a military base, and although I was used to seeing soldiers with guns, these Agency guys dressed all in black looked more intimidating.

I slowed down, feeling less sure of myself. "Are those guards carrying machine guns?" I asked Helen.

"I suppose so. We're not going down that far anyway.

That's where the Agency offices are. I usually stick to the medical block, which is the front block of this building. Occasionally, I'll come down to the Science Division, but this section joins us with the Agency section. That's where General Cavendish works. We don't go there."

"Why not?" I asked.

"Because we might get shot," replied Helen with a straight face.

"Duly noted."

"They never smile. They're not much for conversation, either."

"So I've heard."

"Here we are." Helen opened the door to our right and I followed her in.

The laboratory had worktops in the middle of the room with microscopes and paperwork, shelves and cupboards lining the walls with bottles and jars. Two large refrigerators stood at one end, and several office doors led off from the main area.

An Asian man who looked to be in his sixties came over to meet us.

"Helen, lovely to see you. We don't see enough of you down here," he said.

"Dr Narayan, how is everyone?"

"We are a little subdued, of course. Melissa was distraught; she had to wind down the experiments this morning, so I allowed her to leave early."

"Thank you," said Helen. She turned to me, "Jenna, this is Dr Narayan."

He took my hand. "I am sorry for the loss of your father. I will miss Neil."

"I'll go to my office to call Melissa," said Helen. "Then I'll be outside to collect Jenna in about half an hour."

"That will be perfect," he replied.

Helen left the lab, and Dr Narayan led me to his office. I drew to a halt as I saw that the name on the door next to his was "Dr Neil Banks, Manager, Chemical Testing Lab".

The Doctor turned and walked back to me.

"I am certain we will have time for you to look in on your father's office before you leave." He poked a nearby staff member in a white coat and said, "Make that possible."

"Yes, Dr Narayan," said the young woman, rushing off.

I followed him into his office.

"Jenna..."

"Who is Melissa?" I interrupted.

"Oh. Melissa is...was your father's Lab Assistant."

"Did she know him well? To be so upset, I mean."

"She's only been with us a couple of months, so she doesn't know anyone very well. Of course she's upset, we all are, but your father was running experiments in the basement labs, and according to protocols, someone has to terminate the subjects. That unfortunate job fell to Melissa. She was doing it this morning."

"The subjects?"

"Mice and rats."

"Oh, I see." I'd have been upset too, having to kill a bunch of little creatures for no reason.

He waited for a beat to see if I had anything more to say. I didn't so he continued.

"I'm sure that by now you will be aware of what it is we do at this facility and how important our work is. I imagine this has all been very confusing and possibly a little frightening for you, especially considering the strange phenomena you have been experiencing.

"I wish I could tell you exactly what is happening to you, but in truth, I haven't come across this before. No one has. I am going to suggest a way forward, for which I would like your agreement. If you do not agree, if you are uncomfortable with anything I suggest, we can find an alternative way. You are totally in control at this point."

"What are my options?"

"I will begin with the choice I hope very much that you will not prefer. But you need to know the option is there," said the Doctor. "We can book you in for a little surgery to remove your TGland. That is your Tracking Gland. Following this, you will have no further difficulties with electronic devices, and neither will the rest of us."

"The rest of you?"

"Unfortunately, you wiped out the security card readers in this building on the night you arrived, and no one could get in or out of their offices for several hours."

"Erm...sorry."

"Don't apologise to me. I found it fascinating. Save your apology for Dr Monroe; he had to pee in a bucket in the photocopying room." He laughed, and I felt a little more relaxed.

"If I choose this option, what will happen to me? Will I still live here?"

"I don't know about that. As I understand it, the Faders are hunting you. I'm sure the Principal won't throw you out."

Dr Narayan didn't look convinced about that, though.

"Option two?"

"We can give you an implant immediately. If we take this approach, you will sign a contract to work with us until you are twenty-three. During this time, you can continue your education if you wish. You will be financially supported up to and including PhD level. You will be trained to control your ability and to track Faders."

"So, option three? And I sense you're holding back your favourite until last."

"Indeed I am, Miss Banks. Option three is pretty much the same as option two, but rather than implanting you immediately, I would like a couple of months to study your unique capabilities. You would need to have the procedure within the year for your safety, but I would like to hold off on that for now, for investigative purposes. Of course, you would continue your training, also."

"And what exactly do you mean by studying and investigating?"

"Just inserting a few electrodes into your brain."

"WHAT?"

"Sorry, that's just my little joke."

"That nearly wiped your doors again."

"Oh dear, poor Dr Monroe. I am quite certain he's currently in the photocopying room again.

"The tests would not be invasive. Similar to ECG. Do you know what this is?"

"Yes, I've seen them on TV." I thought for a moment. "What about option four?"

"Option four?"

"I get up and walk off this site today without having my brain messed with or injected or operated on."

"Ahh." He looked awkward. "I'm very sorry, Jenna. There is no option four. As you are now, you are a danger to yourself and others. We have a duty to protect you and anyone who could potentially be hurt by your current condition."

"Who could be hurt?"

"Imagine you have a little event while walking down the road and the traffic lights stop working, or an ambulance loses power on its way to an emergency."

"Okay, okay. I get it. Do I have to give my answer now?"

"No, of course not. Think about it for a day or two."

"Can I see my dad's office now?"

As we walked out of Dr Narayan's office, a man was leaving Dad's office with a bunch of folders. Lying on the top was an ID badge which read "Dr N. Banks. Chemical Testing. European Union". The man looked guiltily at me as he passed.

"Your father was working on a lot of sensitive material which we had to remove before we could give you access to his office."

"I see." I knew that made sense, but it still annoyed me.

"Of course, you can take anything that belonged to your father."

I stopped at the open door and touched the sign with my dad's name. Dr Narayan muttered an excuse and wandered off with a clipboard.

When I stepped in, I breathed in deeply, hoping to inhale the smell of my dad's aftershave, but his office was just sterile. I walked around the desk. It was mostly clear except for personal items and an empty cardboard box. I sat in his black leather chair, which rolled back slightly. Gripping the edge of the desk, I pulled myself towards it and looked at the photographs on there.

One was of me, taken a couple of years ago, sitting on the edge of a fountain in Trafalgar Square. One was of Dad and me in the car at a safari park being photobombed by a giraffe sticking its head through the sunroof. The last one was Dad with Mum in the hospital just after I had been born, a tiny red-faced me in their arms.

I opened the drawers. They were empty except for a dish with paper clips in it which I remember making from clay at school. It was awful, truly terrible. I tipped out the paper clips to reveal the messy "Love U Dad" written on the bottom and put the dish next to the box along with the photographs, adding his nameplate from the desk.

His white lab coat hung from a coat rack by the window. I had been going to leave it when I noticed a tiny glimpse of turquoise peeking out from behind it. I went over to it, lifted it and threw it on the chair.

There, hanging on the rack, was one of Dad's woollen sweaters. I took it down from the hook, held it to my face and inhaled deeply. There you are, Dad. I've missed you.

My eyes stung as I blinked away tears.

I noticed that the lab coat had his name embroidered on it, and a picture ID card with "Dr N. Banks. Chemical Testing, North America" written on it peeked from the pocket. Since Dad's name was on it, I rolled it up with the coat and put it into the box. I placed the pullover, the dish and the pictures on top.

Walking over to the window, I looked out at the view he'd been looking at for the last few years. I could see the Chapel and a little picket-fenced area with trees and flowers. It was the garden of remembrance. He'd been with Mum nearly every day. That was such a comfort, and it was the moment I realised that I wanted to be near them too.

I turned into the office and noticed that on the back of the high-backed leather chair was a note taped in place which read "This is Neil's chair. DO NOT MESS WITH THE SETTINGS".

Why the hell not? I thought. I set the box on the seat and wheeled it out of the office.

When I reached the door, I saw Dr Narayan standing with Helen, and they walked over to me.

"I'm afraid the chair belongs in the office..."

"You said I could have anything that was his." I twirled the chair around to show Dr Narayan the sign on the back.

"Ah yes, but that doesn't mean..."

"I'm struggling with those options, Doctor, really struggling."

"Take the chair." He forced a smile and walked back into his office.

As Helen guided me down the corridor, she muttered, "Well played."

"When I've got this chair far enough away, you can tell him I'm going for option three. That's the lab rat choice," I explained.

I thought about Dad's test subjects and felt slightly uncomfortable with the comparison I'd just drawn.

10

I said goodbye to Helen and pushed the chair out of the front door. Marcus leaped up from the steps to take the chair and roll it along for me, and I grabbed the box with its precious contents.

"Have you been waiting for me all this time?"

"No."

"Yes," came a voice from around the corner. Nathan appeared. "He abandoned me for you, again. I've been bored."

I put my business negotiation face on, also known by Dad as my Monopoly face. "Okay then, how about if we share him during lunch and then you can have him after lunch? Does that work for you?"

Nathan pretended to consider it, and then said, "That works for me."

He shook my hand. Marcus put on a disgusted face.

"What am I, a piece of meat?"

"Well, technically, yes. We all are."

"Smart arse."

Marcus carried the chair up to the dorm room for me

and left the old broken one by the dumpsters. We then walked over to the canteen, picked up some food and sat down with Orla and Zoe. As Orla read her book, Zoe stole Nathan's chips, and Marcus flashed his huge, dimpled, open and honest smile at me, I looked at my new friends and thought, Dad, I think I'm going to be okay.

THE NEXT DAY was a turning point. I woke up for the first time knowing that Dad was gone and he wasn't coming back. I knew I wasn't magically over it, but I had shifted my mind from the past to the future.

I decided to start my training in earnest. I burst out of the dorm filled with confidence, ready for a morning run. A few feet away sat a young man in grey sweats and black t-shirt who was trying very hard to look like he hadn't been waiting for me and was not watching me.

I spent some time warming up and started my run around the campus. After a few minutes of running, I stopped to do some lunges and glanced behind me. Sure enough, there was the young man, also doing lunges. I briefly wondered if he might be a Fader, but as there were other people around, I felt fairly confident that he was a good guy.

The question was, why was he following me around the campus? I figured I could run around in circles for a very long time and I still wouldn't know the answer. Well, now seemed like a good time to ask.

I took a drink from my water bottle and strode over to him. He was over six feet tall with a crew cut and not shabby in the muscle department. He looked to be about twenty.

"Would it be worth my while asking why you're following me?"

"I'm just out for a morning run," he said in a Liverpool accent.

"Then why aren't you running?"

"I stopped to do lunges."

"This must be a trendy place to do lunges."

"Oh, all the runners stop here to lunge. This area is unofficially known as "The Lunge Place"."

"So if I continued with my run, you'd still be here doing your lunges?"

"I'm not sure. I don't do a specific number of lunges. I just move on when it feels right."

"Okay. Well, good luck with that."

I turned and started running again. After five minutes of listening to the man pounding the path behind me, I stopped to stretch out my shoulders. I looked at my back, and there he was, stretching out his shoulders too.

"Don't tell me. This is the shoulder stretching place."

"Why would I tell you? You obviously already know about it."

"You could just tell me, you know."

"Tell you what?"

"Why you're following me."

"I'm running."

"And stretching," I added, helpfully.

"Indeed."

This poor communication was getting me nowhere.

"Okay. Have you been ordered to run with me?"

"They order me to run all the time. I'm in the armed forces, after all."

"But are you though?"

"Am I what?"

"Armed."

"Not at the moment. I'm out for a run. I don't want to risk shooting off something I'd rather keep."

We started to walk around the path.

"Right, we're getting somewhere," I said confidently.

"We are?"

"You're not armed, so you don't think I'm in danger, and you're not here to kill me."

"Excuse me...I'm a little offended now."

"Offended? Why?"

"On two counts. One: that you thought I might have been planning to kill you. I mean, that's just rude. And two: that you assume I couldn't kill you without a weapon. That's pretty insulting to a soldier."

"I apologise for offending your ethics and your professional capabilities."

"Accepted."

"All of which leaves us with only one remaining reason for you following me."

"Which we've established I'm not doing because, as I've explained, I'm just out for a run."

"Oh. Okay then."

I started to pick up the pace.

"Hang on," he called.

I smiled to myself and turned back. "Yes?"

"What's the one remaining reason?"

"You weren't entirely honest, saying that you don't have a weapon, were you?"

"I'm a very honest person."

"Ahh, I see. So how about if I ask if, hypothetically, there might be occasions when you have about your person some medical paraphernalia."

He smiled and chuckled softly. "Maybe, hypothetically."

"They're worried I might have some kind of fit and take

out every electromagnetic device in a fifty-mile radius, aren't they? So you're following me with a hypothetical hypodermic needle in your pocket to put me out of mischief."

"Or a hypothetical tranquilliser gun."

"A *what*? In what way is a tranquilliser gun a piece of medical paraphernalia and not a weapon?"

"In a veterinarian way, hypothetically speaking. But you never heard it from me."

"Well, I didn't. So, what's your name, soldier?"

"Jason."

"Nice to meet you, Jason. Have I got you all day?"

"Pretty much."

"The "running" story would have worn a little thin after a while."

"I hadn't thought that far ahead," Jason admitted.

"Well, let's finish this run. Then I'm going for a shower, after which I'll be going to find the Fader 101 class."

"Don't miss your breakfast. It's the most important meal of the day."

I ran upstairs to the dorm room and headed for the shower. Orla was reading a magazine on her bed. I was pretty sure she'd read it from cover to cover about fifty times. I was pretty sure I'd read it that many times too. As I showered, I mulled things over.

Jason's words had made sense. Dr Narayan had asked me if I would consider moving to another building to make "mishaps more containable". I'd said no. I had new friends, and I was a little frightened of the idea of being isolated. I was also scared that one of these turns would result in me hurting someone. If the price were Jason dropping me like a charging rhino, then I would have to pay it.

Something else occurred to me. If Jason and his pals were covering the outside, who was covering the dorm?

I walked out of the bathroom and Orla was still lounging with her head in that magazine.

"Have you got a tranquilliser gun too?" I asked.

She looked up, and after a beat, she smiled. "Holy feck, no! I have a little hypodermic. Zozo and I have been practising a "sticking and catching" routine, so you don't bang yer crazy head."

"Why didn't you say? You could have practised with me."

"The sweet old Indian doctor with the bald head said we shouldn't tell you because it might cause you to stress and mess up his fancy statistical charts. I said you'd figure it out in less than a week, and it's been just over an hour. You're a gas."

"Have you met Jason?"

"Jason? Oh yes. He's a couple of years older than us. All the girls know Jason. We all swoon as he walks past; you'll have to get in line."

"He is fit," I said.

"Don't be saying that in front of Marcus, he'll be crushed."

"Marcus has got no need to worry. He's fitter, and huge. Have you seen those abs? How does a human get abs like that at sixteen? Plus, he's got the dimples."

"I know. When Marcus smiles, it's like everything's going to be okay. He'd be perfect if it weren't for his personality."

"What's wrong with his personality?"

"He's too much of a joker. It drives me crazy. I can only take so much of him."

"Isn't there any guy that you like here?" I asked.

"Not really. I know I'm moving away, so it's best not to start anything, I suppose. Your man Jason is fine, though. Very nice to look at from behind as he jogged off after you this morning."

We laughed.

"When are you going to your class?" asked Orla.

"Now. Do you want to show me where it is?"

"Why not? Zoe's off with Nathan doing God knows what, and if I look at this magazine one more time, I'll set it on fire. Hey, maybe you can set it on fire with your scary mind." She waved the dog-eared pages in front of my face. "Go on, burn it! Burn it!"

I looked at her.

"You're almost there. You've arched an eyebrow – is that how it starts?"

"That's how getting annoyed starts."

"Okay, let's leave it there for now. Rome wasn't built in a day."

She threw the magazine down on her bed and turned back to me.

"What's it like, though? This thing that happens," she asked.

I sat in Dad's chair with its sign still on the back. "It's like something that gathers inside me when I'm upset or stressed. Sometimes it leaks out in little bits, but other times, if I'm frightened or furious, it just blows like I can't hold it in."

11

My first class was excruciating. It was officially still in the holidays, but the Academy ran this class every week throughout the year for the newly awakened kids. I sat at the back of what was basically a Year Seven class. The desk was too small, so I sat in a chair in the aisle.

It was a small group. There were only eight kids plus me in the large classroom.

The teacher stood at the front and asked, "Who knows what Faders are?"

Eight hands flew into the air. The teacher picked one.

The chosen girl said, "Creatures of unknown origin," like she was reading it from a book.

"Correct, Becky. How long can Faders remain in human shape?"

Again, all hands went in the air.

"As long as they want."

"Correct. Indefinitely."

I raised my hand.

"Yes, Jenna?"

All the children swivelled in their seats to stare at me, which was mortifying.

"Do they ever take the shape of other things? Animals? Like dogs?" I asked.

The children sniggered behind their hands. Once again, all hands went up.

"The Faders never take the shape of lower species," said a boy.

"Because?" the teacher asked him.

Hesitantly, he said, "Is it because there wouldn't be a reason to do it? No benefit?"

"Wrong, Ben." The teacher picked another hand.

"The Fader's brain mimics the brain of the shape they have assumed. If they became a dog or a bird or a worm, they wouldn't have the mental capacity to change themselves back again."

"Jenna, you're very new to this," said the teacher. "Do you have any questions for the class? You can all consider this a test. We'll see what you've learned from your families."

"A test on the first day? That's harsh," I said to the teacher. The children giggled.

"Okay," I turned to the kids, "is there anything they can't fade through, like lead or something?"

"No material has been discovered that Faders can't fade through."

"They look like particles of yellow paint in the air when you blink in. Could a breeze blow them apart?"

"When they are faded, they are not affected by wind or water or fire."

"Or vacuum cleaners," said a girl at the front.

"Why don't they float down into the ground to get away?"

The children just looked at each other.

"There are theories about that, but no one knows," said the teacher.

"What happens to them when you catch them?"

"They are kept in suspended animation. So they can't hurt anyone."

The teacher looked uncomfortable at this point and took back his class with a change of direction.

"How many of you were born to two Tracker parents?"

All eight hands shot up.

"So, just one with a single Tracker parent," he said, looking at me.

On my left, a few seats away a boy whispered, "Mudblood!"

I looked at him, stony-faced. "Really? What are you, twelve?"

He looked straight back at me. "Yes."

I remained quiet for the rest of the period. Orla appeared near the end and sat at the back with me. Zoe and Nathan were waiting outside when we left the classroom.

"How'd it go?" asked Zoe.

"After the kids had gone, I spoke to the teacher. I asked if I could not train with a class of eleven-year-olds. He said I was childish and he wasn't impressed with my attitude."

"Then Jenna added that she would be happy to train with them, but she didn't want to risk the safety of the children when she inadvertently blew in all the windows from pure frustration," added Orla. "He was a bit of an arse about it, but couldn't take the risk of a shockwave in his class."

"You're becoming an urban myth on the campus," said Zoe. "So he didn't need any further persuading?"

"He's printed out the whole term of class notes on 101, and I've still got to complete my homework," I said. "So I'm off the hook."

"Now you've got the lesson plan, we'll work through it with you," said Nathan.

"I'll help," said a voice from a little way off behind us. I turned to find Jason sitting on a bench. "It's mostly meditation and tai-chi. We can get you up to speed."

"Thanks," I said. "We're heading for breakfast now, what with it being the most important meal of the day. Orla's got me covered if you've got anything else you need to do."

"Great, I still haven't showered since our run this morning. I can meet you at eleven in the studio over the gym. That'll give you an hour to digest your breakfast before we start."

"Perfect," said Orla. "We'll see you then." She turned around and started off towards the canteen. Jason watched her walking away, then saw me watching him. He blushed and turned away.

"It's nice of him to help you, isn't it?" said Orla.

"I don't think he's doing it for me," I said pointedly.

"Get away!" she said. "Well, it doesn't matter. He's a lovely lad, and he's fine to look at, but that's all."

MARCUS CAME ALONG to the dance studio at the gym where I learned breathing exercises and movements that were supposed to distribute energy around my body. I felt stupid at first as Jason led us in the exercises, but when I looked around, the others seemed really into it. So I relaxed and went with the flow.

For the rest of the holidays, we met up when the studio wasn't being used and worked on the exercises, adding a couple of new ones every day. Whenever we had to partner up, I was always with Marcus. I think he was a little jealous of Jason, and was certainly annoyed that he was around so much, but I thought that was sweet. I couldn't get the hang of meditating, and every time we attempted it, I just fell asleep and awoke a minute later with everyone looking at me and chuckling.

One disconcerting thing I noticed was Tiffany. I saw her all over the place, either staring at Marcus or staring at me. She kept her distance, but she was always watching. We'd be walking out of a building, and I would know exactly where she was, based solely on where the hairs were standing up on my neck.

I mentioned it to Helen, who just explained that Tiffany was very unwell and was "working through some issues".

AFTER A WEEK, the exercises began to include instructions to blink into the Sight. Everyone else would blink, and so would I, but it just wouldn't come for me. My first sort of success came when Marcus brought his Bluetooth speaker along, insisting that as I hadn't had any incidents for a while, it would be safe to have his iPod in the same room as me. He thought that listening to Enya would help me focus. After about ten minutes, I was finding it annoying and wanted it to stop. I glanced around at the stupid thing and was just about to ask Marcus to turn it off when it made a popping noise and stopped.

Everyone looked at me while Jason and Orla's hands strayed to their pockets.

"Oh nuts! My iPod," said Marcus. I felt dejected. He pulled the iPod out of his pocket and said, "Hey, it's still working. You didn't fry it."

"Did anyone see the lights flicker?" asked Zoe.

They all shook their heads.

"Well done, Grasshopper," said Nate.

"I don't understand."

They were smiling, even Marcus with the busted speaker.

"It looks like you focused on the speaker. It's usually random, isn't it?" asked Jason.

"Oh, I see. I should tell Dr Narayan, I suppose. I'm sorry about your speaker, Marcus."

"Are you kidding? Don't worry about it." He enveloped me in a massive bear hug and lifted me off the ground. Dropping me down, he added, "But next time, if you don't like my taste in music, just tell me."

DR NARAYAN SET up a lab in a separate building and I spent the next few days there, trying to recreate the effect. It brought more frustration, and with that came the flickering bulbs as I'd blink in and out without intending it. The only other positive result was that I was once able to make a light bulb flicker intentionally, but I still couldn't blink into the Sight. That didn't seem to bother the Doctor, but it frustrated the hell out of me.

I sat with my friends for lunch and dinner, and we'd talk about what we wanted to do with our lives. Orla was passionate about horses and wanted to be a vet. Nathan wanted to be a personal fitness trainer, and Zoe said, "I'm not sure, maybe a stripper."

Nathan choked on his sandwich.

"What does the syllabus look like for that?" asked Marcus. "Do you need to practise in front of an audience?"

"Oy!" said Nathan, punching Marcus in the arm.

"Honestly," said Zoe, "I don't really know what I want to do for a job. I'm hoping to study Fine Arts. I like art."

They all seemed like such normal pursuits. I had signed

up to take the same classes as I'd been going to do at my last school, but all I could think about was learning to kill monsters.

DURING THE LAST week of the holidays, I awoke on a cloudy Wednesday to find our bedroom floor littered with envelopes. There must have been about fifty of them. I sat up and stared at them, wondering what they were. Had they been stored above a cupboard and fallen? Did Orla drop them?

I looked across at Orla, who was lying awake and staring at me. She sat up and said, "Happy Birthday, Jenna. I know it won't be the sixteenth birthday you expected to have, but I hope we can make it a good one."

Her arm shot out and in it was a big pink envelope. "You'll be opening mine first, of course. Hang on! Don't get up, I've got breakfast in bed for you."

She ran to her wardrobe and pulled out a shopping bag containing ten bags of strawberry laces, my all-time favourite sweeties.

"Aww! You bought me a diabetic coma. You shouldn't have," I said.

"Well if you don't want them..." Orla started to withdraw the sweeties.

"Hold on, let's not be hasty." I snatched a bag from her hand and ripped it open. As I began knotting the laces end-to-end, Orla swept up and counted sixty-one cards from the floor and dumped them on my bed.

"What in the name of the wee man are you doing?" she asked.

"It's my strawberry lace ritual. I tie them all together and start eating at one end, and don't finish until I get to the other end. Look, no hands."

"Oh Holy God, it's Zozo all over again."

I left a few sweets in the bag for Orla and chewed while opening and reading my cards. I couldn't put most of the names to faces, but they all said such kind things, I felt my eyes stinging by the third card.

When I opened the fourth card, I said, "Oh wow! I've even got one from Tiffany."

"No way!" said Orla. "That's really..."

Her voice ground to a halt as I held up the card with a puppy on it. The puppy's eyes had been stabbed out.

Orla was livid. "I'm giving that to Helen."

"Don't worry about it," I said. "Look, it's not signed. There's no proof it was her."

"Except that we know it was because no one else would do something so messed up.."

"I'm not letting it spoil my day." I threw it in the bin and continued to open cards.

After all of the cards had been opened, Orla gave me a gift bag with a little box in it.

"Don't get too excited," she said. "It's only second hand, what with your record for rendering electrical devices inert."

I opened the box and found a little square iPod Nano.

"It's brilliant, thanks."

I hugged her and we set it up and linked it to my library. It was wonderful to have my songs back again. But she was right, I didn't know how long it would be before I fried my wonderful little gift.

"I'm going to miss you so much," I said.

"Why? Where are you going?" asked Orla.

"I'm not, you are. America, remember?"

"Oh that! I've put that off for a little while. They've said I can move mid-term." She waved her hand dismissively as though that were the end of the discussion.

"But, why?" I asked. "You're not staying for me, are you?"

"No, I'm staying for Marcus's really great jokes," she said. "Of course I'm staying for you. I want to make sure you're good and settled in before I go gallivanting off."

"Orla," I said, "that's so nice." I felt my chin start to wobble.

"Don't you dare cry on your birthday or I'll take all the knots out of your strawberry laces."

I found myself laughing and crying at the same time.

THE SCHOOL TERM STARTED, and all the students were back at the Academy. It amused me to see how many I recognised from my years of being watched.

We held Dad's funeral on the second day of the term. A lot of the students who had been away for six weeks hadn't even heard that he'd died. The cremation had already taken place, and a small wooden box stood on a table surrounded by candles and flowers at the front of the little Chapel. After the service with the Chaplain presiding, we scattered Dad's ashes in the garden, and I took comfort from knowing that he and Mum were together again.

12

Within a few weeks, the term was in full swing. Orla was dividing her time between her academic studies and an Animal Care placement at a vet's office in the town. Zoe was mostly making out with Nathan and ditching everything but her art classes. Nathan was taking his Sports Science and Nutrition courses a little more seriously than Zoe was taking hers. Marcus was finding his Anatomy classes quite tough, but he was keen to follow in his father's footsteps. He had us all bending this way and that as he practised instructing us in various exercises.

Poor Jason was following me around campus every day. He'd grown quite interested in the Computer Aided Design course I attended, and of course, he was very helpful in the self-defence and tai-chi classes, but he was bored by everything else. He didn't do anything else as his current assignment was me.

While I was on the base all day, every day, the others spent several hours a week being driven to various locations for spotting. One day in the middle of October, a week before Orla was due to fly to New York, as she and Zoe prepared to leave on a spotting assignment, I decided I just couldn't bear being stuck at the Academy any longer.

I wandered out of the building and found Marcus.

"At least you're still around," I said.

"Actually, I'm going spotting soon."

"You're kidding! I'm going out of my mind here."

He looked back and saw Jason following at a discreet distance. "Well, you've always got your shadow with you. I don't like the way he looks at you."

"What? He doesn't look at me in any way that I can see. You imagine things."

"I just don't see why he should be following you if I'm around. I can look after you."

This wasn't going the way I'd hoped. I wanted sympathy, not jealous petulance. It annoyed me even more. I felt peevish and frustrated.

I turned to Marcus and said, "Oh, Marcus, grow up," then stormed into my dorm and up to the room I shared with Orla.

"I'm going crazy here," I said through gritted teeth. "Every day, it's the same. Meditating, running, tai-bloody-chi. Why isn't anything working?"

Pacing the room, I spun and caught Zoe and Orla sharing a martyred expression.

"Really?" I asked.

"It takes time," said Zoe. "It's only been a couple of months."

"It's nearly three months and it's not like I haven't managed it."

"You're supposed to be learning to control the Sight," said Orla. "I don't think you can call it a win when it pops out of nowhere in the middle of a rage."

"But at least you know it's still there," added Zoe quickly.

I dropped down on to my bed and placed my head in my hands. "It's this place, you know? It's making me feel claustrophobic."

"Look, we'll bring you some magazines back from town," said Orla. "How about *Heat*? We can gossip about what the reality stars are nearly wearing."

"Why can't I just come to town?" I whined. "It's not fair!"

"We have to go spotting. It's only half a day," said Zoe. "I'll bring something back for you, something fun. Ooh! How about a bath bomb and a bottle of fake tan? We can have a girls" night."

I flopped down on to my back, pulled the pillow over my head and swore liberally into it.

"WOW!" said Zoe. "I don't think I've ever heard a girl say that one before."

"Yes, and there are some surprisingly creative combinations in there too. We'll be back before you know it," said Orla, pushing Zoe out of the room and hastily following.

I wanted to scream, but I knew it was pointless. Getting myself worked up was just going to make me blow again, and I was already pretty unpopular on the campus. I'd knocked the power out and messed up the TV signal so many times now, it wasn't funny.

I sat up at a knock on the window. It was Marcus looking desperate. I opened it so he could climb in.

"You're going to get yourself killed doing that."

"You're a funny colour. Should I go? I don't want you blowing me back out of the window."

"And you're hilarious," I said. "No, really. You should sell tickets."

He climbed in.

"I'm sorry for being stupid over Jason," he said. "But you already looked upset earlier. What's up?"

I sighed. "What's not up? My training is a joke. I'm stuck on my own because everyone's gone into town. Oh, what I wouldn't give to go into town."

"Well, if it's a trip to the shops you want, I might be able to help you." He raised his eyebrows theatrically.

"Go on," I encouraged him.

"Everyone who's going to town is going into a briefing now. In fact, I should be there myself. As far as I can tell, no one is watching the bus."

"You're kidding," I said. "Wouldn't I get shot or something?"

"You can be sincerely apologetic afterwards," he said. "And squeezing a tear out might help."

My trainers were on almost before he had finished the sentence.

I paused. "I'm not climbing out of that window."

"Why on earth would you do that?" He looked perplexed. "I recommend taking the stairs."

We headed down the stairs and walked to the bus parked at the end of the administration building. No one was guarding it.

"Where's the driver?" I asked.

"He'll be in the briefing. I think you should hide under the seats at the back."

"Where are you going?"

"I'm going to the briefing I'm late for," he said with a wink and a dimpled smile. That smile made something, not unpleasant, move inside me, and I smiled as I crawled into the darkness of my hiding space.

As I lay on the floor of the silent bus, my nose started to itch. It really was dusty under the seats. Wondering if there might be spiders and instantly wishing that thought hadn't occurred to me, I began to rethink my impetuous action. Just as I concluded that I was an idiot who needed to get the hell off this bus, the door opened and people piled on.

I heard Marcus call out, "I call the back seat. Come on, Nate!" and feet thundered towards me. Marcus sat above me, and of course, Nate, Orla, and Zoe sat with him. It wasn't a full bus load, and most of the others stayed close to the front.

The bus started up and began to move.

"I feel awful leaving Jenna," said Zoe.

"You could say," said Marcus, "that in a way, she's here with us. In our hearts, I mean."

I almost giggled.

"Marcus, have you hit your head or something?" said Nate.

"She was so upset," said Orla. "They should have let one of us stay with her. Helen was going to look in on her as Jason can't go into the girls" dorm. Maybe that"ll cheer her up."

"Really?" said Marcus. "Oh, I didn't know that."

I could hear a loaded silence above me.

"Marcus, what have you done?" asked Orla.

Marcus lowered his voice. "Jenna's sort of...under the seat."

I chanced a peek out. Orla had hidden her eyes behind a face-palm. Zoe was looking right at me with a huge smile on her face.

"I saw nothing," she whispered.

"This is not so good," muttered Orla as she shook her head. She refused to look at me while Zoe gave me a discrete double thumbs-up.

"I assume," said Orla to Marcus, "that you've worked this out with military precision."

"Of course," said Marcus, somehow managing to sound offended, given the half-arsed way we'd thrown this plan together.

"So she knows how long we'll be there and what time to get back to the bus."

"Oh," said Marcus, "that kind of military precision."

Orla face-palmed again then looked down at me. "We're here for three hours. Back at the bus by sixteen hundred hours. God knows how you're going to get off and on the bus without someone seeing you. I hope you make the most of it because we're probably going to be under dorm arrest for the rest of the year."

I began to feel guilty. I had no right to put my friends in this position; I just hadn't thought the whole thing through. Even so, I was damn well going to make the most of it. I had some cash and the prepaid credit card that Dad had given me for the holidays, which I knew still had a couple of hundred pounds on it.

The bus parked up behind the market square, and everyone began to get off.

Marcus whispered, "Wait for me."

Five minutes later, the door opened, and Marcus called from the other end of the bus, "Freeeeeedommmm," which would have had Mel Gibson glowing with pride.

I rolled out from under the seat, wiped the dust off my jeans and ran down to the door. "Where's the driver?" I asked.

"He's queuing at the pie shop. There are spotters every-where, so you'll probably get caught. Make it count." With that, he removed his baseball cap and plopped it on my head. He turned away, but I reached out impulsively and held on to his jacket.

"I'm sorry I was so bitchy earlier," I said.

"That's okay. I'm sorry I was jealous."

I put my hand on his neck and kissed him. I'd never kissed a boy before and I pulled back to see if I'd had a positive reaction. Marcus was scarlet and grinning. He winked at me, turned and walked away. It seemed to have gone well.

I headed straight for the coffee shop around the corner, bought a caramel latte to go and wandered through the pedestrianised shopping area. I'd almost forgotten there was a normal world out there. Armed with the pre-paid card, I went into a clothes shop and spent an hour choosing tops, jeans, underwear, and pyjamas. I appreciated the clothes other people had given me, but I wanted my own stuff. I would have loved to have got my hair cut, but I knew there wasn't going to be time. Spotters had glanced at me several times, and I'd just ignored it. I wandered around, trying to look like I was supposed to be there, hoping that most of them, if not all, might be unaware that I shouldn't have been.

After putting a huge dent in the card, I left the shop and headed for the nearest bookshop. I'd read everything in sight at the Academy, except the books on grief that Helen had given me. They sat untouched on a shelf in my cupboard. I'd been reading sci-fi and biographies of sports stars, and even, God help me, some romance novels.

I picked up some crime fiction books and the whole set of *Harry Potter*. As I stood waiting to pay, I could see down the road a lot of activity at the clothes shop I'd just left. Two men in jeans, who I guessed were probably Agency guys, were talking to the Spotters, and they were pointing up in the vague direction of where they'd seen me walk. It looked like the gig was up.

I put my card in the reader and entered my PIN. The assistant bagged up my heavy haul and suggested I invest in an e-book reader. I was just about to walk through the exit door when a movement in the window of the charity shop directly opposite drew my attention. Under a mess of wavy hair, a pair of hazel eyes gazed back at me from a serious face.

I ground to a halt and reversed back into the bookshop. He was in a tricky situation – if he walked out of the charity shop, he could be spotted ten times over.

As I watched, he vanished before my eyes. I'd never seen anything like it. I blinked several times, thinking, Work, damn you, work. Nothing!

I should have gone straight out of the front door, but I was now close to the back of the shop. Could he be in the bookshop by now? How fast can they move when they fade? The shopping centre was in a horseshoe shape, so he could have run around the inside of the stores and come through the side wall, avoiding going outside completely. He could be right next to me and I wouldn't know. I looked around frantically, feeling impotent.

As I backed up further, I bumped into someone. Before I could turn around, a man's hand came to my mouth, and I was dragged through the back of the shop into a storage area and out of a metal door in a matter of seconds. The man tossed me into a black Range Rover which tore away immediately down the service road behind the shops and out into the road. Rather than the soldiers I had grown used to over the last few weeks, these men were in black. One wore a dark suit, and the other two wore black chinos with black crew neck sweaters. They looked like Agency, but I couldn't be sure. I wasn't at all certain whose side these men were on.

"Keep her head down," ordered a man I couldn't see in the passenger seat.

A radio chirped, and with relief, I recognised General Cavendish's voice. "The subject has been spotted in the vicinity of the High Street. Do you have the girl?"

"No!" I cried. "He was in the charity shop. It was the boy who killed my dad. He was across the street; he faded. I think he came into the bookshop."

The men ignored me. "We have her," one responded, and they drove on.

"You have to go back. The Fader was there. We could kill him. *I* could kill him." By now I was hysterical, and they still wouldn't let me sit up. The interior light started to flicker, the radio hissed, and the alarm on the car wailed. Everything turned monochrome. *Now* it works, I thought.

"Oh no you don't," said one of the men. He pulled out a hypodermic needle and stuck it in my neck.

I CAME ROUND on a couch in the reception area of the Academy. My head was throbbing and my mouth was dry. Helen was sitting in the chair opposite me.

"Ahh! You're awake." She didn't sound as friendly as before. "Follow me. You should probably see how much trouble you've got your friends into."

When I reached the Principal's office, Orla, Zoe, Nate, and Marcus were all sitting outside. I was frogmarched straight inside.

"Sit," barked Professor Abbott.

"Why are they all out there? They had nothing to do with this," I said.

"So you did all this yourself, did you?" he asked through gritted teeth.

"Yes. I was frustrated at being stuck here. I went for a walk, and the bus was just sitting there with no one watching it. I hid under the bench at the back, waited a couple of minutes until everyone had gone and left." I added, "Lots of Spotters saw me, but I don't think any of them knew I wasn't supposed to be there."

That was enough. No need to embellish.

"I see," said the Professor. "Jennifer, you put yourself and your friends in a lot of danger today."

"I know." I felt so ashamed, but I was still angry that the Agency hadn't caught the Fader. "But all those Spotters. Why didn't anyone get him?"

"We have to be careful in public. You know that. There would be global panic if the general public were to learn of the existence of Faders."

"I'm just saying, we could have got him."

"Or he could have got you. I'm just saying," he countered, mimicking my tone. "Jennifer, this isn't the first sighting of him."

"It's not?" I was dumbfounded.

"We believe he's been in the area for months, since the explosion. We think he's still after you. We don't know why for sure, but we suspect that as he was there when you awakened, he knows there's something special about you. I think you've got them nervous."

"Can't you use me to draw him out?" I was instantly excited. This plan seemed perfect.

"As bait? In a word, no! We want to keep you safe, Jennifer, we owe that to your father. We're moving you to another Academy."

"What? No. That's not fair." I couldn't believe this. How

many times were they going to move me around? How many friends was I going to lose?

"I'm sorry. We have started making arrangements, and it's not up for debate. We had already been considering moving you within the next few weeks, but after today, you'll be going by the end of the week."

I was stunned and sat there, feeling deflated. I didn't have it in me to argue.

"If that's all," I said, getting up, "the others had nothing to do with today."

"For the sake of expediency, I'll accept your version of events."

"Where am I going?" My voice sounded small and pathetic, even to me.

"You'll be joining our Academy in Colorado."

I left the room. I wanted to tell my friends they were off the hook, but I felt so dejected, I couldn't even raise my eyes to meet theirs as I walked away.

When I got back to the dorm, I was surprised to find my shopping bags in the room. They just didn't seem worth the heartache any more. I threw myself on to my bed and cried.

After about half an hour, I heard a click. I turned to the door to see Orla staring at me.

"Jenna," she said, "you should start sorting your stuff out. You'll need to do some laundry before you leave."

"Did you get into trouble?" I asked.

"Of course not. Apparently, we didn't know anything about it, so why would we be in trouble?"

"Oh good. Well, at least that's something."

I opened my wardrobe, took out my laundry bag and filled it, keeping my back turned. I felt so hurt, but I didn't want Orla to see it on my face. It took me a few minutes to realise that I wasn't the only person opening and closing drawers. Orla was also putting stuff into a laundry bag. For a moment, I was confused, but then I remembered that she was due to be moving to New York at the end of the week.

"Are you going to New York now?"

"No. I've told the Academy I don't want to go there any more."

I realised she must be moving up to the penthouse. There would be no reason for her to stay on the third floor now.

"Do you want some help moving your stuff upstairs?"

"Upstairs? What on earth makes you think I'm going upstairs?"

Just then, the door burst open and Zoe staggered in with a full laundry bag, followed by Marcus with the poorest excuse for a John Wayne imitation I'd ever heard.

"Who's ready for Colorado then?"

I burst into tears. Orla handed me the tissue box.

"Don't get too emotional," said Marcus. "You'll bust my iPod and I'll have nothing to listen to on the plane."

I threw the tissue box at him.

"I'm putting this stuff in a washing machine, then I'm going for a bath," said Zoe, and left.

"I could do with a long soak," I sighed. "Those sedatives make me feel like I've been hit by a truck."

Marcus produced a key card. "This might help."

"And just where did you get a girls" block key card?" asked Orla.

"It was Tiff's spare key. She's in the med-block permanently now. Her room's empty." He waved the card in front of my face. "And so is that lovely big bathtub."

"Marcus!" said Orla. "You shouldn't have that. Also, you're a genius."

As Marcus put the card in my hand, Orla ducked into our bathroom and came out with a towel and a bottle.

"Bubbles," she announced, dropping the bottle in my hand. "I'll get the laundry done. You get a spa treat." She turned to Marcus. "And you get out."

"I'm going, I'm going. I can't be gossiping with a bunch of chicks all day. I've got my own manly laundry to do, you know."

He leaped out of range of Orla's boot and disappeared down the corridor.

13

I let myself into Tiffany's old room which was now empty of personal possessions. I was exhausted, and I had the mother of all headaches.

Leaving the bathroom light off, using just the light from the main room, I ran a bath, squirted in some bubble bath, put soft music on my iPod, plugged in my earbuds, and climbed in. I lay back with my head cradled in my hands and a hot flannel over my face, trying not to keep seeing his face through the bookshop window. As I thought about Dad and the fun things we did together, I dozed off.

I CALLED *from the living room, "There's nothing to eat, and I'm starving."*

Dad was in the kitchen. I could hear him opening and closing cupboards. His head popped around the door.

"Do you want me to go shopping then?"

"Yes, please."

"Before I go, would you like beans on toast? Cheese on toast? A tuna sandwich? Or a bowl of soup?"

I rolled my eyes. "You know what I mean, there's nothing I'd make myself."

"What would you make yourself?" he asked.

"Cheetos," I said.

"So what you mean is "We're out of Cheetos"."

"Well, yes."

Dad shook his head and sighed.

A HAND GRIPPED my face over the flannel and forced my head under the water. My hands flew out to claw at my attacker, but my arms were forced down against the back of the bath by the weight of someone's body. I bucked and thrashed my legs, levering the bottom half of my body out of the bath using the taps. My feet were kicked off the taps and back into the water.

He was here. He'd got in here and was finally going to succeed in killing me. My lungs were exploding, and I reflexively gulped for air but sucked in only water. Panic shot through my body, and I forced my legs out again. This time, when he kicked my legs, I hooked both of them around his foot and desperately tried to lever myself out of the water. Instead, my weight pulled him off balance and into the bath.

I got my head above the water. He grabbed at my face again, but only got the facecloth. It came away, and for a fraction of a second, before the lights in the bedroom, and probably the whole base, popped out, I found myself face-to-face with a monochrome Tiffany. Her face was enraged and insane. She grabbed my throat, trying to push me under and strangle me at the same time. I couldn't believe how strong she was. The last time I'd seen her, she'd looked as weak as a kitten.

Suddenly, the door burst open and torch lights flashed around the room. Tiffany was lifted off me and dragged away, screaming, by two uniformed men. I heard the sound of a tranquilliser gun and was relieved to know it wasn't me on the pointy end this time.

A third man put a towel around my shoulders as I hung over the edge of the bath, coughing and shaking. He lifted me from the bath and plonked me on to the toilet seat, ensuring I was covered by the towel.

"Jenna, take breaths. Calm down, or they'll tranq you again." It was Jason. "Are you okay?"

I looked at him, opened my mouth to say yes and vomited soapy water all over his boots.

"Sorry about that," was all I could manage. I was calm now.

"Better out than in," he said, patting my arm.

Two medics entered the room. I was shivering. They put a blanket around me and helped me into the bedroom, sitting me on the bed. The medics were calm and methodical, shining a light into my eyes, taking my pulse.

"Can you tell us your name? Do you know where you are?"

"I know where I am. This place sucks," I said. "I'm only giving it one star on TripAdvisor." And I threw up again.

I knew they'd have taken Tiffany to the med-block, so I flat-out refused to go there. The medics patched up the scratch marks around my face and neck and gave the all-clear for me to go back to my room. Still wrapped in the towel and blanket, I clutched my bundle of clothes to my chest, and Jason, who had stayed outside the room while the medics checked me over, walked me down.

I noticed the lights were back on already. The Academy had developed strategies for dealing with me, and I knew

Orla kept a supply of lightbulbs in her cupboard. Our door was open, and I could hear Orla's voice as I walked towards it.

"Marcus, I told you, when I know something, you'll know. Okay? Don't try to come over. There are uniforms everywhere."

I walked in, and Orla spun around with the phone still at her ear. One look at the pity in her face and I burst into tears.

"She's here. She's fine. I'll call you back."

I could hear Marcus's voice coming out of the phone. "I can hear her cry..." he was saying as she disconnected.

She threw the phone on her bed and enveloped me in a huge hug. "You're okay, Jenna. I've got you."

The door clicked behind us, and Orla just held me as I cried.

"This day has sucked, so much," I said.

"Ah, come on, you got new clothes and ten new books," said Orla. "So it only mostly sucks."

I went into the bathroom to change into my pyjamas, and when I came out, Zoe and Orla were both there with three mugs of tea. I told them everything that had happened.

"I thought it was him," I snorted. "I was somehow less frightened but more annoyed when I realised I was going to be murdered by Tiffany. I mean, who gets murdered by someone called "Tiffany", for God's sake?"

There was a knock at the door and Zoe got up to answer it. Helen popped her head in.

"I wanted to be sure you're alright."

"I'm fine. A bit shaken up. I don't want to think about what might have happened if the Agents hadn't come in," I said. "How did they get there so fast?"

"I've just been speaking to the General. He told me Tiffany tripped an alarm on the fire exit."

Zoe held up her mug. "To Health and Safety."

Orla and I clinked mugs with Zoe. "Health and Safety."

Helen looked at me and smiled. "You're so resilient. Your dad would be so proud of you. Come and see me tomorrow." And she left.

"I guess I should call Marcus before he tries to kill himself scaling the walls," I said. "Does anyone have a phone that works? Oh, and I no longer have music."

"Oh dear," said Orla, "did you fry your iPod?"

"Actually, just for variety, this one drowned."

"I need to get my laundry out of the machine," said Zoe.

"You and your stress related laundry activities," said Orla. "I'll help. Unless you want me to stay, Jenna?"

"No, I'll be okay."

"Here, use my phone," said Orla, reaching up to the top of the wardrobe, "and keep a hold of this. It's like a comfort blanket."

It was a baseball bat.

"Thanks." I hefted the bat and did actually feel some comfort from it.

When Orla and Zoe had left the room, and I heard the door lock click into place, I called Marcus.

"Orla, I've been going nuts here," he said.

"It's me."

"Oh, thank God. Jason told me what happened. Jenna, I'm so sorry about this."

"It wasn't your fault."

"It feels like it was. Maybe if I'd let her down more gently, or never even gone out with her in the first place..."

"Marcus, please," I said, "don't blame yourself. I'm okay.

E. G. BATEMAN

If she hadn't set off an alarm on the fire exit, it might have been another story, but I'm alive."

"There's an alarm on the fire exit?" Marcus blew out air. "That's new. I didn't know they were doing that."

"Wasn't one there before?" I asked.

"No, that's how I got to your window before. I don't climb from the ground. I'm not bloody Spider-Man. I take the fire stairs to the top and shimmy down the drain. The only tricky bit is getting over to your window."

"Well, no more doing that," I said.

"Can you get out to see me?" he asked.

"Not tonight. I'm bruised and tired and still feeling a bit sick."

"I wish I could see you, just for a few seconds. I think you need a magical Marcus hug. Poor Bunny."

"Bunny?" I laughed.

"Yes, you remind me of one of those bunnies in the battery advert. You're unbeatable; you always bounce back."

"Well, I'm sorry. I don't even want to leave the room right now. I'll hop over and see you in the morning."

He laughed. "Okay. Take care, Bunny. I'm thinking of you."

What a weird day it had been, and to end it feeling giggly at being called a bunny.

14

L ater that night, Nathan crept quietly along the outside of the boys" dorm, hugging the wall, staying out of sight of the surveillance cameras. Although the guards had their Sight engaged for Faders, they could still catch him, and then they would have grounded him, especially with all the activities today.

When he was sure no one was around, he sprinted between buildings, and finally made for the aircraft hangers. He was sad that Zoe was leaving. They weren't serious, but they had fun. He liked her, and her sudden change in plans had been a bit of a shock. He was going to be without his almost-girlfriend and his best mate, but his parents lived locally, and they would never have been okay with him moving away.

He stopped at Hangar C to check for guards. He was due to meet Zoe at their usual place: Hanger A. They would sit on a pile of sandbags in the corner of the hanger and make out or just talk.

He heard a shuffle behind him. Expecting to see a

Guard, he turned with a suitably contrite expression on his face.

ZOE SAT on the pile of sandbags, waiting for Nathan. She felt bad about leaving so suddenly. Thinking about the life she was leaving behind, she wondered if anything might have become of her and Nathan's relationship. She didn't think so.

She checked the time on her phone. He was pushing it. The mobile patrols would be checking out the hangers in twenty minutes. She waited another fifteen minutes and decided that was enough. He was probably sulking about being left behind. Hopping down from the sandbags, she crept out and headed back towards the girls" dorm.

Had she looked back and blinked in, she might have seen a yellow mist coalescing into the shape of a boy creeping away into the night.

NATHAN'S EYES STARED UP, unseeing, into the stars as he lay in a forming pool of blood.

15

Dad was banging on the window. He looked terrified as our eyes met through the glass. I opened my mouth to call to him to get out of the house, but darkness exploded into light.

I SHOT UP IN BED, confused. Three men in black with weapons had burst into our room. I looked over at Orla, who seemed as confused as I was. I heard the compression and felt a pain in my neck, and through the terror, I shouted out my overriding thought.

"Really? Again?"

I sank back once more into darkness.

When I woke up again, my head was thumping. I reached back to feel a small lump and gauze at the base of my head. Dr Narayan was sitting on the edge of the bed, telling me not to touch it.

"I'm sorry, Jenna, I had to insert an inhibitor. The guards have told me you have ten minutes to get your belongings into a kit bag."

"What?" I was still dizzy from the dart they'd shot into my neck.

Orla came in from the bathroom. "It's just gone 2 am. I've put all our stuff into bags. You've been out for about twenty minutes. I don't know what's going on, but we have to move."

We were escorted down to the airstrip. I touched the back of my head and glared at Dr Narayan. Feeling violated, I wanted to thump the kind little Indian man.

"If you have a turn during the flight, the plane could crash," he said. I had to give him that one. I had been making progress, but, to be honest, even I wouldn't fly with me.

Agents bundled us into an old, noisy twin-engined death-trap and we flew from the base to Heathrow Airport. We were driven across the runways. No stopping; no dawdling; no airside duty-free shopping. We went straight to a gate which was blocked off to other travellers until we'd boarded a civilian flight at 10 am to Chicago.

On the bright side, we sat in First Class. The four of us and two Agency guys. But the mood was depressed. Security had been high during the whole process. I'd never seen so many soldiers and Agents around, and they looked edgy. None of the soldiers would speak to us. Even the ones Marcus knew well wouldn't explain why we had been woken and moved in the middle of the night. They just told us that they had brought forward the plans to transfer us.

Zoe was sulking because she hadn't been able to say goodbye to Nathan and slept through most of the Chicago flight. The only person who appeared the least bit happy was Marcus, who loved flying and was a geek about anything to do with aeroplanes. As I studied him from across the aisle while he read the leaflet containing the plane's technical data for about the tenth time, he looked positively blissed out. I smiled. He looked up, catching me smiling, and returned a huge dimple-popping grin.

I laughed, "Nerd!", shook my head and went back to my book.

"Are there vomit bags aboard this thing?" an Irish voice piped up beside me. "Because if I keep having to watch the two of you making googly eyes at each other, I'm going to puke."

"It's not like that," I whispered.

"Does he know that?" she whispered back.

"I don't know. I mean, it could be like that. Having Marcus around makes me feel relaxed. I guess I just don't know him well enough yet."

"Well, you'll have plenty of time to find out because he's travelling halfway around the world to keep you safe."

"I'm sure it's not that. It's a great adventure for him, and I think he has a religious experience just being on a plane."

"You might be right about that. He was delirious on that first heap of junk, staring at the propellers all the way to Heathrow."

"So was I. I thought they might fall off."

"You should have seen him when Professor Abbott said you were going to Colorado. He was the first to ask to come along. He demanded it. We just went along with it. We weren't going to be out-friended by the likes of him."

"Do you regret it? If you do, you've got to say. I'm sure they'll still let you go to New York."

"Ahh! Don't be daft. I don't regret a thing. As you say, we're going to have a great adventure in Colorado where we'll ride horses and do other grand American things like eating lobsters on sticks and doing the line dancing and..."

"Drive-by shootings?" added Zoe, still with her eyes closed.

"Maybe not in the first week, Zozo, but I applaud your efforts to embrace the American dream."

At Chicago, we transferred to a connecting flight to Colorado Springs. Marcus sat next to me and nodded off with his head on my shoulder. I didn't mind.

The travelling was taking its toll by the end of that flight. I stood in the doorway and felt my shoulders sag as I forced my exhausted body off the aircraft and down the steps. We arrived at nearly 6 pm local time. After saying goodbye to the Agency guys who had travelled with us, we climbed into a vaguely tank-like black car that was waiting near the plane.

"What is this thing?" I mused.

"It's as wide as it is long," Orla added.

"It's a Humvee," Marcus said as he climbed in next to me looking all curious and perky.

This time, I dropped my head on to his shoulder. I didn't think I'd ever felt so exhausted in my life.

"Ahh, would you look at the two of you," Orla cooed.

"Would you like me to take a picture to remember the moment?" said Zoe.

"Only if you want me to stuff your smartphone..."

"Keep your eyes open, you guys," said a voice from the driving seat.

Suitably chastised, Marcus, Orla, and Zoe blinked in and looked out of their respective windows. I felt useless, as usual, and just kept my eyes closed.

The car took us on the final half hour journey to the base, the location of the Colorado Academy and our home for the next few years. As the car pulled up, I sat up, feeling a little confused. Marcus jumped out and helped me out of the car.

"Where do you get your energy from?" I asked as the rest of us piled out and stood, gazing around.

"I'm manly and fit," he explained, then instantly his bright eyes took in his surroundings. "This place is huge."

"The old place could fit in here fifty times," added Zoe.

I just gawked like an imbecile. The landscape was vastly different to England. While the ground around us was dry and dusty, we were dwarfed by huge green mountains.

I readied myself to swing my kit bag on to my back, but it vanished mid-flight. A big, strapping, handsome soldier had appeared and swept it out of my hands.

"I'll take these up, ma'am," he said, smiling at my effort. "You need to head over to the Administration Building."

I turned to find Marcus scowling with a surly, grumpy face at the man. Zoe and Orla were also watching him, but there were no scowls on their faces. My girlfriends radiated pure admiration for the muscle-bound man who had picked up all four kit bags and was sauntering off as though he hadn't a care in the world.

"I'm finding this America place is beautiful, as are many of its contents," said Orla.

Zoe nodded her agreement.

I took Marcus's arm and we followed the driver towards the Administration Building. I expected the building to be almost empty as it was nearly 7 pm and already dark, but the office was a hive of activity. A soldier guided us to a glass-walled meeting room at the end of the open plan office. Some people glanced at us as we walked by, but most of them, with their noses in their laptops, appeared not to have noticed us.

We sat alone in the meeting room. Marcus reached into

the middle of the table for a bottle of water and began to fill four glasses.

"Yuk! Sparkling. Pretentious crap," he said.

"Chuck some over here, you'll hear no complaints from me," said Orla.

Then the chat petered out. We were all pretty tired.

A man in fatigues strode into the room and sat at the top of the table.

"I'm Major Tomowski. The kids here call me Major Tom, as you might expect. It's good to see you got here okay. Cavendish made the right call moving up your extraction since everything's gone to hell back at Hilltop."

"What do you mean?" asked Orla.

The Major paused. He apparently thought we knew something we didn't, and he seemed to be gauging how much to say now.

He sighed. "You had a Fader attack. Two of the students were killed, Nathan and Tiffany."

Zoe shrieked. Her hands flew up to her mouth. Orla was out of her seat in a second as she moved to comfort Zoe. Marcus froze with his eyes on the Major.

"Not Nate," Marcus whispered. "And Tiff? How?" He dropped his head into his hands.

I hadn't moved from my seat. I couldn't even work out how I felt about Tiffany. I knew Zoe had been seeing Nathan, but my mind flooded with scenes from the past weeks. Nate and Marcus, playing one-on-one basketball, Tops Trumps and Xbox games. I thought of them calling each other Brother. It broke my heart to know that Marcus had lost another important person in his life. His hand had balled into a fist in his lap. I reached across and covered it with my own. I could feel him shaking.

"Do they know who did it?" Marcus asked.

"A Fader," the Major repeated.

"Which one?" I asked. "Did they see it?"

"They didn't see it, just the usual signs. I didn't know they hadn't told you. I'm sorry. I guess they were concentrating on getting you out of there."

The office outside had gone quiet. I looked out to see the faces that had turned towards us, noticing a bearded man wearing an unbuttoned lab coat over chinos and a polo shirt standing awkwardly at the door, like he'd been in the process of coming in but now wasn't sure what to do. He wore an ID on his lab coat, but it was too far away to read.

"It's getting late, and I guess you need to settle in," said the Major. "I have to visit Capitol Hill so I won't be around for a few days."

He nodded to the man at the door who entered the room and stood with his hands in his coat pockets.

"Dr Philipson, thank you for waiting."

I looked again at the ID clipped to the man's lab coat. It said, "Dr S. Philipson. Director SciMed".

"No trouble at all. Is everything okay?" he asked, looking at Zoe, who was sitting with her head in her hands while Orla stroked her arm.

The Major said, "The kids were unaware of the events at Hilltop. Nathan Parker was their friend."

"I'm sorry for your loss," he said, looking at the middle of the table.

"This is Dr Philipson. He teaches at the Academy."

"Stuart Philipson. Everyone just calls me Doc," said the man, still standing.

I smiled briefly at him. He looked awkward. I felt sorry for him.

"Doctor, these kids need to get settled in, and Miss Banks here looks like she's gonna keel over with exhaustion."

He was right. It had been a long, sad day and I just wanted to sleep.

"Sure, I can help with that. If you'd like to follow me."

We filed out of the office, past the staff who were once again concentrating on their work and over to the accommodation block.

Dr Philipson sidled up to me awkwardly and said, "I was very sorry to hear about your father. We met several times when he came over here for projects and meetings. He was well respected."

I realised these projects and meetings must have been the "TED Conferences" Dad went to.

The accommodation here was set out similarly to Hilltop with the boys" and girls" blocks facing each other across a courtyard. Dr Philipson gave Marcus a key card and asked one of the security guards to show him to his room.

Marcus paused and turned to Zoe. "I'm sorry, Zozo."

She said, "I'm sorry for you, too. Let's talk tomorrow."

Marcus looked at me. He didn't seem to know what to say, so he covered the space between us and took me into a big hug. Then he stepped back, turned and marched away. I felt a lump in my throat, and my eyes stung as I watched him walk off alone.

We were moved straight into sixth form rooms, which were called the "Senior High" dorms in Colorado. Orla took the key card for her door, but went in with Zoe. I wanted to follow, but Orla said, "You're dead on your feet. Get some sleep."

She was right. I could feel myself swaying slightly with weakness. I gave them both a hug and went into my room.

The Faders had now murdered three people I knew. Even after Dad had died, after the Fader had tried to get me at the bookshop, I had felt somehow detached from the true, relentless horror of what these creatures were. I couldn't bring myself to think about it. All I could focus on was the bed.

I stumbled into it, fully dressed, and fell immediately into a deep sleep.

16

I woke up confused and checked the clock for the time. It was II pm. I felt fully rested and wondered if I had slept for an entire day. When I double-checked with my phone, I saw that only three hours had passed. I wondered if this was jet-lag; never having experienced it before, I was unsure. I figured I'd pay for it later.

More importantly, I was hungry. I went into the bathroom, washed my face, pocketed my key card and left the room. I paused by Zoe's door, hearing her sobbing quietly and Orla's soft whispers. Then I continued along the corridor, occasionally hearing quiet music in the rooms.

At the end of the hallway, I found a door ajar, the flickering light and sound of a TV coming from behind it. I walked in to find a girl sprawled across a sofa in the dark, watching *Glee*. She had long dark hair and dark-rimmed rectangular glasses. Glancing up at me, she frowned, not recognising me.

She blinked in and out, then smiled and said, "Hi."

"Hi," I said. "Erm...I'm looking for food. Please show me the direction to get food."

She laughed. "You're English? That's awesome! I'm Hannah."

"Jenna." I smiled.

"OK, Jenna. About face, and head through the door across the hall."

I turned around and walked into a room with a few tables, microwaves and vending machines. Inside the vending machines were sandwiches, tortilla wraps, burgers, and drinks. I immediately realised that I didn't have any US currency.

I pressed my forehead against the glass, about three inches from a bag of Cheetos, and sighed. "So near and yet so far."

"Key card," came a voice from behind me.

I turned and looked at Hannah. She was wearing, of all things, a pair of One Direction pyjamas. I suddenly felt like I wasn't so far from home and smiled again.

"You can use your key card to get the Cheetos. You don't have to smash through the glass with your face."

All business, I immediately got to work. Within a minute, I was sitting with a chicken tortilla wrap, a bottle of coke and the bag of Cheetos. I had hovered over the burger, but decided against it.

Hannah joined me at the table.

"I've got the *Glee* box set too," I said. "Well, I had it," I corrected myself after remembering the explosion.

Hannah chatted away about the show while I devoured the food. She reminded me of Gill, and I ached to speak to my best friend from my old life.

After I'd finished eating, I asked, "Where is everyone? It's pretty quiet around here."

"We're supposed to be in our rooms by twenty-two hundred, but I was monitoring the juniors. My shift just ended. I need to get to bed; the security guys will be around soon, and they don't seem to like *Glee*."

"Harsh!"

"I know, right?"

I threw my food wrappers into the bin, plugged my card into a machine and pulled out a bottle of chilled water. Then we made our way back along the hall. Zoe's room was now silent. Hannah's room was two doors down from mine, so we said goodnight and went into our rooms. This time, I showered and changed for bed.

I woke up briefly after an upsetting dream about Nathan, but went straight back to sleep when I realised I couldn't hear alarms or TVs on the fritz.

THE NEXT MORNING, I awoke to a knock at my door at nine-thirty. I had a vague awareness that there had been some noises earlier, but I had resolutely slept through whatever was going on. I left my room at around ten and found Orla and Zoe in the kitchen, drinking coffee and eating bagels from the vending machine. Zoe's eyes were puffy and red, but her hair was standing on end in full do-not-mess-with-me spikes.

"Dr Philipson has been around, and he's going to meet us downstairs at midday," said Orla. "And we met your friend, Hannah. She divulged the key card secret of the vending machines. Wonderful girl."

I glanced at Zoe who looked hollowed out. I wanted to say something, but Orla discreetly shook her head. As I joined them at the table, I absently poked at the slight lump on the back of my neck where Dr Narayan had injected the slow release hormone capsule.

"Don't fuss with it. It might get infected, and you'll have a big bag of pus hanging off the back of your head," Orla scolded.

"That's so disgusting," I said, getting up to fetch a bagel and drink from the machine.

"Just so you know," said Orla, "the tea's fecking rank."

WE MET Dr Philipson as arranged.

"Have you experienced any unusual activity since having the, erm..."

"If you mean, since Dr Narayan microchipped me like a puppy, then no, nothing," I said.

"It's not a microchip..."

"I know. It's a slow release hormone designed to combat the unwanted effects of being a freak."

"You calling me a freak, Banks?" said Marcus, walking up to us. "We've all got them, you know."

He looked like he hadn't slept. He gave Orla and me a brief hug and enveloped Zoe in his arms, but she pulled away.

"I'm okay," she said, her shoulders stiff.

"I'm not," said Marcus.

Zoe's shoulders dropped and she returned Marcus's embrace.

"All the weird activity has stopped," I said to Dr Philipson. "No more electronic equipment went on the junk pile last night."

"That's good news," said the Doc, but he did look a little disappointed. "I am still very interested in understanding more about your curious ability."

"Oh, that's easy," I said. "Next time you're with a group of good friends, just take all their mobile phones and smash them with a hammer and watch their faces fall. Then you'll understand."

I knew he would want to take the inhibitor out and continue with Dr Narayan's studies, but my only real motivation for playing ball on that had been to stay near Mum and Dad in the Garden of Remembrance.

"Doc, for now, I just want to fit in with the people around me, find some normality and wreak terrible vengeance upon the monsters that killed my dad and Nate.

The Doc took us to see the counsellor, Uber-Perky-Cassidy. We each spent half an hour with her. I expected her to want me to talk about Dad and Nate.

"I understand you've been on a path to study Environment and Design," she said.

"I'm thinking of joining the military," I said.

"Oh! That's not going to be possible straight away."

"Why not? They said it was an option at Hilltop."

"You're in the US now. You're here on a student visa. you'd need a Green Card to join the military." She could see my disappointment. "Can I make a suggestion?"

"Go on," I said. It was a good job they'd stuck this thing in my neck or the whole building would have been in a blackout.

"You will be spending a certain amount of time in physical activities every day anyway. We can include weapons and survival skills training in your curriculum. Your previous school reports say you excelled at Design. Keep that up for now. When you're going through big changes, it's healthy to stay in touch with something you're familiar with. Give yourself a chance to settle in."

It sounded reasonable. I nodded my agreement.

· · ·

I SPENT every day in physical activities: tai-chi, self-defence, weapons training, survival skills. Marcus was right there beside me. November went by in a blur as we trained and meditated together in the evenings.

When Orla wasn't out spotting, she worked on her Veterinarian studies and spent her spare time assisting the vet down at the stables with the horses.

Zoe became titanium. For a few weeks, Hannah was the only person she would let near her. It was understandable. Hannah was patient and empathetic, and seemed to have an instinct for knowing how to relate to Zoe when she was raging or seemed lost. I thought that might hurt Orla, but she could see that Hannah was good for Zoe and we made space for her in our little circle.

It was hard not to get caught up in the enthusiasm for Thanksgiving. The cafeteria on the base served a Thanksgiving turkey meal to those of us who didn't have family to visit. It was a testament to how much Hannah had become one of us that we were all a little sad that she had gone home.

My first Christmas without Dad was painful, and I knew that Marcus and Zoe would be missing Nathan terribly. Knowing that their daughter's new friends were far away from family or had no family at all, Hannah's parents, Mr and Mrs Deschene, invited us all to spend the holidays with them. They were both part Navajo and provided a beautiful mix of Christmas and Navajo traditions. Hannah's father held a healing ceremony which involved passing around and drinking a tea made from cactus. He said the ceremony was to heal our bereavement, not for those who had passed because they were on a great journey. I was so deeply touched and honoured by their understanding, something in me did feel at peace.

I finally had my breakthrough in January just after school began. I had been meditating with Marcus, and as usual, I had fallen asleep.

I woke up suddenly, feeling like I was in danger. My eyes snapped open and I gasped.

"Sorry," said Marcus, pulling his hand away.

"For what?" I asked.

"I don't know," he said. "I nodded off. I thought maybe my hand had strayed somewhere it shouldn't." He blushed.

"Something's not right." I jumped up too quickly and swayed a little. I shook it off and looked around the room.

"You must have been dreaming," he said.

"No. I don't know." I was sleepy and confused.

I blinked automatically, trying to blink in as I had tried a thousand times before, and it just happened. Everything was monochrome. I looked at Marcus. He was looking around us too. I blinked again, and he was back to normal.

I tried it again, and it worked.

"Oh my God!"

"What?" he said, looking at me. "We're safe. I've looked; I can't see anything."

I smiled a huge grin. "I know, neither can I."

"You blinked in? Are you kidding me? You did it?"

"Yes, you gorgeous monochrome man."

"Can you do it again?"

I tried again. I blinked in and out, perfectly. "Monochrome, colour, monochrome, colour."

Marcus leaped up and pulled me into him. I felt dizzy with excitement.

"Jenna, you little star! My clever Bunny!"

He hugged me, lifted me off the ground, held me in his arms and swung me around as my feet dangled in the air. I laughed like an idiot. When he put me down, I swayed again, still feeling like my head was in a fog. I realised I must have been in a deep sleep on the floor.

He caught me in his arms and said, "I'm going to kiss you. If that's a problem, you need to say so now."

"Well, about time!" I said.

He lowered his face to mine and kissed me for a full minute. He smelled like spicy citrus; I guessed it was a shower gel or deodorant. His face was a little scratchy, but I didn't mind.

Just as he had nearly taken my breath away, he pulled back.

"I need to tell Orla and Zoe," I said.

"That we kissed?"

I looked at him with an eyebrow raised.

"Oh right, yes, the other thing," he mumbled and blushed.

We had one more kiss outside the dorms, then he wandered off to the boys" block. I raced into the girls" dorm. It was just as well I'd gone back – I'd missed curfew by half an hour. It's a wonder the guards hadn't caught us.

I ran up to my floor and listened at Orla's door. Nothing. I put my ear to Zoe's door. Silence. How frustrating. I desperately wanted to tell someone.

As I walked along the dark corridor, I heard the sound of *Glee* in the TV room. Awesome, Hannah was still up. She'd do.

I walked in to find the room in darkness except for the light of the TV as usual. Hannah was there on the sofa as I'd hoped, but I hadn't expected to find Zoe lying on top of her, and both of them in a state of undress.

I looked at them, and they looked at me, and I couldn't tell who was more surprised. I tried to think of something to say that would distract us all from the mortification of the situation. All I could come up with was, "Marcus kissed me."

Zoe said, "Cool! About time! Hannah kissed me."

"Cool!" I said and went to bed.

THE NEXT MORNING, I awoke to the sound of banging on my door.

"Let us in, ya eejit," Orla called.

I leaped out of bed and opened the door. Orla, Zoe, and Hannah piled in and smothered me in a group hug.

"Marcus kissed you? Seriously? That was all you wanted to say?" said Hannah with a huge smile on her face.

"I found Marcus sitting outside the dorm like a puppy. He's been there since 6 am waiting for you. He told me you blinked in," said Zoe.

I looked at Zoe and Hannah. I didn't know what to say in front of Orla. "It was late, I didn't want to disturb you."

"Oh, I know about that now too," added Orla, looking at Zoe and Hannah. "A day for fecking surprises indeed."

Hannah was blushing, but Zoe just giggled. "Jenna, blink in," she said.

I had a momentary flutter of fear that it wouldn't work again. I deliberately closed my eyes, told my brain what I expected of it, then opened them again. My three mono-chrome friends stared back at me.

"Yep, still works," I said with relief.

"Okay," said Orla, "now get dressed and see the pining puppy outside."

The three of them hugged me again and piled out of the room. I went to a drawer, pulled out a zip-lock bag, opened it and breathed in the scent of dad's aftershave from the turquoise jumper. I carefully sealed it again, replaced it and went to take a shower.

I GRABBED a coffee and bagel to go and headed down to find Marcus. When he saw me, he jumped to his feet but didn't move towards me.

"Does it still work?" he asked.

"Yep!" I confirmed.

"And, are we okay? With the other thing?"

"Yep!"

He walked towards me and kissed me on the nose.

"Let's go and see Dr Philipson. I was thinking, tell him you have some fantastic news, he'll think your superpower has come back all by itself, and we can watch his face fall when he realises it hasn't."

"You're evil!"

"Meh!" he conceded, shrugging.

"I'm not doing that. It's mean," I said through a mouthful of bagel.

We went to see Dr Philipson, and his response was lukewarm.

"That's very good news, Jenna," he said. He was clearly disappointed, but didn't seem all that surprised. He must have anticipated it. I think he'd been hoping that I wouldn't succeed in developing the Sight so he could use it as an excuse to remove the implant.

"We've got a lot of Spotters and Trackers here. Don't you think it would be better to work on this other talent you might have?" he asked. "Have you considered that you might be able to do a lot more than break consumer goods?"

"What do you mean?" I asked.

"The reports of your awakening specified that furniture in the vicinity was toppled over. That's incredible."

"I'm not rejecting that as an option, Doc. I just want to get the hang of using the Sight first."

He looked doubtful.

"Look. I have the Sight. I see the Faders now. I want to go out with the others," I pleaded.

He sighed and passed me medically to work with the Spotters. I felt a little bad for him, but it wasn't going to spoil my day. I had already passed my self-defence class, and I'd started firearms training. As far as the Academy was concerned, I was ready to go spotting, and I was excited.

17

S potting was boring. It was great to get off the base and visit a few of the local towns and actually see America, but spotting was incredibly dull. I had hoped that Aaron, my Section Leader, would assign me to watching pre awakened kids for signs of awakening, but because my own experience had been atypical, he decided that wouldn't be appropriate. I was disappointed about that because I felt sure I would have done a much better job than the people who had been watching me all those years.

Instead, a few of us would roll up at a busy outlet mall and hang out, eating pizza, trying cosmetics and perfumes, browsing through CDs or books or clothes. Basically doing whatever kids did. I know, that all sounds fun, but while I did slightly extend my wardrobe and hugely extend my book collection, after a while, it was boring.

It was a cold March day on what felt like my fiftieth trip out, led by Aaron, with Vicky, Jenny and Sarah who were all a year or so younger than me. I slid off, mid-shift, to use the bathroom. As I walked in, I blinked in and found myself in the middle of a yellow mist aiming towards a stall with an

Out-Of-Order sign on the door. It was all I could do not to scream and run.

As naturally as possible, I entered the closest stall. I stayed blinked in on the toilet while I watched the yellow haze around the cubical until it disappeared. Flushing and walking out of the cubicle, I stayed in the bathroom, brushing my hair. A couple of minutes later, an attractive young woman walked out of the cubicle and started freshening her makeup.

As I washed my hands, I smiled at her in the mirror while she put on her lipstick and she smiled back. As usual, the real world had turned a hazy monochrome, and in human form, the woman looked no different to anyone else. I blinked back out, and she was still staring at me in the mirror, but her expression had changed. I realised that the smile had frozen on my face.

I faked the most shallow-sounding accent I could muster and said, "Nice colour." My heart hammered as I walked past her to the hand dryer. I stood with my back to her, drying my hands, expecting to be attacked from behind and trying to remember my self-defence moves.

I walked out of the bathroom without a backward glance, rejoined the team and tried to look like I wasn't completely freaked. I picked up a magazine and flicked through it casually as I told them about the woman. One of the girls took the magazine from my hands as it was rustling so loudly, they couldn't hear me correctly.

Aaron texted the backup team. I had to stop watching the door of the ladies" room, waiting for her to emerge, but I kept it in my peripheral view. The backup team arrived and ordered us back to the vehicle. I was given a tablet and told to type up a report describing her. Of course, there was no one there when the Agents entered the room. I knew it was my fault that she'd got away.

The Agents put the mall on a watch list, and more advanced Spotter and Tracker teams would take over that location.

"I'm off to your mall tomorrow," said Orla, later that night.

"Good luck! She's probably miles away now," I replied.

"Not always. There could be a nest nearby. Sometimes they have jobs."

"What kind of jobs?" That was news to me. "I thought they stole whatever they needed."

"Usually, jobs to help them get something they want. They can't get everything from fading. Sometimes they need information. Just because they're standing faded behind someone all day doesn't mean that person is going to access the right screens on a computer to get them the information. We find them in banks, travel agencies. One was found working in a kindergarten once. I've no idea why."

I was horrified at the very thought. What would the Faders want with babies? I was chilled.

My dreams that night were bombarded with terrible images of bright yellow shadows engulfing babies. Through the whole nightmare, the woman stalked, looking so human with her lovely lipstick, navy skirt, cream coloured blouse and company lanyard. I woke up soaked with sweat, suddenly realising what the dream had been telling me. What I already knew. I threw on my sweatpants and t-shirt and pounded on Orla's door.

"Orla? Orla!"

No response. I ran down to the kitchen – empty. I charged down the flights of stairs in my bare feet and burst out into the morning sun. Orla, Hannah and a couple of other girls were climbing into an SUV.

"Orla, wait."

I was out of breath.

"The Fader," I said as I gulped in air.

"Slow down, girl," said Hannah.

I took two breaths.

"She was wearing a company lanyard, from the cosmetics store. But it wasn't in the inventory. She must have flushed it. She works at the cosmetics store."

The driver got on to his radio and after a minute turned to us.

"Okay, ladies. We'll have a tactical team joining us today. We need to move out."

"Take care," I said to them as they pulled away, "and buy me something pretty."

I WAITED around all day for them to come back. I couldn't focus enough to do yoga or tai-chi, I was too tired to meditate, and I certainly wasn't going to attempt firearms training while I was this jittery. I'd probably blow my face off.

Finally, when I was several discs into Hannah's *Glee* collection, they returned. Orla burst into the TV room and ran at me with a high-five.

"We got it!" she shouted.

I punched the air.

"Tell me everything."

"You were right. It was working at the cosmetics counter. First, we checked the security cameras and saw it enter the bathroom about half an hour before you did, but it never came out. It must"ve left the clothes in the stall and put the

Out-Of-Order sign on the door so it wouldn't be disturbed. Then it faded off somewhere. We saw you go in and come back out, though. When you came out, you'd got this wild look on your face."

"Yeah, I'd seen a monster," I said.

"We went in the store for a look around and identified its location."

"If you'd confirmed what it looked like with the CCTV, why did you need to go in there?"

"We made sure there weren't any more around, faded. But it was alone. We left the store, and the backup team moved in."

"Didn't that cause a stir?" I asked.

"It was discretely incapacitated, and one of the guys shouted, "She just fainted." He picked it up and offered to carry it to the staff room, and when they got out back, they flashed IDs, announcing themselves as Homeland Security. They said it was a terrorist and took it out back. They chucked it into a black van and off we went. The van turned off towards the mountain just before we got back.

"Anyway, here's your something pretty." Orla handed me a set of eyeshadows with "Smokey Glitter Eyes" written on it. "It was very polite," she said.

"Hey, thanks," I said, then I let my jaw drop. "It served you? On the cosmetics counter?"

She nodded.

"Oh my God! You are so hardcore."

"Well, I'm going for a shower," said Orla. "Good luck with the Smokey Glitter look."

My mind was spinning. I couldn't believe I'd been instrumental in catching a Fader.

I thought, That's one for you, Dad.

It was the proudest moment of my life.

I sat happily in front of the mirror and attempted the Smokey Glitter Eyes look. Twenty minutes later, Orla stepped out of the bathroom. I looked up at her.

"What do you think?" I asked.

She looked at me and took a step back.

"Holy Mother of God," she said. "You look like you've been punched in the face by Tinkerbell."

"Yeah, I think it's going to take some practice," I agreed.

WE WERE in a meeting with Major Tom. Also in the room was a tall, athletic and ridiculously handsome guy with dark skin and bright blue eyes. He reminded me of Nathan. I glanced at Zoe, whose eyes were down and cheeks were red.

"This is Alejandro. He's originally from Cuba. He's just transferred from the Brazilian Academy."

We all said, "Hi."

"You can call me Al," he said. "Like the song."

The Major chuckled, but we just looked around at each other.

"Unless you don't know the song, I guess," said Al, looking embarrassed.

"That's one for Spotify," said Marcus.

"I'd like you to show him around," said Major Tom. "Zoe, I've teamed you up with Alejandro for spotting. He has a unique approach which I think you might appreciate."

"But I spot with Hannah," Zoe said. "And the others," she added.

"Indulge me," said the Major, putting an end to the discussion.

Marcus showed Alejandro to his accommodation, then we took him around the base and to the diner in the evening.

"What made you decide to come here?" I asked.

"I believe that we are blessed to be able to do what we do," said Al. "So I am happy to serve in any way I can, but also I like to travel. So why not? I'm hoping to visit Europe too, some day."

"I guess you're right," said Orla. "It's easy to forget how lucky we are."

The next day, I watched out of the window as Zoe and Al went off in a different car. Al had what looked like a toolbox with him and Zoe looked sullen.

Marcus, Hannah and I were part of a team spotting at a cinema. We were seated at the back, watching an action movie, which wasn't really my thing, and taking turns to blink in. Hannah was watching the screen, Marcus had his arm around me and I was nodding off.

I was suddenly aware that Marcus had tensed. Instantly, I blinked in to see a yellow mist moving into the middle of the room. I froze. Hannah had also become aware and blinked in.

Hannah took out her phone. "Damn it! No signal," she whispered. "I'll go out to call."

She moved to the end of the row and left the room.

After a minute, the mist moved back to the side of the room and down towards the fire exit near the screen. It disappeared through the door.

Marcus whispered, "Wait for Hannah," jumped up and ran down towards the exit, opened it and flew through it.

I didn't know what to do. I waited a minute, but worried that Marcus could be running into some kind of trap, I got up and ran down to the exit.

The hallway turned to the right on the other side of the door. I followed the yellow mist to the end and left. Marcus was at the end of the hallway, bent over double.

He was standing by the wall where the yellow trail ended abruptly.

"Marcus, are you okay?" I called as I ran to his side.

"Went through the wall here," he puffed. "Shouldn't have had the hot dog and nachos."

"You dope! You could have got yourself killed. What if that had been a trap?" I was angry and relieved all at once.

We made our way back through the hallways to the cinema screen room and found Hannah standing at the back.

"Where the hell did you two go?" she asked.

"Genius here decided to go cloud chasing," I said, thumping Marcus's arm. His eyes were bright and unrepentant.

"That's the most exciting thing to happen to me in weeks," he said.

"Great!" said Hannah. "You're gonna love the paperwork." She rolled her eyes and we headed out.

When we arrived back at the base, Zoe was animated.

"Al's a street artist," she said. "He works with chalks. His art is amazing, and get this – he makes money. I sat there with a hat for the tips, getting a good look at all the people passing by, and Al drew the most amazing picture. Here, I took photos."

Zoe passed her phone around. His drawing looked like a hole in the ground with cute smiling beavers and rabbits poking their heads out of it. She was right, he was really good.

A FEW DAYS LATER, the Major called us into the briefing room to announce that the April Showers Music Festival was going to be held at a local vacation park. I was horrified.

"The ice is barely off the ground. In fact, I think we might get another frost. Why would they hold a festival at this time of year?" I hated the cold.

Major Tom ignored me. "Festivals are a great place to find Faders. If there's something a Fader loves, then it's fading into events for free."

"And we're bound to get one," Said Orla. "They're like buses. They always come in threes."

As we left the meeting, Orla said, "What's the matter with you? You're looking distracted. You can't be that afraid of the cold."

"It's not that," I said. "It just never occurred to me that the monsters would like music. I don't know; it disturbs me."

"Pah! I bet they're not there for the free music. They probably steal pretzels and hot dogs and rob people's wallets."

"I wonder how they do it if even their clothes evaporate when they fade," I said.

"They're sneaky buggers. That's how," said Orla.

As we walked towards the accommodation blocks, I looked up at Cheyenne Mountain.

"What do you think's up there?" I asked.

"Everyone knows what's up there. It's the Stargate," said Marcus.

"Very funny." I'd seen a few convoys heading up that way on the way back from spotting exercises. "It must be where they keep them."

"You think they keep them? Alive? That's risky. What if they got away?" Marcus visibly shuddered. "What if there's thousands of them up there and they all got away? We'd be the first thing in their path."

"You're probably right. It would be too dangerous."

Later, I found Al sitting alone in the diner, looking sombre.

"Are you okay, Al?"

"I've just come from the Chapel."

I wasn't surprised. He seemed to be in the Chapel every day.

"My grandmother is dying. I was saying a prayer for her."

"That's awful. Can you go visit her?"

"I said goodbye before I left and I have important work to do here. All I can do is pray for her. So I do that."

He looked sad and I didn't know what to say.

"Do you think Zoe likes me?" He asked, out of the blue.

"How do you mean "likes"? You know that she and Hannah are together don't you?"

"But that's not real, is it? They are not a man and a woman. I like her, she has the soul of an artist. I think we should be together."

Five seconds before I had been full of sympathy for Al. Now he was starting to sound like a bit of a dick.

"Erm... I think she likes Hannah. Anyway, I have to be somewhere. Take care, Al."

I left the diner.

There was a banging on my door. I opened it and Hannah stormed through in tears.

"What's wrong?"

"She's got another one of his pictures on her wall. This one's of her. He's drawing her!"

"Well, is she dressed in these pictures?" I asked.

"Of course she's dressed. If she wasn't, I'd have his head in my hands."

"I think he's just got a bit of a crush on her. It would probably be best to just ignore it."

"Do you really think there's something going on?"

"Yes. No. Oh, I don't know." She sagged on to my chair. "I know he looks like Nathan."

"Have you asked her about it?"

"No," she replied. "I'm frightened what the answer will be."

"He's only just got here. Just tell her how you feel. Zoe would probably be upset if she knew you were feeling so insecure."

"I know. But I don't want to tell her. I sort of feel like I'm being stupid."

"You're only being stupid if you let yourself get upset over something that probably isn't happening and will never happen. Just ask her."

"No, I think I got it out of my system talking to you. I'm good."

I gave her a hug and she left looking no happier.

IT WAS early evening on the first night at the festival camp. We were staying in a wooden cabin in a small copse of trees, near the fields where the festival was taking place. We had been going out in shifts to check the live performances or around the cabins and tents. Al had a stall selling his art. He was doing really well.

Zoe and Hannah were currently wandering around smiling, holding hands and blinking in. They weren't due back for another hour, so I was surprised when a shadow fluttered across the window.

"Marcus," I said, "something's moving around out there."

Orla flicked off the lights and blinked in, looking out of the windows. I blinked in too, looking in the room, and Marcus checked the bathroom.

Whoever it was, it wasn't Faders.

Something moved again.

"Who's there?" shouted Orla. "What are you up to?"

"I'm just out for a run," said a familiar Liverpool accent from the darkness. "I hear this is a good spot for lunges."

Orla's eyes grew wide, and she couldn't hide the grin on her face.

"Oh great!" said Marcus, rolling his eyes and not sounding happy at all.

We opened the door to find Jason leaning lazily against the porch.

"Gonna invite me in or will I have to sleep out here with the creepy crawlies?"

"Can we think about it?" asked Marcus.

Orla and I reached out and dragged him in while Marcus gave him a suspicious assessing look.

"Why are you here? Is Jenna in danger again?" he asked.

"No, nothing like that," Jason assured us. "General Cavendish is at the base for a conference, and I just manoeuvred myself into the team. I wanted to see how you were all doing."

He glanced over at Orla as he said this, then looked immediately around the room. "Nice digs. Very...rustic," he said.

"Don't knock it," I said. "It's better than a tent."

"Accommodation like this would cost thousands at Glastonbury," added Orla.

"Where's the little spiky one?" asked Jason.

"She's off doing the rounds. Tonight is our first night here. It's been boring so far; we've not seen a spec of yellow."

"It's like that sometimes." Jason shrugged. "What have you got to eat? I'm starving."

"We're a bit low on rations," said Orla. "Someone's been

eating us out of house and home," looking directly at Marcus.

Marcus walked up behind me and, quite territorially, wrapped me in a huge bear hug.

"I keep telling you I'm a growing boy."

"Zozo and Hannah will be back soon," said Orla. "Let's go and get something to eat then."

We ate burgers, dogs, and fries from a van in the Unplugged field as we listened to a band playing fiddles and banjos. The vaguely Irish sound of the music seemed to take Orla to another planet, and she danced like a woman possessed with her auburn hair flying out around her. Jason watched her with a look of pure rapture on his face. He had it bad.

We all stood and danced for the last song of the night, including Marcus who complained of a full stomach as he was dragged up by Zoe and Hannah. As the crowd roared at the end, Jason leaned towards me and whispered, "I need to get a private word with you soon. There's something you need to know."

Before I could respond, he was off cheering for the band as though he'd never said a thing.

I WOKE up on my camp bed the next morning, listening to Marcus's snoring. I looked over at Jason. He was awake and looking right back at me. The others were all asleep.

I poked Marcus. "I'm going for a run. Do you want to join me?"

He opened one eye and looked at me.

"You're nuts!" he said and turned over, immediately snoring, as I had known he would.

Just before I walked out the door, Jason said, "Hang on, I'll come."

I'd been expecting this, too. He slipped his trainers on, pulled a hoodie over the t-shirt he'd slept in and walked out with me.

We ran for about half a mile, then Jason took out what looked like a mobile phone and pressed a button on it as he slowed down. I blinked in and out periodically as we walked, and I knew Jason would be doing it too.

"Well?" I asked.

"Cavendish is here about you," he said. "Apparently, there are plans to inject you with a new inhibitor. This one is a little microchip. They can remotely deactivate it so they can continue to study you."

"They *what*? How do you know?"

"I just know. I can't give up my sources." He tapped the side of his nose with a finger.

"How am I going to get out of this?" I asked.

"I'm sure we'll think of something. Let's finish our run. There should be a bathroom block at the end of this track, I saw it on the map."

"Really? I don't remember seeing it there."

He'd already taken off, and I followed.

The building at the end of the track looked abandoned.

"Are you sure this is a toilet block?"

I blinked in as we jogged towards the building and instantly I could see a yellow haze of Fader activity right across my field of vision. Grinding to a halt, I called to Jason.

"Faders! Oh, my God, the mist trails, they're everywhere."

I turned to him, and he was just standing there, staring at me with a nervous face.

"Jason, what's going on?"

"I'm sorry, Jenna, I had to get you here somehow."

"Are you working for the Faders?"

"Well, kinda."

I whirled around to bolt back to the trees and ran straight into someone who had come up behind me. My training kicked in, and my fist was nearly at his throat when I froze, looking into the eyes of someone I thought I would never see again.

"Hello, Little Duck."

18

Neil Banks stood in the hallway of his home, listening to a sound coming from the kitchen. His heart hammered as he walked with the cat in his arms into the room to see the microwave with something large and metal revolving and sparking inside. Everything happened so fast. One moment, he was staring at the microwave, then the world melted away.

After a blur, he was sitting on the floor in Mrs Cowan's house, which was separated from his home by two garages and two solid external house walls. A moment later, the house shook, and Mrs Cowan's decorative cat plates fell off the wall.

As he looked about himself, a boy of about eighteen suddenly appeared, lying on the carpet next to him.

"Holy crap, that was close," said the boy.

Neil jumped up. "What the hell have you done?"

"Saved your life. You're welcome," the boy drawled with a lazy southern American accent. He got up, went to the window and smiled, muttering, "One down, one to go."

"I don't understand," said Neil. "I can't fade. How did you do that?"

"I can fade anything or anyone I'm touching. That's why we still have our clothes on. Otherwise this would look like a whole different situation if that little old lady walked in."

"What? I've never heard of that being possible."

"you'd be amazed by the things you don't know."

"You're the boy who tried to kidnap Jenna. What the hell did you do to my house?"

"Okay. I can see we're off to a rocky start here. I'm Connor, pleased to make your acquaintance. I didn't do anything to your house. That was your people, not us. You called us last night, and I was in the area. I guess your guys had your phone or your house bugged and decided it would be best to take you out of the picture so they could control your daughter. When you went to the van for boxes, the moving guy took out something nasty-looking and stuck it in your microwave.

"And I wasn't kidnapping your daughter. I could see she was about to awaken and I was trying to get her somewhere safe. You know they were watching her, right? I didn't know she was going to go nuclear. I've never seen anything like that. Damn, nearly scared the crap out of me.

"Dude, I don't want to be rude, but I think we should get the hell out of here. This place will be crawling with Agents and Trackers. I reckon your neighbour won't take too kindly to us smashing up her kitty plate collection, and that cat looks like it's about to rip my eyes out."

Neil looked at Felix. He was a long-haired breed, and every hair was standing straight out as he made wild, strangled hissing noises at the Fader.

"I need to get Jenna," said Neil.

"I don't think we'll get near her right now. They'll be all

over her. We need a plan. They won't believe you're dead for long."

Neil started to get up, but sat straight back down. "I don't feel too well."

"Yeah, it kind of makes you seasick the first time," said Connor.

CONNOR SAT in the back of the black van as it crawled into New York City from the Airport. It was the worst time of the day to be traversing New York, and Brooklyn had been a nightmare. They had flown over in a cargo plane owned by a small family company. It hadn't been comfortable, but it was safe. The problem wasn't just that the traffic bummed him out as much as it would anyone else. It wasn't safe for him to be so enclosed. If he had to fade and Trackers spotted him, he might not be able to get away so easily. It made him uneasy.

The men in the front of the van and Neil Banks, sitting next to him, didn't have those concerns. They were just regular people; they didn't have to worry about leaving a bright yellow trail wherever they went.

The van reached its destination, a parking garage on the Upper East Side. It was driven down into the sub-levels and parked. Making their way to the stairway entrance, instead of climbing the stairs, he and Neil went through a service door halfway down a long passageway lined on one side with pipes. The men from the front of the van went through another door into a poorly lit office.

Connor wondered how much crap would hit the fan. He'd messed up, and he knew it. He should have got the girl first. She was the primary mission. His instructions had been clear. Get the dad if you can, but make sure you get the girl. His boss didn't take failure well. No, that was an understatement. His boss was a total bitch.

A girl typing on a laptop glanced up at them and murmured, "She's waiting for you."

"Great! Honey, can you find some food for this?" The Fader dumped the cat basket on to the desk and guided Neil straight for the inner office without waiting for a response.

A woman stood with her back to them, studying a map on the wall dotted with coloured pins. Her grey hair was pulled back into a severe bun. She pushed another pin into the map and turned around. Neil looked thoughtfully at her face. He felt like he should know her.

Connor attempted an introduction. "Boss, this is..."

"You can leave us now, Connor. I know who he is. He's my son-in-law. Welcome to the United States, Neil. My name is Vanessa Harvey."

Neil Banks was stunned, but as he stared, he recognised the familiar facial features from his wife's old photo collection.

"I thought you were dead," he said.

"Apparently, a lot of people are pretending to be dead these days, Neil."

Neil sat across the desk from his mother-in-law.

"I don't understand. Tessa's whole life, she thought you were dead."

"It was for her safety. The truth killed my husband. I didn't want it to kill Theresa too."

"But what happened?"

"I was captured by Faders. The Agency had told us horror stories about what they did to Trackers. The most important thing they taught us was to take a cyanide pill before the Faders could interrogate us. It's a cruel but effective form of information control."

"And now you're working with them? That kid saved my life. He said it was the Agency who tried to kill me, but he hasn't been too forthcoming since so I don't understand what's going on here, Vanessa. I do know that Faders killed your husband in the Washington State Massacre."

"All lies. While Tom was there, some Faders made contact with a Tracker and were able to convince him of the truth about what Faders are – what the Agency is hiding. The Tracker agreed to share the message with others at the Academy. The Agency got wind of it almost immediately and killed everyone to stop the truth from getting out, even the children, and, of course, my Tom.

"What truth? What was this message?"

"Neil, Trackers *are* Faders."

"What? But that can't be. Trackers can't fade."

"You will have seen scans of the gland at the base of the skull they call the Tracker Gland. It activates at puberty, allowing a newly awakened Fader to identify other Faders – to find their tribe, so to speak."

Neil leaned forward, nodding. He'd seen many such scans.

"If left to mature unhindered, roughly a year later, the gland begins emitting, occasionally creating the yellow aura. Then shortly after that, the gland fully matures, allowing them to fade."

Neil was outraged. "My daughter is a human. She's my own daughter, I should know that."

"We are all human. We think it's just a step in evolution," Vanessa said. "When I was captured, I was injected with a solution that neutralised the effect of the red inhibitor pills. It stung like a bitch. I don't mind telling you, I screamed. Of course, I didn't believe what they were telling me: that I was a Fader. The very idea disgusted me.

They were my enemy; they were monsters. I wasn't a monster. Within a few days, however, I began emitting. I blinked in and I could see my body awash with yellow, and I knew it was true.

"The truth is, the Agency uses young Faders to track their own kind. They used to give us the little red pills, but these days, they inject the slow-release capsule which stops Faders from emitting and fading. After Washington State, the Agency decided it was too dangerous to risk Trackers coming into contact with Faders. When the Trackers were out in the world, they were too difficult to control and monitor.

"The Agency fabricated a tale about the tracking gland becoming unstable, and they would remove it while the Tracker was still young enough to be easily manipulated. Also, the gland is a little powerhouse of energy. The Agency has been trying to find out how to harvest and use that energy for years."

"But I've worked alongside the Agency for most of my adult life. How can this be true?"

"What level of access did you have? Did you ever feel like you'd never progress beyond a certain level? I imagine the fact that you married a Tracker – a Fader – closed the door to any chance of working within the Agency, if it had ever been open. Have you noticed that Agents don't seem to be very friendly people?"

"You can't miss it. I was told they were trained to keep emotionally distant."

"When they're recruiting Agents, the number one quality the Agency looks for, if you can call it a quality, is bigotry. They find bitter, angry people with a chip on their shoulder; people who are looking for someone to blame. They put these people through intense training, which is more like brainwashing, and tell them exactly who they can blame for everything that's wrong with their lives."

Neil's shoulders sagged. He'd been trying to get access to information for years, but it was always beyond his security clearance level. Removing the gland would have been the best way to protect Jenna from this life once and for all, but it had never been a safe option without access to the right information. He couldn't just have gone digging into his daughter's head and hoping for the best.

Vanessa stood up from her chair behind the desk, came around and sat next to him.

"Neil, how did my daughter...how did she die?"

Neil sat back in the chair, gathering his thoughts and preparing to relive the most tragic days of his life. He stared into the middle distance, unable to recount the story without seeing it.

"Tessa knew. I see that now, she must have known. A week before her death, she returned from a tracking assignment. She seemed edgy. She told me that something had happened; she didn't trust the Agency any more. I'm not sure she trusted me. She wouldn't say what had spooked her.

"I found her going through my papers in the office at home. When I walked in, I swear, she looked like she thought I was going to hurt her or something. I told her I've never had any secrets from her and she could look at anything she wanted. I left her to it.

"The next day, I told my boss I was worried about her and he said they'd get her in for a psych evaluation. She wouldn't even talk to the junior counsellor, and that was her best friend. When they told us they were going to check her TGland, she just lost it and had to be tranquillised. She said they were going to kill her. She thought I was going to kill her. The doctors suspected that the Sight was failing. Some Trackers get paranoid and think they are surrounded by Faders when this happens. They tried inserting another inhibitor to calm everything down.

"That evening, back at the house, she locked herself in the bathroom, and we talked for hours through the door. I talked about anything I thought might bring her back to me – our wedding; when Jenna was born; when we first started seeing each other, sneaking around trying not to get caught.

"In the end, she let me in. I could hardly see her at first. The shower had been on all the time she'd been in there, and the room was thick with steam. My Tessa was curled in a ball in the corner, shaking.

"She wouldn't let me turn the shower off. She said "they" were listening. She made me swear I'd find some way to stop Jenna from awakening. I swore, and that was that. I couldn't swear and not mean it; she'd have known. And I couldn't go back on my word, even though I thought she was wrong to ask. She was so desperate for me to promise.

"As we curled up together on the floor, she pushed a piece of paper with a phone number on it into my hand, and said, "If it happens." I understood that I'd have to call the number if Jenna ever awakened. She wouldn't say any more about it. She fell asleep on that bathroom floor in my arms.

"When she wouldn't wake up, I called the medics. They took her straight to the med centre and started tests. They found that her TGland had a tumour. She died two days later."

Neil blinked away tears and looked at his wife's mother. He could see the same raw pain reflected in the lines of her face. Neil calculated that she must have been in her sixties by now. He couldn't imagine how hard it would be to stay away from Jenna. He suddenly feared that she was going to ask that from him.

"I'm not leaving Jenna with those people."

"I have no intention of abandoning Jenna. That's why you're here, Neil, we're going to get her back," Vanessa said. "We had someone on the inside at Hilltop. Unfortunately, Jenna was moved too suddenly for any plans to be made, but we know she's now in Colorado."

"Colorado?" Neil sat with his head in his hands. "On the doorstep of the Cheyenne Facility? I've been there several times. She might as well be in Fort Knox."

"This situation is not without its challenges, but it's not going to deter me, and I'm quite certain it's not going to deter you."

"You're right about that."

"Does Jenna have any reason to think that you're alive?"

"As far as I know, none at all. Connor and I have been hiding out in an empty apartment above the local shopping centre. He called me to say he'd seen Jenna in a bookshop and I tried to get there, but an Agent recognised me, and we had to run for it. I had hoped that maybe one of the kids had seen me, and word might get back to her, but I didn't even make it into the pedestrian shopping centre where they were spotting."

"What do you know about Jenna's awakening?" asked Vanessa.

"I've never seen or heard of anything like it. She emitted a shockwave – well, I'm sure Connor must have told you about it. He was standing right there when it happened. I arrived a few seconds later. The wave had knocked over furniture in the vicinity. It was the damnedest thing."

"It was in Connor's report, but I just wanted a second

opinion. You should rest. Connor will take you to the safe house. We'll be heading across the country in a few days."

Neil stood up to leave, but paused. "How can people not know?"

"The Agency will have you believe that Faders are an organised group of terrorist monsters. It's just not like that. Some Faders don't even know what they are. They might awaken without ever realising they are different, without even learning how to blink in. They walk around in their everyday lives, going to work at the office or waiting on tables without a clue that when they occasionally emit, they are a bright yellow target for those who have been trained to see."

"I worked there for all those years on the hormones used in the inhibitor," said Neil with his head in his hands. "I was a teacher to those kids."

"I tracked down my people for more years than I care to remember," said Vanessa. "I can't imagine how many of them died because of me, and the people who died because of Theresa? Well, that's on me, too. We need to get to Jenna before she has to carry this burden."

19

I stared, not daring to believe, waiting for the features to slide into something, someone else.

"Is this real?" I asked.

Dad had tears in his eyes as he nodded. He had a beard. I hadn't seen him with a beard since I was a little girl. I reached out a hand and touched his face. He put his hand over mine, and I knew it was real.

I flew into his arms.

"I'm sorry, Jenna. I'm sorry you thought I was...I'm sorry you had to go through that. But we need to get you out of sight. We have to talk."

I let my dad guide me to a transit van parked in the clearing.

"Are you okay? Have they hurt you?" I asked.

"Jeez," said a voice from the front of the van that turned my blood to ice, "we get the worst press."

My head snapped in the direction of the hazel-eyed boy. He was still wearing the same denim jacket. I was confused. I hated him; he'd killed my dad...but, my dad was right here.

"He killed Nate..."

"I know he didn't kill Nathan," said Dad. "He was busy keeping me alive at the time. We'll explain everything, but we need to get you out of here. It's not safe for you here any more."

"We don't know who killed Nathan and Tiffany," added Jason. "Nate was found by a patrol within a few minutes of being attacked. The back of his neck had a cut. The implant had been removed and was just lying on the ground beside him. I don't think that was the cause of his death, but the Agents are not saying. It was definitely a Fader because there was a fade-trail heading back towards the compound, but it just stopped and completely disappeared in the middle of nowhere. That's pretty much unheard of with a recent trail, and that's why they got you out. They couldn't risk losing you."

"Stay down. I think someone's coming through the trees. We need to go," said hazel eyes.

"Okay, Connor," said Dad. "Move it."

"If that was a Tracker, there's gonna be choppers above us within a half hour."

As the van sped away, Dad talked while I just clung to him. I couldn't bring myself to unwrap my arms from him.

Connor's phone rang. He listened, sighed and announced, "Choppers are in the air. Plan B."

After a few minutes of Dad talking furiously fast, the van screeched to a halt and he hugged me.

"Jenna, we're not going to be able to get you away this time. You have to go back."

"Dad, I can't let you go now."

"It's okay. Just go along with whatever Jason says. I have to get out of here; they can't know you've seen me, or they'll kill you. We'll get you out, I promise. You mustn't let anyone know what I've told you. You have to keep it to yourself.

They listen to everything. They watch everything. I love you, sweetheart."

With that, Dad kissed my head, jumped out of the van and ran to a car parked on the side of the road.

I looked at Jason, feeling myself starting to meltdown. "What if they stop him?"

"They won't. Everyone will be scanning for Faders. Your dad will be on the freeway in minutes."

"Okay, man," said Connor, "it's your turn."

"Make it realistic, but don't kill me, dude." To me, Jason said, "We stopped for a rest. You were scanning in front of us, so you didn't see him appear behind me and knock me out," he glanced at Connor, "but not kill me.

"He knocked you out with a non-hypothetical dart, so you don't know anything. When you wake up, I will have done some brave soldier stuff that you missed and won't have to describe to anyone, and the evil Fader will have disappeared into the night."

At this point, I heard a loud crack and Jason hit the floor.

"Jesus, you might have killed him." I looked suspiciously at Connor, who rolled his eyes. Remembering myself, I added sincerely, if belatedly, "You saved my dad. Thank you."

He took a step towards me, looking straight at me with those mysterious green-hazel eyes. His lips turned into a gentle smile as he tucked my hair behind my ear.

"Good luck, beautiful," he said with a wink and shot me with a dart.

"Not again!" I moaned as he gently laid me on the floor of the van. He faded in front of me. I blinked in to see him disappear through the side of the van and I was gone...again.

.   .   .

I woke up to a penlight shining into my eyes. I groaned and tried to wave it away.

"She's coming round," said the medic.

My first thought was of my dad. I was just about to call out for him when I heard General Cavendish, and my mouth snapped shut.

"You have a remarkable capacity for getting yourself into trouble, Miss Banks."

"General? What happened? Something...did something happen to Jason?"

"I'm okay," said a voice. I turned to see Jason being treated by another medic. He gave me a weak wave without looking up.

After listening to Jason give a fictitious account of what had happened and false descriptions of the assailants to the Agents, I was bundled into a helicopter with him, flown back to the base and taken straight to the medical centre. I tried to insist that I was alright; I didn't want to go into that med-block. I knew what the Doc was going to do to me in there, but I wasn't supposed to know, so I couldn't risk making any further fuss over it.

I looked around the triage room. A hypodermic sat on a shiny metal tray on the desk. I was beginning to despise the sight of those things.

Jason and I were alone in the ER. I looked at him and opened my mouth to speak, but he shook his head almost imperceptibly and rubbed his ear, reminding me that they were listening and watching. I thought, and used the opportunity to reinforce my story.

"I'm sorry, Jason. I just didn't see it coming."

We continued a conversation as though we didn't know they were listening.

"You're not the only one," he said. "At least neither of us

is dead. God knows what they'd have done with us. Look on the bright side: if I'd had any idea they were there before they knocked me out, I'd have taken my pill and told you to take yours. We'd be dead now. But, we've learned something important – they're still after you."

"But what happened? Why didn't they get us?" I asked.

"I came round in the back of the van. Apparently, they don't like dealing with us when we're awake. I punched one of them; they just stopped the van and vanished. Cowards."

"It doesn't bear thinking about," I said. "I should buy you a coffee. How long are you going to be here?"

"Until the General's meetings are over, not long. Then back to England."

"Oh. Orla will be disappointed."

He brightened up. "You really think so?"

"You never heard that from me," I said. "It's been great to see another familiar face. For all of us."

"Ha! Not all of you. Your big boyfriend doesn't like me."

"He's just protective," I said.

"Well he might have a point. I nearly got you killed today."

"It was my idea to go for a run."

"And I joined you to make sure you were safe. It's a shame you're not still blowing things up with your freaky brain. That could be a useful defence."

I glanced up at him and saw his eyebrow go up a fraction of an inch. I thought about it. It was pretty obvious the Agents were going to do this to me anyway. Perhaps I should appear to welcome it.

"You're right. I might have been able to help us both out there today. I've been selfish about that. Too scared of being different, of the way people looked at me." I sounded sincere because I was. If I had an edge against these people, I should learn to use it. Now more than ever.

He smiled. "Are you keeping up with your meditations, exercises and having a proper breakfast?"

"I am. You helped me a lot back in England with all of that, thanks."

Five minutes later, Dr Philipson returned. Jason had been right. He'd clearly been listening. The Doc looked excited; he was almost vibrating. He discharged Jason immediately, dropping a bottle of Advil into his hand and almost shoving him out of the door. When the two of us were alone, he opened a cupboard on the wall, placed the hypodermic inside and closed the door. He wouldn't need it any more.

He pulled up a stool next to me. "Jenna," he began, "we've been working on a great new piece of tech which I hope will interest you. It's totally okay if you don't want to go for it, we're not going to force you into anything you're not comfortable with."

"Really? What is it?" I asked, looking, I hoped, curious and bewildered.

20

The Doc wanted the procedure to take place the next day, but I asked for a few days" rest, explaining that I was feeling nauseous from the tranquilliser. General Cavendish agreed this would be okay, but was clearly irritated by the delay. He didn't want to leave until the procedure had taken place. But, and I know this is bad under the circumstances, I wanted some matchmaking time with Orla and Jason.

Once again, the Agents confined me to base, which was fast becoming the story of my life. Back in my room, I desperately wanted to tell my friends the truth, but Dad had said I couldn't risk it. He had told me a very different version of the events that had taken place in Washington State in the seventies, so I knew I couldn't be careless. Over the years I had developed a sixth sense for when someone was physically watching me, but I couldn't tell if my room was bugged. I would have liked one of the little signal jamming machines that Jason had, but that would have been a giveaway, too. I had to get through my days without letting people know that my heart was soaring at the thought of my dad being alive. At least, I hoped he was still alive.

Activity had gone into overdrive on and off the base. The Spotters and Trackers were visiting every town in a radius of three hundred miles. They always had armed backup units with them, and teams had been brought in from across the country. I couldn't wait for each group to get back and deliver news, or rather no news, which is what I wanted.

I needn't have worried about matchmaking. Jason and Orla were working and travelling together for three days non-stop. When they finally returned, I had an inkling that something had happened, but neither shared so I didn't ask.

On day four, there was no more putting it off. I had the procedure. The Doc removed my implant and put a new one in its place. As soon as I came round, I tried blinking in and did it with no trouble, but I didn't know whether the implant had been activated or not. I asked Dr Philipson, but he just told me to rest.

The next day, General Cavendish was due to leave. As Jason was about to jump into the SUV, he turned around, took three strides to Orla, swept her into him with one arm and delivered a kiss worthy of a Hollywood epic.

"Oh!" said Marcus with his arm around me. "I thought he was after you."

I elbowed him in the ribs. "You Muppet!"

He nibbled my ear, and my knees went weak.

A FEW DAYS LATER, as I sat in the kitchen drinking coffee and waiting for a word from the Doc to start the experiments, I heard feet thundering on the stairs. It was Zoe and Orla. They flew past the kitchen towards my room, and I began to feel panic.

They ground to a halt a few steps after the kitchen door-way, realising they'd just run past me, and bolted into the room.

"Jenna!" panted Zoe. "You won't believe it."

"We got the monster!" burst Orla.

I was too shocked to speak.

"Your indie with the pretty face," she added, helpfully.

"I...I can't believe it," I said. "Is he..." please let him not be, "...is it dead?"

"Nope," said Zoe. "We got it alive."

"I have to be sure. I want to see it. Is it up there?" I asked, nodding towards the mountain. I couldn't imagine any way I could get up there.

"No. They've got top brass visiting up there so they carted it off, unconscious, to the medical building."

"I saw it," said Zoe, "and I kicked it in the balls after the backup team knocked it out. I hope they kill it slowly." Zoe leaped at me and hugged me fiercely. "We've avenged your dad and Nate," she sobbed.

I thought I was going to throw up.

I wanted to make an impassioned plea to Dr Philipson. To explain that I needed to see, for the sake of my sanity, that they had captured my father's and Nate's killer. Knowing he wouldn't budge anyway, I didn't attempt it. It wasn't worth the risk of drawing attention to myself at this point without a plan in place. I wondered what condition Connor was in. On a previous visit to the med centre, I'd glimpsed the machine the Agency used to keep Faders unconscious so they couldn't fade. It delivered a constant dose of drugs and monitored them.

They would be moving him in the morning. I had to think fast.

This deception had gone too far. I had to find a way to

tell the others. I was frantically trying to think of a way, but nowhere on the base was safe. Any code I could come up with would be pointless; the Agency had experts here. I considered writing it all down and showing it to Orla, but where were the cameras? Could I rip it up and eat it before they burst in with their bloody dart guns? Or real guns? I couldn't risk getting my friends killed too.

Before the Doc had implanted me, the stress of this would have sent every TV in the building haywire...and that gave me an idea. Knowing Agents might be watching me, I sat and rubbed at the back of my neck for about ten minutes, as though it was bothering me.

Eventually, "Oww!"

I sighed audibly and rubbed it again. Winced.

"Ahh!"

I rubbed it hard a few more times, got up, put my shoes on and knocked on Orla's door.

"What's up, sweetie?" she asked.

I leaned against the wall. "I don't know. This implant feels hot. I don't feel well."

She looked at the back of my neck. "Jenna, your neck is really red. I think you should see Dr Philipson. The site could be infected."

"It's been throbbing all day," I said, "but through all this stuff with the monster, I didn't say anything."

"Come and sit down. I'll get my shoes on, and we'll go over to the med centre."

I walked into Orla's room and glanced out of the window. It was dark in the courtyard, apart from some low lights along the pathway. No people; no vehicles.

As we left her room, I tried to think of a reason to bring Zoe and Hannah because I didn't want to have this problem all over again. I couldn't think of a legitimate reason, so as we walked along the corridor, I yelped with pain, clutching my neck and stumbling into Zoe's door. If she was in there, that would get her out.

There was no sound from her room, but a moment later, Hannah's door opened, and two heads popped out. By this time, I was sweating with nerves, which only served to support my fake illness.

Of course, there was no holding back Zoe, and where she went, Hannah went. Into the lift we all lurched, and down. If I'd had any doubts that the Agents were watching us, they went when the doors opened and a Jeep was parked right outside with its headlights illuminating the previously darkened courtyard.

As we burst through the door, Orla muttered something about the luck of the Irish and demanded that the Jeep should take us to the med centre immediately. Of course, the gentleman driving, who was in black chinos and crew neck sweater, rather than a standard Airforce uniform, was only too happy to oblige. I slumped weakly against Orla, feeling guilty as she looked at me with such compassion like she thought I might die.

The Agent tried to take ownership of my body on arrival, but my friends insisted on helping to prop me up as we went into the med centre and the guards buzzed us straight through to the examination room I'd been in a few days before.

Dr Philipson was waiting for me. All of my friends tried to speak at once.

"Perhaps you ladies should wait outside," he said.

Hannah moved obediently towards the door. I gripped Orla's hand and burst into tears.

"Don't leave me."

Honestly, I don't know where all this stuff was coming from, but I was working it.

Orla stood resolutely at my side, Zoe by hers, and Hannah by Zoe's. Dr Philipson rolled his eyes.

He moved to the back of my neck. "It's quite red and warm to the touch."

There was a filing cabinet in the corner standing open and a file out on his desk. I was pretty sure it would be mine. He walked back in front of me and I looked away from the file. He took out his stethoscope and announced that my heart rate was up.

No shit! I thought.

He took out an ear thermometer and found that my temperature was also up a little.

The power of positive thinking, I thought.

"It's been throbbing for most of the day. I'm sorry, I should have mentioned it earlier," I said.

"I suspect you might have a small infection from the insertion. I'll give you some antibiotics, that should clear it up."

Suddenly this was not going to plan.

"But it feels hot in there. Burning hot, like it's overheating or something."

"It's on, but it shouldn't overheat. I'm sure it shouldn't."

He seemed not to know.

I said weakly, "Is there any way we can find out if having it switched on could be making it overheat?"

Come on, I thought, it's not rocket science. You can get there.

"Well," he said, "we could try turning it off, give it ten minutes and see if it cools down. I'll have to give you something to relax you. We don't want any accidents."

"Thanks, Doc," I said, suddenly feeling nervous.

The Doctor injected my arm.

"How long will this take to start working?" I asked.

"A few minutes."

I counted ninety seconds, said, "Woah! Good stuff," and sighed, relaxing onto Orla's shoulder.

"That was quick," said the Doc.

"She's a snowflake," said Zoe.

The Doc went over to his computer, and immediately I began some meditation techniques to calm myself in preparation. The drug hadn't really kicked in yet and I couldn't have everything going crazy straight away.

"There, it's off. Does it feel any different?" he asked.

I quickly blinked in and out. That answered one question: the Sight was here to stay.

"Not yet," I said. "My mouth's parched. Can I get some water, please?"

Hannah offered to go, but the Doc stopped her. "We can't have you wandering around here on your own at night. I'll ask one of the guards."

The Doc walked over to the door and, holding it open, called a guard. I worried that this wasn't going to work, trying not to panic.

The guard must have returned to the front desk and couldn't hear him. The Doc had to walk further out to the other side of the corridor, and the door swung closed. I heard the electronic click of its security mechanism.

Then I let it all in. I thought about Connor, either dead or drugged in the other room. I thought about the Agents killing him. He didn't deserve such an awful fate. I thought about how he'd saved my dad's life. I thought about Dad, out there risking his life trying to save me.

That did it. The lights started to flicker.

"Oh no!" said Zoe. "Jenna, calm down. It's going to be okay. Orla, have you got your tranq?"

"No, it's in my room."

The lights got bright, and the Doc's computer made funny noises. Footsteps came running, but they weren't quick enough. The room and the whole building plunged into darkness. I could hear the Doc on the other side of the door trying his key card in the reader, but it was too late.

Everything was off, including anything that could be monitoring or recording us. The only light was from the street lighting across the road.

I turned to the girls. They were looking at each other.

Orla looked at me with pity. "Don't worry, sweetie, it's not your fault."

"Oh yes it bloody is," I whispered. "We don't have long. You have to listen to me carefully before this sedative takes hold."

I told them about my dad being alive. I told them the Fader boy in this building somewhere had saved his life, and I told them the hardest truth they would ever hear. Our Governments were using us as weapons against our own people. Not monsters, just humans with an ability. I told them the truth of the Washington State facility. I told them as much as I could in the time we had.

They didn't want to believe; I didn't force them to. I gave the girls the information and reminded them that after this we would be watched even more closely. We could not give the Agents any reason to think we knew the truth, or they'd kill us. Beyond this room, the girls would have to come to their own conclusions.

Zoe was angry about Connor. She wanted him to be Nate's killer. She had to get her head around that.

I looked through the open door to the Doc's office. The

file was still on the desk with a picture on the front. I'd guessed it was mine, but with only the light from the street, I couldn't see from where I was.

"Is that my file?" I asked. "Can someone have a quick look at it? I'm feeling too wobbly to get up."

Orla walked over to it, stood by the window and flicked through it.

"Yes, it's you. Height, weight. There's stuff about your scary mind, but it's a bit technical. Oh! You and Marcus are a seventy-one per cent match. That's gross – why would they even need to know that?"

"I wonder what our files say about us," said Zoe to Hannah.

Orla returned to the cabinet and tried to open a drawer.

"It's locked, sorry." She turned away to look at Zoe, who was poking through the overstuffed in-tray on the desk. About halfway down, she pulled out a sheet of paper.

"Well there's bureaucracy for you. The head of the Science and Medical Division has to confirm your dad's deceased before they'll delete his security access. Dr Philipson is way behind on his paperwork."

She looked at me, shrugged, folded the sheet and shoved it in her pocket. As she opened her mouth to say something more, both she and Orla jumped as a loud click came from the filing cabinet.

Orla blinked in and gasped. "Oh, dear God. Your Fader's in here," she said. "He just jemmied the lock on the cabinet."

The others blinked in, but I was too sleepy. They turned their heads, following his path through the room. They stopped, staring at me for a moment, then looked towards the far wall.

"He's gone," said Hannah.

"That was so strange. He stopped in front of you, and I'd swear he stroked your face," said Zoe.

I thought of those hazel eyes and crooked smile, and wondered what my compatibility rating would be with him. Then I thought of Marcus and felt guilty.

Orla opened the cabinet and took out a couple of other folders. She flicked through her own.

"Well that's insultingly thin."

She opened the second folder. After reading for a few seconds, she said, "Zoe, I think you should see this."

Zoe took the file and held it up to the street light to read.

"The bastards! There's a whole section here on my sexual orientation." She read further. "No!"

We heard a rattling at the outer door. The Agents weren't waiting for the power to be reset.

Zoe looked at the door and back at Hannah.

"You're not going to believe this. They brought Al here intentionally to break us up. Apparently mine and Al's compatibility is ninety-two per cent. "His physical attributes and artistic leanings along with his dedication to the future of the Tracker program and strongly held conservative beliefs make him an ideal candidate to disrupt her current relationship. Alejandro has reported that Zoe is showing signs of closeness and trust. This is confirmed by video and audio recordings. Hannah has begun to show signs of jealousy and insecurity." He agreed to this? I feel sick. I'm going to kill him."

"You can't do anything," I said. "If they know we know, we're dead."

We heard the sound of the outer door being breached. Orla took the folder from Zoe and tidied it before returning all the folders to the cabinet. The Agents were at the door to the room and we could hear muffled discussions on the other side.

"This is going to look very suspicious, you blowing the security when he's in the building," said Zoe to me. She wandered through the room, opening and closing drawers and cupboards, then returned to the gurney where I was sitting. She looked at me; she looked angry. How could she not be, when I had just destroyed her world? I had told them all that they're the baddies and they might as well be working on the Death Star.

She jabbed me in the neck with a hypodermic.

Orla was pushing closed the cabinet drawer.

As quietly as possible, Hannah said to Orla, "Jenna's was on the desk."

"Shite," said Orla, pulling out the folder and placing it on the desk. She then pushed the drawer closed and gave it a quick tug to ensure it had locked again. It stayed shut. She stepped back into the room as the door splintered in. I drifted off to the sound of Orla shouting.

"Thank God! I need a wee, right now."

21

S ome time later, possibly only a few minutes, I roused briefly at the sound of the perimeter siren. I sighed. Hopefully, Connor had escaped. I'd done what I could to help him.

I awoke, still in the medical block, but it was morning. My friends were gone, if they were still my friends. I was alone with the Doc.

I gripped my head. "Did I get tranquillised again?"

"I'm afraid so. You had an episode in the lab last night. I was locked out, and your friends didn't get to you quickly enough."

"They'll be disappointed. They've been practising. I thought it was down to a fine art," I said. "What happened?"

"Well, Jenna, I'm in deep, deep trouble, but on the bright side, you didn't die."

"You're in trouble? Why?"

"That doesn't matter now. Your heart rate and body temperature have returned to normal. I've given you an antibiotic shot, just in case. We're ready to start working on your talent. If I can get some good results and fast, I might keep my job."

I almost pitied him.

I touched the back of my neck to find it covered with gauze.

"You knocked out your inhibitor last night. You're lucky it didn't kill you. You pretty much killed everything in here. I swapped your chip for the spare." He blushed. "It seemed a shame to let a good sedative go to waste."

I just wanted to be out of his sight. "I'm glad you had a spare. I hope the broken one wasn't expensive."

I smiled ruefully at him, wanting to smash him in the teeth.

"About a million dollars," he sighed.

"Oops! Can I go now?"

"Of course, Jenna. Your implant is switched on. Shall we start at twelve?"

I figured if I made it back to the residence block without getting shot in the back, my friends and I were probably going to be okay. I found the three of them in the kitchen, nursing cold cups of coffee. They looked like they hadn't slept, and they all looked at me like I'd ruined their lives. I suppose I had. I had revealed them to be accessories to... what? Murder? Torture? Now they knew the truth, and they were powerless to change anything. They were even unable to discuss it for fear of being murdered themselves.

Choosing my words as carefully as I could, looking at them each in turn, I said, "I'm sorry you had to knock me out. You all look like you feel awful, but I know you were just doing your job. I can't have made it easy for you." I hoped they'd understand what I was trying to say. Then I looked just at Orla. "If you prefer, I can move down to the med lab or something."

I went to my room to change. There was a new key card in an envelope taped to my door. Of course, I would have wiped the magnetic strip on our cards in the lab. I took out the new one and let myself in.

Thirty seconds later, there was a knock at the door. I opened it, and Orla stood there, still looking haunted. She stepped in and hugged me.

"We're sorry...for sedating you. It was all for the best, though. We still love you, you daft mare."

"I don't imagine it will be the last time. I'm starting my X-Men trials at twelve."

"On an empty stomach?" asked Orla. "Over my dead body!"

That statement gave me chills. Orla dragged me back to the kitchen, gave me a bagel and refreshed the coffees.

"Have you all been sitting here all night?" I asked.

"Mostly. Although Zoe did what Zoe does when she gets stressed," said Hannah.

"Ah! Laundry," I said. "I hate doing laundry. I don't understand how that relaxes you."

"I left a tissue in my pocket and the whole wash was covered in white bits. I had to do it twice," said Zoe, looking straight at me.

She'd disposed of the piece of paper she'd taken from the office. That was a relief.

"So you're twice as relaxed?" I asked.

"Not so much," Zoe said as she dropped her head on to her arms on the table.

We drank and ate and chatted about safe things: *Glee* and *Buffy* and which X-Man we'd rather be. Dr Philipson appeared at the door and looked suspiciously at our maudlin group.

Orla looked up and said, "Doc, would you like to join our

coffee group for the terminally sleepy? None of us slept a wink last night, we were so worried about Jenna."

To me, he said, "I expect your friends have told you about the Fader. You mustn't blame yourself."

I nearly lied and said they had, but the Agents would have been listening to every word we had said.

"No," I said. I looked around at the girls, more to break eye contact with the Doc than anything. Rather than put the others through the trial of faking a response, I just acted like I'd put two and two together. "Oh NO!" I put my head into my hands. Orla hugged me. Zoe burst into tears and ran out of the room, and Hannah went after her. I don't think there was anything fake about Zoe's reaction.

"Jenna, we caught it once, we'll get it again." He patted my shoulder awkwardly. "Anyway, I came to tell you we won't be starting until late afternoon. The team is still setting up. We lost some equipment in the med centre last night and we're waiting on replacements."

Good! I thought.

WHEN I ARRIVED at the lab, Dr Philipson was waiting for me next to an SUV. An Agency man was in the driver's seat and a couple of lab assistants were there too. I started to feel nervous. Was this it? Were they going to take me somewhere quiet and shoot me in the head? Would a scientist even oversee something like that?

"I think it'll be best if we go to work somewhere a little quieter," Doc said brightly.

That statement did not make me feel any safer.

He continued, "We can't risk the security of the site again, so we're going to use another building."

The word "building" was particularly generous. It was a

hastily thrown together container park, probably as far from the main complex as it could get while remaining on the property. I could even hear the highway.

I wandered around the small compound while the Doc and his assistants set up. There were three mobile units, like Portakabins, placed in an open-ended square. On the right was a toilet block with entrances at each end for men and women. The middle cabin had its door closed, and the left side cabin appeared to be a mobile lab. Three small square plastic tables were set out in the middle, along with a few chairs. Two stadium lights on scaffolding towers rose up either side of the central unit and faced down towards the centre. They appeared to be connected to a noisy generator at the back of the toilet block. No regular military people were here, just the Agency guys. Welcome to Stalag 19, I thought.

When the Doc was ready for me, I was led into the lab unit which separated into two sections – or rather, one area inside another. I was led into the inner room, which contained only a chair and table and a mess of wires with metal studs at the ends. These were similar to the equipment Dr Narayan had been using. The wires plugged into machines along the wall and out of the other side into a computer on a desk. The computer was attached to a screen, but I could only see the back of the monitor.

The Perspex wall around me had fine metal wire threaded through the middle of it. I sat in the chair while a technician taped electronic sticky pads to my body in various places. A band around my chest and a skullcap for my head seemed to be held in place by the electronic sticky pads.

As the first pad was attached, the Tech called out, "Pad One."

The second Tech at the computer called back, "Pad One confirmed."

"Jenna," said the Doc, "you mustn't blink in while we're doing the experiments. It could affect the readings and we'll have to repeat the tests. So, as soon as you're in that chair, no blinking in."

"Okay, Doc, I got it."

I learned that the two assistants were Manuel and Vera. I thought of them as Nerd 1: Manuel and Nerd 2: Vera. They weren't particularly friendly, but perhaps that might just have been my perspective now that things had changed. I worried that my friends were experiencing the same paranoia.

"Are we ready to turn off the inhibitor?" asked Vera. The Doc glanced at the lights on the wall by the door to my little plastic cell; the lights were red. I guessed that meant it was locked. I didn't like that. He nodded, and Vera paused at the keyboard looking at the Agency guard in the corner, whose name I didn't know.

The moment drew out, and I got annoyed.

"Oh for God's sake, just get on with it. I've got a date tonight."

Vera gave me a look of withering contempt and pressed a few keys on the keyboard. I observed, for the first time, that under their white lab coats, both Techs were wearing neck to feet black. They were Agency.

The machines around the lab sprang to life. Dials which had been sitting at zero now bounced up a little.

"How are you feeling, Jenna?" asked the Doc in a matter-of-fact but kind voice.

"Nervous," I responded.

"Can you pinpoint why, specifically, that is?" he asked.

"I'm thousands of miles away from my home, which isn't

there any more. My dad and a friend have died because of me, I'm a medical freak, and I'm hooked up to creepy machines in the middle of nowhere."

"That makes sense. But what about the Fader? You didn't mention it. Are you worried about that?"

Oops! I thought. I should have said that first.

I began to get more nervous because of my omission, and I could see the needles on the dials rising a little higher around me.

"I am now. Thanks for that."

"So you're going on a date? With Marcus?" the Doc asked.

"Dinner and a movie, sort of. We're going to the diner on the base, and then we'll watch something on TV or a DVD." I imagined being snuggled up on a sofa, watching TV with Marcus. I looked at the dials; they were all flat. It was interesting that thinking about Marcus seemed to calm me. Useful to know.

Dr Philipson was scribbling in a notepad. I could see he had observed that too. I didn't feel comfortable with him knowing so much about me, but I couldn't think of a way that I could investigate this without him.

"Do you miss your father, Jenna?" the Doctor asked.

I'd been expecting it. I thought immediately about the Agency trying to kill my dad. The needle bounced up, and the lights began to flicker. I didn't blink in and out; I had a much better handle on that now. Suddenly, the dials all dropped down, and I realised the Doc had engaged the implant.

I looked at the Doc. "Of course I miss him." I could feel my eyes stinging with tears. It was pure outrage, but he wouldn't have known that.

"Are there any foods you miss from home?" he asked.

I was confused by this new direction.

"Yes, fish and chips. I miss them, and real Cadbury's chocolate. I've had it here, but it doesn't taste the same."

"Okay," said the Doc, "let's call it a day. We were just calibrating the machines anyway. We've got everything we need to begin tomorrow."

After being detached from the wires, I sat on one of the plastic chairs outside while the others wrapped up. I had a lot to consider. I thought about Nate, about how he'd died. I now knew that he had been a Fader, just like the rest of us. Did that make any difference to the situation? A Fader who didn't have an implant had pulled Nate's out. Why would they do that?

I wondered what the Agents were going to do to me. I now understood why they only had a small window to study me. If they kept turning off my implant to carry out their experiments, eventually, I'd start emitting random yellow pulses. They couldn't let that happen. I had a horrible feeling that they'd find some other ways to experiment on me, and I might not need to be alive.

As I sat in the back of the Jeep going back to the compound, I started to wonder about the Trackers who were supposedly asked to join the Agency – the ones who"d been recruited and had disappeared. Surely the Agents couldn't risk having Trackers working directly within their organisation. I concluded that those Trackers were probably dead. They were considered a threat, suspected of knowing too much, maybe? How credible did the threat need to be for the Agents to act on it? Were we in immediate danger? Were they weighing up the odds on whether to keep us alive or not?

I had too many questions and not enough answers.

22

A balled up piece of paper hit me on the side of the head.

"She shoots, she scores!" cried Orla, as she pumped her fist into the air.

I just looked at her through the mirror with my eyebrows raised.

"You've been staring at yourself in the mirror with one eyebrow pencilled for five minutes."

"Sorry. Miles away."

"What's on your mind? I mean, besides all the stuff that's, you know, on your mind."

"I'm considering the problem of Marcus."

"I thought you liked him."

"I do." I looked at her. "But we're so different in a lot of ways. We have different beliefs. I'm not always sure of the best way to talk to him."

She knew what I was saying. Marcus hadn't been there in the med lab last night. He didn't know what we knew.

She thought for a moment. "I see your problem. Men are

from Mars. These things have a way of sorting themselves out, though. This place doesn't help, does it? Having monsters chasing after you."

We both knew who the monsters were, and it wasn't the Faders.

I finished my makeup. "I can't believe I have to go on a date wearing jeans," I said. "I wasted those trips to the mall. I should have been looking for Faders in the changing rooms."

"You haven't said what happened in your brain experiments. Have you been sworn to secrecy?" asked Orla.

"No. It was just not very interesting. Dr Philipson said stuff to get me upset."

"What happened?"

"I got upset and the dials on their machine flipped. Then Cheery Vera, the Tech, pressed a button and it stopped. Well, the dials stopped. Not so much the upset. Doc asked me one unexpected question. He asked what I missed from home."

"What did you say?"

"I told him I miss fish and chips and Cadbury's chocolate."

"Oh my God! Fish and chips, and oh. My. God! Chocolate." Orla rolled around on her bed with her hands on her belly. "Now I miss them too."

"Well, time for date night," I said, throwing my lipstick and phone into my pockets.

"Where's he taking you?"

"You're kidding, right?"

"Yep! Enjoy the diner."

It was a ten-minute walk to the diner. Marcus met me outside the block and offered his arm.

"Are you going to take it this time?"

"You know what? I think I am." I took his arm, and we strolled to the diner.

The board outside said "Fish & Chip Night".

"Wait, what?" I said, staring at it. "Why would Dr Philipson arrange this?"

"Maybe he didn't," said Marcus.

"Seriously? You got the Doc to plant questions for your nefarious intentions?"

"Nefarious is a bit strong," he said defensively. "More like, nefarious adjacent."

I smiled broadly. It was time to give myself the night off worrying about a situation I couldn't currently change.

"Okay, Marcus, let's see how the Americans have interpreted your request."

"Oh Jeez," he said. "Now I'm nervous."

As we walked in, the Manager was explaining to a couple of young Trackers, "No, they're not like a pack of potato chips. They're British chips. British chips are like fat fries."

He spied Marcus and said, "Dude, you owe me. This is, like, the twentieth time I've had to explain it."

"Dude," replied Marcus, "to be fair, I had to explain it to you about twenty times. Just change the board to say "British Fish & Fat Fries"."

"I'm doing that. I'm doing that right now." He started to walk off, and then spun back around to me. "Welcome to The Hickory Shack's British Night. Your table awaits."

"Thank you," I giggled.

Marcus led us to a booth in the back of the diner. We sat, but I noticed him looking around nervously.

"Are you okay?" I asked.

"Yes, great." He beamed.

"But?" I prompted.

"I'm a bit worried about what the mushy peas are going to be like."

To Marcus's horror, I took out my mobile and called Orla. "Orla, there's fish and chips on the menu. Just letting you know." I didn't wait for an answer; I disconnected immediately and turned the phone off.

"Is that some code for when a date's turning out badly?" Marcus asked.

"You shouldn't be surprised to hear we were talking about fish and chips earlier. I'm not the only one missing them. Orla would never forgive me if I didn't let her know."

Ten minutes later, Orla, Zoe, Hannah and Al turned up and sat discreetly at the opposite end of the diner from us. Even Nerd 1 and Nerd 2 were in – their curiosity piqued, perhaps? Or spying on me. Probably the latter.

The fish and chips were very nice. The mushy peas were interesting.

FOR THE NEXT TWO WEEKS, I trundled down the desert road on the base that led to the lab. The Doc continued with his experiments, and I resumed mine. He was trying to get me to focus my efforts in one direction. He knew I'd done it before because I'd stupidly told Dr Narayan when I popped Marcus's Bluetooth speaker and nothing else in the room.

This time, however, I was intentionally giving my efforts a more scattergun approach. I was learning how to control them without appearing to, although I couldn't see how that was going to help me.

It was getting easier for Doc to get me riled, though. As the days went by, I started to feel isolated and a little stir crazy. I was worried about the others; they were going out on patrols every day. There had been no sign of Faders yet, but I felt strongly that at some point, the Agency was going to test their loyalty. Also, the vibe between us felt different, and I was worried the Agency would pick up on it. Marcus could tell something was different. I'd been praying he wouldn't say anything, but of course, he did.

We were playing pool in the rec room when Marcus finally piped up.

"What's wrong with you lot? You used to be so enthusiastic about Tracking, but you all look so miserable now."

It seemed Orla had also been expecting this. She leaped in.

"I think it's the Fader getting away. I don't know about anyone else, but I've just felt demoralised since then. No offence, Jenna. No one blames you; you know that, right?"

"I know," I said. "I thought they might have caught it again. If I could do it over, I'd stay away from the med centre and let that implant fry my brain."

"You can't think like that," said Marcus. "None of you can. We have to stay positive, and we have to support each other." He walked up behind me, wrapped his arms around me and spoke into my neck. "I hardly ever see you these days. I miss you."

I turned around in his arms and faced him. "I'm sorry," I said. "The days at that camp exhaust me. It's emotionally draining, and sometimes it's upsetting."

"Then that's when you need me the most," he said, kissing my nose.

"That's true. Your hugs are like magic. I feel so relaxed when I'm with you."

"You should experience one of my massages."

"You give massages?"

"I'm studying to be a Physio. Of course, I do."

"We need to discuss this in depth."

"We do!" he agreed. "But first I need to trounce you at pool."

IN THE FOURTH week at the mobile camp, we stopped for lunch. As ever, the Doc ate with the Nerds. Rather than sit at my usual plastic table in the shade, I took my water and my wrap and went mooching around the area.

I could see for miles back towards the compound, but a rocky outcrop surrounded the trailers at the rear. It was only a couple of metres high, so I climbed it and sat at the top. The landscape sloped down away from me. Off to my right, I could see a little of the road I'd been hearing. It went around a bend so that only a small curve was visible, but there were currently no cars on it. More interestingly, I could see the fence with its warnings of electrocution every few metres.

My eyes tracked the fence in both directions and came to rest at a small metal cabin with a green light on top and two doors on the front, covered, again, with electrocution warning signs. A Greyhound bus appeared briefly over the distant horizon in the shimmering heat of an unexpectedly warm spell late in May. It disappeared moments later around the bend. I couldn't see where it was going, but I was jealous.

I felt I was being watched and turned my attention slowly across the horizon while eating my lunch. Moments later, Dr Philipson was next to me.

"I'm not sure we should be up here." The Doc looked around. "What's so interesting?" he asked.

"Freedom," I sighed. I rolled up my lunch packaging and stood up, wiping dust from my jeans.

"Your nose is getting burned. You should be wearing a hat out here."

I smiled up at him and thought, you'd be okay if you weren't a murdering psychopath.

We went back to work, an idea trying unsuccessfully to form in my mind. I needed some quiet time.

———

23

When I woke the next morning, I had an idea about what I wanted to achieve, but I needed to think out a plan. I didn't want to spend the day at that awful little camp again. I needed time to myself.

I trudged into the bathroom and looked in the mirror. My forehead, nose, cheeks, and chin were all bright red with sunburn. I sighed and walked away, then stopped and went back to the mirror. This was perfect. I didn't smile, but I wanted to.

I met the others in the kitchen, still in my pyjamas and sipping on a bottle of water. I dropped into a chair and closed my eyes.

"Jenna, are you okay?"

"Not really. I've got a terrible headache, and I feel a bit sick."

"Your face is sunburned," said Hannah. "Were you in the sun yesterday without a hat and sunblock?"

"For about twenty minutes at lunchtime," I said.

"That's ten minutes longer than it can take to get sunstroke," said Zoe.

"You need to take some painkillers, drink plenty of water and get back to bed, young lady," said Orla. "And we need to get off. I'll tell your driver you're not well."

I stood at the window and watched them leave, recognising my Agency driver sitting in the Jeep waiting for me. Orla diverted from the others getting into their vehicle and strode across to him, spoke a few words and headed back to the car. As the car pulled away, she glanced up at my window, her face grave and questioning. She clearly knew I was pulling a sickie and wanted to know why. It must have been maddening for her.

As I watched them drive away, a movement caught my eye. My Agency driver raised his phone to his face as his eyes tracked their departure. I assumed he was telling the Doc I wouldn't be coming in, but the conversation seemed to go on for longer than that would take. Then he locked up his car and leaned against it, waiting for something.

Suddenly aware that while I had been watching him, someone was likely to have been looking at me, I sighed and moved away from the window to refill my water bottle. I took two Advil from the bottle in the kitchen cupboard and downed them. I didn't want to leave the kitchen because it had the best view of the road outside and my bedroom window looked out in the opposite direction, so I sat with my head cradled in my arms on the kitchen table for a few minutes, periodically sipping my water.

After a while, I heard an engine outside. I got up to tip my bottle into the sink and looked out. Another car had stopped and picked up my driver. No day off for him. I was just turning away when I noticed that the surly Agent who usually watched me at the camp, whose name I'd learned was Merl, was also in the car. They sped off towards the exit. Something seemed off.

I refilled my water and padded back to my room.

In bed, I texted Orla. I had to be careful with how I worded it. The Agency would obviously be monitoring our communications.

"Hi – it's a shame I'm not working today."

"Why?"

"I just saw Miserable Merl heading out somewhere in a car, just a few minutes after you. Today would have been much more pleasant in work without his face glaring at me all day. Look behind you. If he's still on the same road, perhaps you could stick your arm out and give him the finger for me."

"LOL! Not a chance. The moody bugger would probably shoot it off. Get to bed!"

"I'm in bed! I took pills. Sleep now."

"Take care, Sweetie x"

"You take care too x"

I dropped my phone onto the table, visibly shivered and pulled my covers up over my head. Then I started thinking, and then I started planning.

THE OTHERS CAME BACK a little earlier than normal, and the atmosphere in the kitchen was one of forced enthusiasm.

"How did it go today?"

"We finally got one," said Orla with a victorious tone I could see she didn't feel.

"Fantastic! What happened?"

"We went to a different location this time. After about three hours, I spotted a man walking through the mall with a suit and briefcase emitting a bright yellow trail. I called the team leader, and the backup team was there in minutes. I think we must have been an additional team at a site they were already working. you'd think they'd be a bit more forthcoming with the information, though, wouldn't you? I guess these Americans do things differently."

"Was Miserable Merl the backup?" I asked.

"Yeah. They must have reassigned him after I told them you were sick. No wonder he's miserable, he can't catch a break."

We laughed.

"Yeah, I guess. Well done, though. It sounds like it was a textbook takedown. Maybe you'll get a bonus."

"As if! How are you feeling now? Did you get some rest?" asked Orla.

"I'm feeling good now," I said. "I seem to have slept it off."

Orla and I were getting excellent at reading between the lines. She knew I'd stayed in bed for my own reasons and we both knew the Agency had been testing them today. If she hadn't called in the Fader sighting, my friends would probably be dead by now. I hoped the Agency felt they had proven their loyalty. The Agents must have already known about that poor Fader. Whether or not Orla had called it in, he would have been captured.

We all knew we were playing a dangerous game.

Zoe and Hannah came in. Hannah looked like she was just about keeping it together. I glanced at Zoe, and she looked worried.

"Okay," I said, "we need to go out and celebrate tonight. The problem is, this resort has too many places to choose from."

"Where do you want to go?" asked Zoe.

"Well, we could go to that place up the road. The red and chrome place," said Orla of the only diner on site.

"Oh, the Hickory something?" Zoe asked.

Orla and I both said, "The Hickory Shack!"

"I suppose I'd better get my hair done. As we're going to the Hickory Shack, I'm pushing the boat out and wearing my fancy jeans."

The silliness wasn't forced. It was a welcome relief, something we all needed.

MONDAY MORNING, I went out to the car, and Marcus was sitting in it.

"I thought this was my car."

"It is," Marcus said. "I'm helping you today."

"I don't understand."

"Neither do I, to be honest, but the Doc seems to think it will help you, so..."

"Okay," I said, still not getting it.

When we arrived, Marcus hopped out of the Jeep and looked around. "So this is where you've been coming every day for weeks."

"This is it," I said, expansively sweeping my arm.

"Jenna," said Marcus.

"Yes?"

"This place is dismal. No wonder you've been so depressed."

"Well, it's a little brighter today."

"Ahh! The lovebirds are here," said Dr Philipson, coming out of the central lab. "Jenna, if you could hop into the lab, they'll set you up. Marcus, can you follow me?"

"Okey dokey, Doc." Marcus did a little salute and followed him into the second mobile unit.

I watched him go in, starting to feel a bit nervous as I entered the lab. Manuel attached the pads and electrodes, calling out, "Pad One, Pad Two," and so on as he went along.

Vera was at the console. "Pad One confirmed, Pad Two confirmed."

At Pad Seven, I heard, "SON OF A BITCH!" yelled from the second unit. I jumped.

"It's a good job we hadn't switched off the chip. The look on your face, you'd have fried the whole place," said Manuel.

Five minutes later, Marcus came in looking a little pale.

"Marcus, take the seat next to Jenna. Remember what I said about no blinking in, okay? It's important," said the Doc.

"I remember, Doc," said Marcus with another salute.

I wondered why the Doc was so insistent that we didn't blink in during these tests.

I blinked in.

"The things we do for love," Marcus said, and winked at me.

I smiled nervously at him. I was worried and scared. But, holy smoke, did he just say the "L" word?

"What's wrong with your neck?" I asked, having seen a patch of gauze over the back of it.

"Jenna, Marcus now has a similar chip to you," said Dr Philipson.

"One that you can switch off?" I asked.

"That's the only difference. It's less complex than yours. It stays on permanently."

"Then what's the point of it?"

I already thought I knew where this was going. I could feel my heart racing, one of the machines matching the beats.

"I think you might get better results if you're more emotionally invested in our tests," the Doc explained. "Marcus has agreed to offer some incentive in helping you refine your skills."

"What? You can't do this. It's barbaric."

"Jenna, I think it will be better if you get a hold of your emotions."

Marcus was looking nervous now too. He'd let the Doc put that chip in him, not even realising what was going to happen.

Merl was standing by the door with his hand not too far from his gun. They had apparently run out of patience, and this was a last ditch attempt.

Marcus sat next to me in the inner room. "So, can we have a fish and chips "last meal" thing?" he said. No one laughed.

"Cutting the switch," began Vera, "in three, two, one."

I got a grip.

"I imagine you're quite upset with me," said Dr Philipson.

"Ya think?" I asked without a hint of humour. "This is unprofessional and irresponsible."

The light overhead started to flicker.

"Erm..." said Marcus, looking nervous.

Vera's hand poised over the keyboard, and I worried she wouldn't stop it in time.

"Concentrate on the tape machine in front of you."

Manuel switched the music on.

"Seriously?" asked Marcus with a nervous laugh. "Enya again? Oh God, I'm truly going to die."

Then something happened. Something unexpected. I realised that having Marcus here, holding my hand, was having a calming effect. While I was still absolutely as mad as hell, I was more in control than ever. Not from fear of hurting him, but as always, because he relaxed me. It was like the anger that had built up in me had dissipated just enough to allow me to control it. I found that I was able to focus on the tape machine.

I thought, Just stop, and I loosened my hold on the energy. The speaker popped, fizzled and was silent.

The Tech tapped the keyboard, engaging my chip and I let out a breath.

"Great!" said Marcus, giving the Doc a thumbs up. "Could you maybe take this thing out of my head now?"

"It won't hurt if we leave it in there for now," said the Doc.

"I so hoped you wouldn't say that," said Marcus.

"Let's break for a while and we'll study the data," said the Doc.

I hadn't observed that blinking in had made any noticeable difference so I blinked out again.

Marcus and I moved a couple of chairs into the shade to wait. He was so excited.

"That was unbelievable. That was just, wow!" His eyes were like saucers.

"I can't believe you let them do that to you," I said.

"In my defence, I didn't know what they were going to do."

"I can't believe you let them do that to you without knowing exactly what they were planning to do."

"Yeah, you've got me there," Marcus said. "Seriously, though, what you can do is amazing. I'm sure there will be ways you can help the Agency with it. You're going to be their most valuable weapon."

"Don't call me a weapon," I said, horrified at the thought. "But yes, I know. They are never going to let me go anywhere again. I'll never see the inside of a Cheesecake Factory. No more clothes shopping. My great American adventure and

I'll never see anything outside of this place." I sighed. "I don't want to belong to them, Marcus. I want to belong to me."

I could feel my eyes starting to sting.

"Jenna, it's not going to be like that," Marcus said. "Sure, things are difficult at the moment because of this situation with the Fader, but it will be different. You won't be able to use your superpowers here. They'll need you out there eventually, and I'll be beside you every step of the way." He took my hand and kissed it. "I'll make sure you get all the cheesecake you want."

After nearly an hour, Merl appeared and told us to get our stuff together. It was going to take the rest of the day for them to extrapolate meaningful information from the data.

I couldn't get away fast enough.

24

A nother day, another tape machine. I went to the camp alone. The problem was, I wanted to continue to experiment myself, but I didn't want Dr Philipson to know I was doing it. Also, it was going to be a lot more complicated to achieve my goal. I needed to control the data coming from all of the electrodes on my head so that I could concentrate on yet another thing.

The threat was there now. The Doc hadn't taken the chip out of Marcus; he could bring him in anytime. I had to give results. At first, I struggled to contain the energy the way I had when Marcus had been there. I'd somehow been able to reduce it to a manageable level, but I hadn't focused on how I had done it. I remembered the feeling of it draining away, and that helped.

After a few false starts and a threat from Dr Philipson to bring Marcus back, I just let go.

Finally, I felt ready for a little experiment of my own. Dr Philipson was asking me to concentrate on the tape machine. I stared at it, but I wasn't concentrating on just that. I was thinking about one of the electrodes on my head,

Number Three. It would usually pulse and make waves on the screen, and I thought how great it would be if it stayed still for a few seconds. I pushed that thought out. Of course, all the other dials rose as soon as I did that.

The tape machine popped.

"Excellent. I think we've turned a corner," said Dr Philipson. "Let's take a look at the data."

"Can I go to the bathroom?" I asked. "And I think one of these pads is loose." I reached round the back of my neck and pulled off a sticky pad. "This one's been moving around a bit."

Manuel came in and unclipped the electrodes from the sticky pads and looked at where the loose one had been.

"Number Three," he said to the others.

"Ah yes," said the Doc, "it stopped transmitting just before it cut out. Thank you, Jenna. We'll fix it after your break."

I wanted to punch the air. I'd done it. I'd concentrated on not just one thing, but two, and eliminated everything else.

I was exhausted, so I let everything go haywire for the rest of the day. I suffered the Doc's questions, and then he let me go back to the base. I realised I wasn't going to get away with messing with the electrodes again; I'd have to find other ways to practise.

The tests continued through June and July. My birthday in August almost went by without me even noticing. By mid-September, I'd built up my capacity for disrupting or increasing the electrical current in small things around me. The others didn't notice as they were all looking at me or their screens.

On the wall of my little room were two tiny LEDs, one on each side of the door. The lights were green when the door was open and red when it was closed. Finally, one morning, I was ready to give it a try. I concentrated on making the electrodes transmit a standard response on the screen. Without looking at them, I directed my mental focus towards the little lights in my peripheral vision on the wall. The light on my side was simple. I had it flicking red and green, and no one noticed.

Frustratingly, I couldn't get the light outside the door to budge. All through my attempts, I kept the electrodes sending their lazy rhythm to the screen. When I thought I was nearly ready, it didn't seem wise. I couldn't risk blowing one thing in the lab, so I sacrificed my iPod for the greater good.

I flickered the light. Looking at the Doc, I periodically nodded while zoning him out. I could see the screen reflected in Vera's glasses. I kept concentrating on the electrodes staying relatively even and simultaneously tried to direct the energy at the iPod. It got hotter in my pocket.

I started worrying that I was going to burn my bum, so I stopped thinking about the iPod. I realised the Doc was talking about Dad, so I looked upset and relaxed my control over the electrodes and popped another cassette recorder.

I had been discreetly blinking in and out during the tests over the summer, and on this occasion I discovered why the Doc had told me I shouldn't. I found myself sitting in the middle of a pool of yellow mist. My first thought was that there was someone in the inner room with me. Before I could stop myself, I jumped up from the chair.

"Bloody hell!"

"Jenna, what's wrong?" asked the Doc.

I hopped around from one foot to another.

"Cramp in my calf," I said, relieved that I had recovered so quickly. I limped around for another minute then settled back into the seat.

So I had started emitting. I didn't know much about it. I knew it was something that Faders did occasionally, sometimes for seconds or minutes. I didn't know how frequently it happened.

As usual, the Nerds flicked the switch and started working on their data. I stopped emitting the second the chip came back on. I was pleased by how I'd been progressing and felt that I might only be a couple of weeks from feeling confident enough to put my plan into action.

As I waited to be disconnected, the Doc stood beside me.

"Jenna," he said, "I know you've been bored on the base. I've got some good news for you."

I couldn't believe I was finally going to be allowed off the base. I was delighted. I smiled up at the Doc, encouraging him to continue.

"Did you know that some Trackers who are considered particularly talented are offered a position working for the Agency?"

The smile was still frozen to my face.

"I had heard that, but all I've done is a little spotting. I won't even start tracking until I'm eighteen."

It was a good job the Nerds had switched the chip back on and removed the pads. I was terrified.

"Well, I think you know that you have other talents. Just think about it for a day or two. It's very exciting work."

"Would I stay here?"

"you'd probably be working all over the world," he said, confirming my worst fears.

"I'll think about it, thanks," I said and went outside, putting my hat on as I went.

"Flee the cage, little bird," said the Doc as I exited the room.

Yeah, whatever, I thought.

I spent five minutes in the sun on top of the rocks, then sat and ate my lunch in the shade. I was going to have to move up my plans. I didn't think the Agents were going to kill me yet, but they were definitely planning to isolate me from my friends and everyone else.

I looked at the landscape as I ate. I had in mind what I wanted to do, but I wasn't even sure it was possible.

Something about what the Doc had said to me as I left bothered me. It seemed a funny thing to say, given that I still felt like I was in a cage. I felt like that all the time. Did he know what I was planning? Why would he say that? The cage.

After half an hour, the Doc's head popped around the corner.

"Okay, back to work."

As I walked back into the lab, what he had meant suddenly hit me. It was all I could do not to swear out loud.

As the Nerds hooked me up to the machines, I asked, "Can you leave the door open, please? I'm starting to find it claustrophobic in here."

"Sorry, Jenna. We can't begin testing unless we close the door," said the Doc. "It's protocol."

"Okay. It's no biggie."

I shrugged.

We carried on with the tests.

"Why do we do the same thing over and over?" I asked.

"We have to get a reliable baseline before we can alter the tests. It's just how this works. I know it seems boring for you, but we're doing world-changing stuff here, Jenna."

"It's not boring. I still can't quite believe it's my head that's doing this. It's just...well, I'm in the middle of this, but in some ways, I feel like I'm not involved at all. I want to understand this too."

"I promise, when we understand what's going on, you'll be the first to know."

I sat quietly thinking while the Doc and his Nerds continued their work. It made sense now. This little room was a Faraday cage built inside the lab. It became fully activated when the door closed. The red light above the door indicated that the cage was working. And that's why I couldn't affect the light on the other side of the door. I could manipulate the monitors because I was controlling the electrodes at this end.

I needed to figure out how to disable the cage.

When I got back to the accommodation block, I found Orla.

"Oh my God, Orla, you're not going to believe this." I forced excitement into my voice. "I think they're going to ask me to join the Agency. The Doc was feeling me out about it today."

Orla knew what this meant. She froze. This was bad; we were being watched. I clicked my fingers in front of her face.

"Did you hear me?"

"Yes," she said. "Honestly, I don't know what to say. This means you'll be going off, not allowed to contact us. I'll miss you. Also, I'm a bit jealous. It's a lot to process."

She'd made a good recovery. I was relieved.

"I haven't said yes or no yet," I added.

"I've never heard of anyone turning them down. What do you think you'll do?"

"I don't know. I've got a lot of thinking to do. Watch this space!"

A FEW DAYS LATER, I nearly killed myself.

I walked into the kitchen in the morning to a discussion

on the benefits of skin care regimes. Hannah was reading out descriptions of various overpriced potions, and Orla was saying, "All you need is a good face cloth. You need heat to open the pores, exfoliate with the cloth and use cold water to close your pores. That's it. None of your fancy, expensive Hollywood creams."

That evening, I was getting ready to meet Marcus at the diner. I stepped out of the shower – a steamy bathroom was the only way I could bring myself to get naked, knowing Agents were probably watching me – and wrapped a towel around myself. I was about to start drying my hair when I looked at the hairdryer and thought, Why the hell not? My plan was to accidentally on purpose drop the hairdryer into the sink and cause a short in the electrics.

I plugged in the hairdryer, putting it on the side while I filled the sink with cold water. Splashing the water on to my face, I patted it dry, leaving the sink full of water. I picked up the hairdryer and started to dry my hair, then flipped my head around like I was a supermodel going for extra lift at the roots. At this point, I "accidentally" dropped the hairdryer into the sink. Unfortunately, before the electricity shorted, it travelled up my wet hair which had been trailing in the water. I'd been method acting again, got carried away, and electrocuted myself.

The journey from standing at the sink to lying on the floor was a mystery. I sat up. I seemed to be okay, but for some reason, I burst into tears. There was a hammering at my door, and I wobbled across the room and opened it. Zoe burst in.

"What happened? Are you okay?"

"I had an accident in the bathroom with the hairdryer."

"Are you okay? You're as white as a sheet."

"I'm alright, I think."

"You didn't fry your chip, did you? I mean, as well as all the electrics. Dr Philipson will go nuts."

It hadn't occurred to me that was a possibility. I glanced at my phone and tried to make the screen glow, but nothing happened.

"I think it's alright. I'm sure the whole place would have been in chaos by now."

Zoe looked a little disappointed. "What were you doing?"

"The cold water toning thing, then drying my hair but not thinking to empty the sink," I admitted. "It's not like I did it deliberately," I said, looking straight at her. She needed to know that things were moving along.

One of her eyebrows raised a fraction of an inch. "Of course not. But jeez, Jenna, if something can go wrong, it will go wrong with you. Why would anyone give a dope like you superpowers?"

"I know, right?"

I laughed weakly, and then the Security guys turned up. They took one look in the bathroom and one look at me. Closing the bathroom door, one of them barked, "Don't go in there." Then they left.

I dried and dressed, took my pen and notepad from my desk and wrote a random to do list, beginning with "buy a new hair dryer". I didn't know where the cameras were or even if anyone bothered to look at them, but I couldn't risk it, so I wandered around the room, looking in drawers. Sighing, I dropped the piece of paper on the bed next to me and waited.

An hour later, the electrician turned up. While he fixed the socket, I had another scout around while holding the piece of paper.

I asked, "Do you, by any chance, have a roll of Sellotape?"

"Huh?"

"Sticky tape."

He reached into his toolbox. "Will this do?" he asked as he held up a roll of insulating tape.

"Thanks, I'm sure it"ll do the trick."

I tore off two pieces and stuck the list to my wardrobe door with one of them. The other short length of tape remained adhered to my hand inside my pocket.

I returned the tape. "Thanks."

25

"You don't need to worry about the Faders," said the Doc the next day. "I think you're doing an excellent job of trying to kill yourself."

"Yes, it's looking that way, isn't it," I said, doing my best to look sheepish.

"Are you sure you're up to this?"

"Honestly, I'm not feeling the best, but I was worried I might have done something to the chip so came along anyway."

"No need to worry, the chip's insulated from regular electrical shocks."

I put my bag down on the floor with my water bottle sticking out of it then walked into the cage and flopped down on to the chair for Vera to hook me up. She walked out, closing the door behind her. Now that I was aware of the cage, I could clearly see the connecting points along the door's edge before it swung closed.

As the Doc walked back to the screens, I discreetly peeled the black insulating tape from my black watch strap and waited. I didn't know if this would even work. I could only cover up one of the contact points, so I prayed it would stop the whole cage from working.

"In three, two, one," said Vera.

"Okay, Jenna, you'll see there are two tape machines in with you today. I am going to start you on trying to focus the energy on two objects."

"Two objects?" I said. "You think I could do that?" I let the electrodes wobble a bit, for effect.

"It's alright. You don't have to try if you're not feeling up to it," he assured me. "The bosses have been impressed with how you're progressing. General Cavendish is coming out to see you, but you don't need to overtax yourself today."

Me, being the trouper I am, said, "I'll give it a go. I can try." I pondered momentarily on the injustice of knowing I'd never get an Academy Award for my recent performances.

I leaped from the chair and opened the door, reaching down to get my bottle of water. The Doc and Manuel moved towards me; Merl's hand moved towards his gun; I pretended not to notice that. Vera headed for the laptop to switch my chip back on.

I ducked straight back into the room, holding up the bottle. "Forgot my water."

The door clicked back into place, and the Doc said, "You shouldn't do that, Jenna. Someone could have passed it to you." He looked up to see the lights either side of the door flicker from green to red.

I resumed my place and took a drink from my bottle. "Sorry, you all looked busy."

I gave a stellar performance, trying so hard to focus simultaneously in two directions at once.

"How can you afford to keep going through tape machines like this? We must have blown at least fifty of them," I asked.

"You've blown over seventy recorders, but they're obso-
lete. We don't use them any more. These tests seem as good
a demise for them as any," said the Doc. "You might say
they're going out with a bang."

I wasn't listening to his side of the conversation. I was
doing what I'd come here today to do.

I visualised the electrical box outside and hoped that
what I was doing wasn't going to be loud. Sometimes, the
things I did were quite noisy. Finally, with that completed, I
realised I was going to have a problem. Vera usually
switched my chip back on while I was still sitting in the
chair. They were going to notice the door lights changing
colour, indicating that the cage was inactive.

I said, "Doc, I'm feeling sick." I got up and opened the
door, allowing the lights to go green. Vera was on the
machine and activated my chip while I hung on to the door
frame. "Can you get this stuff off me? I'm not feeling too
healthy at all."

The Doc came over to me and guided me back to the
chair. The door swung closed, and both lights went red
again.

"Take deep breaths," he said as he reached for my water.
The tape was back on my watch strap by the time I took the
water.

Dr Philipson looked disappointed. "I should have let you
rest today after last night. Do you still feel sick?"

"I don't think it's imminent, but my stomach's churning."

The Nerds put me in the Jeep, and the Doc said, "Make
sure you get some rest tonight."

"Thanks," I said, "I will."

But I had plans for the night that didn't involve rest.

Back in the kitchen, I waited until the others returned.

"How was your day?" I asked.

"Nada again," said Hannah.

"Maybe we've got them all, and there's none left," said Zoe.

"Now wouldn't that be a thing!" said Orla. "We'd all have to go and get real jobs."

"I don't know how to do anything else," said Hannah with horror, the thought only just having occurred to her.

"You're studying to be an engineer," said Zoe. "I think you'll be fine."

"That's years away. What about now?"

"It's okay," said Orla, "they'd have to give us retraining as part of our redundancy package."

"Can I train to be a mystery passenger on a cruise?" asked Zoe.

"Sure you can," said Orla. "Why not?"

We all seemed to realise at the same time that this conversation was getting a little dangerous.

"Don't even talk like that. I'm only just getting the hang of this stuff, and I don't like the idea that some Tracker might have killed my monster."

"Our monster," said Zoe reflexively.

"Our monster," I confirmed.

"Anyway," said Orla, signalling an end to that conversation, "how are you, Sparks?"

She was looking at me.

"Sparks?" I asked.

"Sure, that's your new nickname."

"Well, I suppose it's better than The Sporker," I said.

"Huh?" said Hannah.

"Nothing. It was a lifetime ago. I'm under strict instructions to unwind tonight," I told them. Not an accurate quotation, but close enough, I figured. "I think we should go to the diner."

"Text Marcus and see if he's free. He's been playing basketball with the guys lately."

"Orla," I said, "Dr Philipson said the General was coming to visit. He might already be here, and you know what that means." I raised my eyebrows suggestively.

"I think I'd know if Jason were coming."

"You never know, though. What if the plane's just landed and Jason was going to sleep, not realising that you were in the diner pining for him."

"Pining?" asked Orla.

"Just message him, tell him we're going out tonight in case he's in the area. It would be great to catch up, wouldn't it? God knows, I need a night out. If I see another Grey-hound bus going somewhere I can't, I'm going to scream. At least we finished before those awful stadium lights came on today. They give me a headache."

"God, it would be awesome if he were here. I've missed him so much. Okay, I'll text him now."

"General Cavendish?" asked a perplexed Hannah.

"No, Jason!" we all chorused.

Orla: "Hi"

Jason: "Well hello there!"

Orla: "We're going out tonight. If you're around, then you could come and give us a lift :)"

Jason: "Sorry, beautiful, still in England. We're coming in a few days though."

Orla: "Poor me. I'll have to walk it. And in these heels too."

Jason: "You could wait, and I'll come out with you at the weekend."

Orla: "Sorry, there will be no waiting. Jenna is going stir crazy. Apparently, she's been gazing hungrily at Greyhound buses and getting headaches from stadium lights (she's a real moaner!). Anyway, she needs a night out. Plus she tried to murder herself with a hairdryer last night."

Jason: "Oh dear, death by bad hair. Have a pleasant evening. I'm sure someone will give you a lift. I'll see you soon."

"Well, he's not here. He's coming in a few days. I'm all disappointed now," said Orla.

"I'm just waiting for Marcus to text back. Oh, speak of the devil," I said.

Marcus: "Okay, Sparks, meet at the diner?"

Jenna: "Don't you start with the Sparks thing too! I've had a stressful day. Can you borrow a Jeep and pick us up? Also, Orla in heels. I don't want to carry her."

Marcus: "Ha! I'd love to see that! Will pinch a Jeep."

"There we go," I said. "Marcus is coming, and he's committing GTA for us."

"That's a good man you've got there, Jenna," said Orla. "Let's get ready then, ladies. Remember, it's forecast to be pretty cool this evening and Marcus isn't a hundred per cent reliable and might turn up on a bicycle."

"What happened to the "good man"?" I asked.

"I mean he has good intentions," she said. "He's a man with good intentions."

"And the road to hell?" I asked.

"Well, yes," she said. "He does his fair share of manual labour."

"I have no idea what you two are saying," said Hannah.

"The road to hell is paved with good intentions," said Orla.

"Ah! That's the truest thing I ever heard," Hannah replied, and we all silently agreed.

I went back to my room and started getting ready. I tried on pretty much everything I had, flinging clothes all over the place. In the end, I wore the inevitable pair of jeans with low heeled ankle boots and a turquoise V-neck sweater that was several sizes too big for me. I wrapped a big belt around it and let it hang off one shoulder. There had been a lanyard tucked inside it which I had discretely popped into my bag. I pocketed my phone and put my duffle coat over my arm, took a look around the room and walked out.

I met the others, as usual, at the kitchen.

"Where's Zoe?" I asked.

"She ran over to ask Al something," said Hannah. "Apparently it couldn't wait." She managed to sound suitably irritated.

A few minutes later, Zoe was back, slamming the door to her room. We all looked at each other. Fewer than sixty seconds later, she was back out with her coat on.

"Are we going or what?" she asked.

"What's wrong?" Orla asked. "You've a face like a smacked arse."

"It's not me who got the slap," Zoe said. "I went to ask Al a question about the chalks he uses. We were chatting in his room and he tried to kiss me. So I punched him."

"Why would he do that?" I asked.

"He must have got the wrong idea. I was being friendly, but not *that* friendly."

"Do you think he'll come to the diner tonight?" asked Hannah.

"I wouldn't think so. I told him I didn't want to see his face again."

I wanted to laugh. She must have been giving him all kinds of subtle signals to encourage him to try it on just so she could stop him from coming with us tonight.

I looked at all three of them. We hadn't spoken a word of the plan, but they had all got the message. They knew we weren't coming back here. No one was overloaded enough to make it obvious to observers, but we knew.

The beep of a horn told us that Marcus had arrived. We stepped into the lift.

"I can't believe he stole a Jeep. He's not going to get into trouble, is he?" asked Hannah.

"I doubt he stole it. He probably borrowed it or swapped it or something," I said as we walked out.

"Ladies, your chariot awaits," Marcus announced.

We looked at the giant Humvee.

"Oh my God, Marcus," I said. "You're going to jail."

"It'll be one of those American penitentiaries," said Orla. "You'll be smashing rocks in a quarry."

"On a chain gang," added Zoe.

"I couldn't let Orla destroy her feet in those...Orla, what are you wearing on your feet?" he asked.

"I so very much wanted to wear the heels, they're beautiful, but...Marcus, have you ever put your feet in a pair of UGGs? There's no comparison," said Orla. "Plus, they're cursed. Once they were on, I couldn't take them off."

I took his arm. "I'm still tired from my stressful day, and feeling sick from electrocuting myself," I said. "Marcus, we need this Humvee. We deserve it. Also, you've nicked it now, and you'll be in the slammer tomorrow. You can't let it go to waste."

"Fair enough, Bunny. In you hop."

We piled into the car and trundled up to the diner.

Dinner was burger and chips and five dollar shakes all round. We sat back in the booth after our meal while the waiter cleared our plates.

"I don't understand why these five dollar shakes are only three dollars," said Marcus to the waiter.

"The diner's subsidised by the Government," the waiter replied.

"God Bless America," was Marcus's enthusiastic response.

Now was the time to start making things happen. I looked briefly at the girls, each in turn. They seemed to be expecting it, all looking back at me.

"Marcus," I began, "tell the girls how horrible Stalag 19 is."

"It's pretty awful. It's in the middle of nowhere, and Jenna spends her days with sour-faced Agents and Techs and a Doctor who tells rubbish jokes."

"That sounds miserable," said Zoe as we exited the diner and walked to the big car.

"No, Zoe, you can't possibly know how bad it is without seeing it," I said. "Marcus! Let's show them the camp of boredom."

"Are you nuts?" he said as we climbed in.

"But, I've got this," Orla stage-whispered as she produced a full bottle of vodka.

Marcus stared at it. "Where the hell did you get that from?"

"Hannah has connections," said Zoe, giggling.

"Can we go, Marcus? Please?"

"Please," we all said, laying it on thick. "Pretty please?"

"Well," he said, "they do say it's easier to ask for forgiveness than permission."

He started the car, and we headed down the road, past the accommodations and on to the darkened property of the base. After a few miles and a few turns, we were there.

"How we didn't get stopped is beyond me," said Marcus.

We climbed out of the car and looked around. The only light was from the almost full moon.

"It's a bit creepy at night, and without the lights on," I said. I was annoyed that I hadn't considered how dark it would be. I'd dropped massive hints about the stadium lights, but we'd left early that day, so they weren't switched on. I couldn't believe how stupid I'd been. If the moon hadn't been out, we'd have been in complete darkness.

As it was, the moon was casting an eerie light on to the portable buildings and the landscape around them. I worried that there would be a night guard there, or that the Agents had discovered what I'd done and were waiting for us. Oh God! I thought. What if Merl was here, skulking around in the dark with his itchy trigger finger? I shivered.

"I think I'm going to need a slug of that vodka. I can't imagine how much trouble we're going to get into," said Marcus.

"Oh, I don't think we need to worry about that," I said. "Not right now, anyway. Let's climb my little hill."

We all climbed and sat down on top of the rocks.

"You can see a little bit of the main road down there, and just for a few seconds, a Greyhound bus comes into sight, but then it's gone again."

"Jenna, it's pitch black out here. We can't see anything," said Marcus.

"You have to use your imagination," said Hannah.

Marcus looked around and then at me. "You are feeling isolated here, aren't you." He lifted my chin and kissed me. "Look at the stars. There are millions of them. It's like a different sky from home."

He tipped the bottle to his mouth, took a sip of the vodka and began to cough. "Oh my God, that's disgusting."

I tried a sip but spluttered. "Oh dear. That's a disappointment." I passed the bottle to Orla, who just screwed the top back on.

A cloud drifted across the moon, and the landscape was gone.

"Well, now it's pitch black. Literally. This plan might be the most ill-conceived plan in the history of plans," said Marcus.

Hannah put the torch of her phone on and shone it out into the darkness. "Nope, can't see a thing."

As we looked out, a light flashed three times in the distance. Orla and Zoe looked at each other, as best they could in the darkness, turned and started back down the hill with Hannah.

"Did you see that?" said Marcus, sitting up. "That light?"

"Maybe it's that Greyhound bus," I said.

"Maybe," He looked troubled.

I got up and started walking towards the fence. It was about twenty feet away.

"Keep back from the fence, Bunny, or you'll be getting your second shock in twenty-four hours."

"Not an episode I'd care to repeat," I admitted.

Even out here, in the middle of nowhere, I was too scared to speak the truth. I was frightened that the Agency could still hear me. It was ridiculous, but I felt deeply that they would hear anything I said.

Suddenly, the revving of an engine broke the silence. Marcus jumped up at the sound just as the Humvee appeared at the top of the little hill.

"Oh my God! These things can sure move," said Zoe from behind the wheel.

Marcus was stunned. "What? Are you insane? What are you doing? Even being here is bad enough, but you're going to get us chucked out of the Academy."

"Hannah wants to get going," said Zoe. "I was just coming to pick you up."

Zoe, Hannah and Orla were all in the front of the car with seatbelts on.

"Go on, lovebirds. You can have the rear seat," said Orla.

"I think I should..."

"Ooh, good idea. Come on to the back seat and smooch with me." I climbed in, and Marcus reluctantly followed me.

Zoe looked at me, and I inclined my head forward. She got the message.

"Put your seatbelts on, boys and girls. It"ll be a bit bumpy getting down from here."

We put our belts on as Marcus said, "You should be okay, just reverse slowly down the way you came up."

Zoe put the car into drive and floored it.

"Zoe, no, you're going forward..."

"That I am, Marcus, that I am." As she raced towards the fence, her voice vibrating from the rough terrain, Zoe said, "It was thoughtful of you to get us a Humvee. I don't know how this would have worked in a little Jeep."

"Zoe, the fence, it's electrified," said Marcus.

"Not if I've done my job right, sweetheart," I said, putting my hand in his.

Orla looked back. "What do you mean, "if"?"

We hit the fence at speed and tore straight through it, carrying on downhill almost to the road. Zoe had already started to brake, but unfortunately, we met a four-foot drop into a ditch with a tree sticking out of it, and came to an abrupt stop at a jaunty angle.

"Everyone okay?" asked Zoe. We all answered in the affirmative.

"What the hell is going on?" shouted Marcus, apoplectic with rage. "What have you done?"

"Everything exactly right," said a voice from the window beside him.

Marcus turned and looked right into my dad's face. "Mr Banks?" He was so shocked that he couldn't find any more words.

"Hello, Marcus. I hope you've been looking after my little girl."

Marcus looked poleaxed.

"Oh, I don't approve of that at all," said Dad, looking at the bottle of vodka still in Marcus's hand. He dropped it immediately, and it thudded to the floor.

"Hello, Little Duck," Dad said to me.

"Hello, Dad."

"I think we need to get out of here."

"Smashing idea," said Orla. "Nice to see you all alive and safe, Mr B."

"Nice to see you too, Orla. How are the equine studies going?"

"Well, I think they'll have ground to a halt after tonight, Mr B."

"I'm sure we can sort something out for you."

Out of the vehicle, we started off towards a car parked by the road. After a few steps, I turned around to find Marcus still standing by the ditch with indecision on his face.

"Tell you what, Marcus," said Dad, "come along. Hear what we have to say, and if you want to go back, you're welcome to."

It seemed unfair that Dad was missing out the fact that the Agents would kill Marcus in a heartbeat once he knew the truth, but I said nothing.

We stopped briefly to disable all mobile phones and drop them into a ditch. As we walked to the car, it was clear that Marcus had blinked-in and was looking around.

"There are no Faders here, Marcus," said Dad.

We climbed into an SUV and Dad started to drive,

talking to Marcus as he did so. The hairs were standing up on the back of my neck until we reached the highway and anonymity of being just another car in a sea of headlights.

WE PULLED into a gas station just outside of Colorado City where a minivan and its driver were waiting for us. The driver was Connor. There was a change of clothes waiting for us. We went into the small bathroom in the back of the station to change. I was talking to Dad, so Marcus went in with Orla, then Hannah and Zoe changed.

I didn't want to leave Dad's sweater. It had felt like the only thing that connected me to him over all these months.

Dad hugged me and said, "Sweetheart, it's just a bloody jumper."

Connor walked into the station with me and waited while I changed. I cleared out my duffle coat and shoved a handful of tissues and other junk into the pocket of the parka Dad had brought for me. As I shoved my feet into a pair of trainers, there was a knock at the door.

"Jenna!" whispered Connor.

I opened the door. He rushed into the stall with his finger over his lips, signalling silence, and locked the door behind him.

"An Agency car has just pulled into the station. The others had to drive out. We need to get out of here. The back exit is at the end of this hallway. We must move, fast."

26

I followed Connor down the hallway to the back exit. He tried the door, and it swung outwards. As we silently closed it, the buzzer sounded to indicate that someone was coming in through the front door. The Agency car was filling up on the right side of the building, so we ran across the road in the darkness to a diner on the opposite side. We walked in and took a booth at the back.

"Why didn't you just fade us out through the bathroom wall?"

"I'd have left a trail for them if they've got a Tracker with them. I don't think they're looking for us. They didn't look at the van twice as it took off."

"Will they be able to come back for us?" I felt a little frightened.

"We can't hook up with them for a few days." He looked at me. "Jenna, it's not a problem. Well, it's kind of inconvenient, but I don't think we're in any danger. We do need to get out of sight, though."

"What can I get you?" asked the waitress, following this with a memorised list of specials.

"Two coffees, please," said Connor. "Just a minute, what was that about pie?"

"Cherry pie, pumpkin pie, apple pie."

"Pumpkin pie sounds great." He looked at me. "Honey?"

"Just the coffee for me." I smiled.

"I hear ya, sister," said the waitress. She slapped her full hip, then filled our cups and walked away, chuckling.

Sixty seconds later, she was back with the pumpkin pie.

"Thank you, ma'am," said Connor, all southern and polite.

"You enjoy that, sweet cakes." Then to me, she said, "See if you can steal a bite. It's really divine."

When she had gone, I said, "I thought we had to get out of sight."

"Yes, but pie." His hazel-green eyes twinkled.

We sat in silence in our booth which had an excellent line of sight over the front door, the back door, and the gas station through the side windows. We could also see the SUV I'd just travelled in with the others. It was parked up at the closest side of the gas station, but didn't seem to have been observed by the Agents.

"Have they gone?" I asked.

"I can't see. Hang tight." He got up and walked to the front where the waitress intercepted him. Her arm pointed to the opposite back corner. He turned around, glancing out of the windows as he turned, and then made his way through the door clearly labelled "Bathrooms".

He came back to the table a few minutes later.

"Their car is gone."

"And the waitress thinks you were running out on the bill," I said. "She hasn't taken her eyes off me since you walked out of that door."

Connor took a ten dollar note and a couple of ones out of his pocket and dropped them on the table.

"Let's get out of here," he said.

"Where to?"

"There's a motel across the road."

As we left the diner, Connor gave the waitress another "Thank you, ma'am."

I started to walk towards the road, but Connor veered me back in the direction of the SUV and dangled the keys out.

I breathed a sigh of relief. "I thought we were on foot."

We drove the short distance to the motel, but then turned off towards what looked like an industrial estate where he parked the car out of sight. From there we went on foot to the motel and stood in the dark at the rear of the building.

"Wait here," he said and began to fade. It was the first time I'd seen it up close, while fully conscious and in control of all my faculties. Suddenly, he wasn't so solid. Then, as he faded I could see the wall through his face, and his face was gone. I blinked in to see a cloud of yellow disappear through the wall.

After a few minutes, he returned and solidified into a human again.

"I've found an empty room," he said. "I'm going to fade you so we can get to it. Are you okay with that?"

"I guess so," I said, even though I had a thousand questions. What if I flew apart and didn't come back together again? What if the chip stopped me from fading? Oh My God, what if my clothes disappeared? It was too late; he put his arm around me, and I began to fade.

It didn't feel like anything. I felt like I was still standing there. In fact, I looked down, and I could see myself. I hadn't dissipated into a million molecules. I looked at Connor. There was a bright yellow shape and a haze of yellow around us, but everything else was monochrome.

I tried blinking in and out, but it didn't seem to make a difference. I felt the pressure of his hand on my back as he moved me through the wall. It didn't feel like I was sliding into a wall; it was like walking through a hologram. It was nothing.

We were in the hallway. He led me to room 106, and we walked through the door. Connor removed his arm from around me, and everything went back to normal again.

Connor looked at me with an edgy expression on his face. "You're white. You're not going to faint, are you? Or puke?"

"No, I don't think so. Oh! Actually, I'm not so sure." I sat on the edge of the bed, then slid on to the floor and put my head between my legs while trying to regulate my breathing.

Connor went into the bathroom and came back with a glass of water and a wet towel. I drank the water and wiped the towel across my face.

"So, what now?" I asked.

"Now we wait. We are nowhere near as far as I'd like to be from the base. We're still on the same main road that goes straight to Colorado Springs, and as you can see, it's used pretty regularly by the Agency and other uniforms. Those Agents weren't looking for you, but that could change any minute. It wouldn't be safe to be on the road now. The others will be at the first safe house by now. I think we're going to hang tight for a couple of days and catch up to them at another planned stop. We should get some sleep."

"I think you might be right." I yawned as the thought of sleep came to me. I climbed on to the bed closest to me and pulled the covers over me. "Thanks for saving my dad, Connor."

"You already thanked me for that," he said as he lay down on top of the other bed.

"Yes, but I thought I was hallucinating that time."

He chuckled softly. "You're welcome."

As I AWOKE, my nose sifted through the smells. Coffee, bacon and...and...donuts? I opened my eyes to find take-out bags on the table beside me and a large cup of coffee.

"Coffee, bacon and donuts," Connor announced as if I hadn't guessed.

"Oh great! Three of my five-a-day," I said, licking my lips. "Is it too early to profess my undying love for you?" I was looking at the food, but even I wasn't sure whom or what I was speaking to.

"I don't think your boyfriend would be too thrilled about that," Connor replied.

"Oh right. Yes. Good point." I was clearly a cheap harlot, ready to give up my Marcus for the promise of bacon.

"What's the plan for today?" I asked.

"Sit quietly and hope they don't let the room while we're in here."

"Does that mean I can't have a shower?"

"I think we can manage that. I'll keep an eye out after we've eaten to be sure no staff is coming down the hall so you can get a shower."

After we had eaten, I took a quick shower and Connor washed. We sat on the beds staring at the TV, which was on silent with the subtitles switched on. When the maid came to clean the rooms, I stood with everything gathered next to Connor while he faded to stick his head through the door.

He was ready to fade me if she came in, but she just walked past. We didn't rest until she'd cleaned all the rooms she was going to clean and walked away with her trolley.

I blew out a breath and settled back on to the bed.

The man in the next room had left early, so Connor had popped through the wall and dropped our breakfast garbage into his wastepaper basket. At least we didn't have to sit and smell our breakfast all day.

"Connor?" I asked. "What happened when you awakened? Did your parents have to explain everything to you? Did they have to warn you about the Trackers?"

"My parents weren't Faders," he said.

"What? I thought you had to have at least one parent with the ability." I was shocked. "Were you adopted?"

I realised that was an inappropriate question. "Sorry," I said.

"No, I wasn't adopted. I was born in New Orleans, Louisiana. In the Bible Belt of the USA. My father was a preacher of the evangelical kind, which is pretty much the only kind in that neck of the woods. The first time I faded, I told him about it. I tried to explain to him what had happened to me and he took his belt to me for lying. After that, I kept it to myself. When I was fourteen, he saw it. He said the Devil was in me and he was going to beat it out of me. I faded in that very instant and ran away. I never went back."

The thought of a boy going through all that and then running away so young was heartbreaking.

"Where did you go?"

"I pretty much looked after myself. You know the Faders they warn you about? The ones who break into places and steal? That was me.

"I wouldn't steal millions or even thousands. Just enough

to get by. Sometimes food, clothes. Hotel rooms like this. I didn't know about the Trackers until a year later. I was faded, moving through a mall when I realised a bunch of kids could see me. I could see they were nervous, making calls. I faded through a few walls to lose them and walked back towards them un-faded. I was really nervous; I thought if they had seen me faded, they might still know it was me, but they didn't even notice me. Of course, I know now that's because I wasn't bare-ass naked."

I smiled.

"I hung around a little longer and watched them all file out. I didn't dare follow them in case it was too obvious. A few minutes later, there were a couple of guys dressed in black cargos and black sports shirts and jackets. They weren't in uniform as such, but you could tell they were military. I figured it was about time for me to move on."

"So you hadn't even known there were others like you?"

"After that day, I figured there must be. That operation couldn't just have been set up for me; it looked too big."

"Was that the last time you came across Trackers? Before here, I mean," I asked.

"There was one other time. I was in Los Angeles, staying at the Beverley Wilshire Hotel."

"Isn't that the famous one where the stars stay?"

"The very same. I'd been staying there for a couple of days when I got the vibe that they were on to me again. You know when people are looking at you but pretend they're not?"

"I think I can picture that, yes," I replied.

"I had managed to fade out of my room and down to the lobby, but the Agents were everywhere. Just as I thought I was screwed, Taylor Swift stepped out of an elevator with all her security around her and started walking through the lobby. I stayed faded and walked with her. I kept with her step by step until we were out of the door. The Paparazzi were flashing their cameras at the front of the hotel, and I just floated into her car with her. Obviously, the Agents couldn't do a thing. I hopped out in the middle of the traffic. Into a car, a cab, a bus and lost them. It really scared me, though."

Connor got up from his bed, poured a glass of water and handed it to me, then poured one for himself. He began to speak again as he sat back down.

"I didn't fade again for months," he said. "I'd made my way to New York. As I said, I was trying to get by without fading, but I was hungry. A woman was sitting on a seat in Central Park; her purse was open next to her. I decided it was worth it. I faded and walked over. I put my hand in her purse, and she turned to look me straight in the face. She said, "We need to talk. You're not safe." Then she faded too. Her clothes, I mean everything, dropped to the ground. She said, "Get those, would you?" and started to move away."

Connor's face showed the excitement he must have felt at the time. It made his telling of the story all the more compelling.

"I grabbed her stuff and followed her to a café on the edge of the park. I dropped her stuff in the women's bathroom, and walked out of the men's room. I sat at a table waiting for her, terrified she'd just disappear. After seven agonising minutes – yes, I counted them – she appeared, ordered coffee and bagels for two, and watched as I ate mine, then hers.

"The first question I asked was how come all her clothes fell off." He laughed at the memory. "She told me that most Faders' clothes disappear when they fade. Hers just drop to the ground and that's considered unusual. She'd never seen someone who could fade and keep their clothes on, or fade other things as I could.

"Then she quietly told me who she was," he continued. "She told me what she was. She told me about Trackers and the Agency. She said she had a place I could stay and that was that. I had a home; I had a family."

"I'm sorry you got caught. I know that was because of me," I said.

"It was going to happen eventually. I take risks I shouldn't. It wasn't your fault. You risked a lot to get me out of there. I woke up, lying inside some kind of machine. There were people standing near workstations on the other side of a Perspex wall. The room was really dark, but I could see they were trying to get out of the little room they were in and couldn't get through the door. When I moved, I realised I had needles in my arms."

He rubbed his arm unconsciously.

"I guess they had been keeping me asleep. I faded instantly and got the hell out of there. It was pure luck that I wandered through a wall and found you sitting there."

He smiled then. A warm, genuine smile which made me think of Marcus and feel guilty.

THE NEXT MORNING was Monday morning.

"Will fading make me feel sick every time?" I asked.

"No, it usually only happens the first time," he said.

"Could I...Would it be okay for me to have another go?"

"Sure. I guess the room will be refreshed by house-keeping today. We'll have to fade then anyway."

We made the beds and gathered our coats and bags together. By the time the housekeeper had come into the room, we had faded again. We stood in the centre of the room while she walked around and through us.

I was terrified when she walked through me because I thought I might see her internal organs and freak out. I was relieved that it just went dark for a moment, like when I'd walked through the wall. She spent a few minutes cleaning and preparing the room, then left.

I waited for Connor to take his hand off me, but he didn't straight away. He held up his hand. I watched. He touched my hand then held his up again. I got the picture and held up my hand, palm towards him. I could still only see him as a bright yellow person-shaped blob in the centre of a haze of yellow. He moved his hand closer and closer to mine. I started to feel something. It was like the energy I had been experimenting with. Instead of blasting out, it was flowing from him and from me, and where our hands drew closer together, the energy pulsed and rippled between us. I felt alive from the top of my head to the tips of my toes.

Suddenly, I felt wrong. Like this was too nice, too intimate, and I'd forgotten about Marcus who was, no doubt, freaking out about what might have happened to me.

I pulled my hand away, and Connor took his other hand from my back.

"Did you feel the energy?" he asked. "How awesome is that?"

He turned away to sit on his bed, but not quickly enough. I knew that he had felt something else too. Something more. I saw it on his face. He looked conflicted.

I sat back on to my bed and stared at the silent TV. I couldn't have told you what I was watching; my mind was racing from the strange experience I had just had.

27

A t lunchtime, several cars turned up at the motel. It was clear that our free room was no longer going to be available. We gathered what little we had and walked out of the motel, across the road to where we'd left the car. As we hit the rush hour traffic, I lay down on the back seat of the car under a blanket in the hope that no traffic cameras or Agency cars would spot me.

We turned off at Albuquerque and stayed in another motel for one night.

The following day, we drove to the outskirts of Sedona, Arizona, and on to a quiet unlit road. We approached a secluded house and drove straight into its open garage. There were no lights on, and Connor made me stay in the car while he had a look around. I watched him as he took a bicycle and basketball from the garage and dropped them on the lawn. He picked up a skateboard from the lawn and dropped it in the garage, then signalled me to come out of the car.

"What was all that about?" I asked, pointing at the bike.

"Choppers. They fly over occasionally, searching. It's best

to make the place look like there's a family living in it. Anyway, it looks like the others aren't here yet," he said.

"Are they supposed to be? Could something have happened to them?"

"No. We've missed a couple of safe houses out. They're due to be here tonight. I can't guess what time, though. There is *someone* here who's been waiting to see you."

I walked through the open plan living area into the kitchen, and a streak of black and white fur flew at me and landed in my arms.

"Felix!" I cried and hugged my cat to my chest, bursting into tears.

"He got dropped off today. He should have already been fed." Connor stuck his head around the kitchen door into the utility and confirmed, "Food, water, poop tray and poop, all present and correct."

An hour later, I heard a car pull up into the garage.

"Thank God!" I heard Dad's voice. He must have seen the car and realised we'd arrived.

As I walked to the internal garage door, I could hear Marcus's voice.

"Whose place is this?" he asked. As I looked through the door I saw him squinting into the darkness outside, no doubt blinking in and looking for Faders.

"I can't tell you," said Dad.

"How are we supposed to trust you if you're going to keep secrets?"

"Marcus!" said Zoe. "It's Jenna's dad. It's Mr B. We already trust him, don't we?"

"Marcus," said Dad, "I literally can't tell you. Connor booked it through Airbnb."

Orla barked a laugh.

Zoe and Hannah turned towards the door first, both

running to hug me. "I'm sorry we drove away. I'm so sorry," said Zoe.

"It's okay," I said. "I wasn't alone. It was fine."

Orla came over, and the relief on her face was excruciating. I could see she had been worried.

"Jenna, Marcus has been a total nightmare. An unbelievable grumpy storm of a man." She reached me and hugged me fiercely. "I missed you too."

Marcus stopped to look at me.

"Hello, Grumpy," I said.

He walked to me and wrapped me in a bear hug that made me weak at the knees. "Hello, Bunny. I don't think you could have any comprehension of what being apart from you has done to me."

"Oh, that's easy," said Orla. "It's made him a fecking ogre."

We walked into the kitchen, and Connor busied himself with his back to us. Dad followed us in, and I went to hug him too.

"Did the other thing go okay?" Dad asked Connor.

"I haven't heard," said Connor.

"And what's this other thing?" asked Marcus.

Dad and Connor looked at each other and at Orla.

"It's Jason," said Dad. "We haven't heard if he got out okay."

"Oh...well, I smell coffee, thank the heavens," said Orla, trying to hide her watering eyes by walking away quickly.

"It's in the pot and fresh," said Connor. "Sit down, I'll bring it over. Did everything go to plan?"

"Like clockwork," Dad said.

At the same time, Marcus said, "I wouldn't know!"

"How did you manage to stop the Agency from hearing you plan your escape?" asked Connor.

"We didn't discuss it, we just did it," said Zoe.

"Hasn't Jenna told you all this? What else did you find to talk about?" said Marcus, sounding a little hostile towards Connor. I could understand why he was so belligerent.

"We didn't do much talking," said Connor and walked out of the room.

Oh, that sounds great! Thanks a bunch, I thought.

"We had to stay quiet. Connor faded us into an empty motel room." As soon as I'd said the word "motel", I realised I'd probably just made things worse. Luckily, Orla saved me.

"You faded? Oh my God! What was it like?"

"Were you naked?" asked Zoe with horror on her face.

"It didn't feel any different and I wasn't naked. I was still there, except that I wasn't. But I did feel faint afterwards."

"I do that to all the girls," called Connor from the other room.

Marcus's face was red. I needed to have a word with Connor.

"I threw up," said Dad, "all over Mrs Cowan's carpet."

My jaw dropped. "Dad!"

"I know. I just hope she thought it was one of her cats."

Marcus was still looking like he might kill Connor. Orla took one look at him and launched into her story.

"We knew the Agency was monitoring us, that they were listening and watching. It made planning tough. The night Jenna faked being sick to get into the med-block, she told us, briefly, what was going on. That you were alive, Mr B, and what we are." Orla glanced nervously at Connor as he came back into the room. "She told us they were listening. We couldn't be sure how or where. We just assumed that every-where on base, even when we were out spotting, was compromised.

"Jenna had been behaving oddly. I tried to pay attention. When she suggested going out that night, a look in her eyes seemed to say that we were getting out for good. We just went along with everything as Jenna manoeuvred us with the occasional comment. Even Marcus went along, and he hadn't a clue of what was going on.

"She seemed to need me to let Jason know that we were going out. And she mentioned a Greyhound bus and stadium lights, so I mentioned them to him. I guess that's how you knew where we were. I was expecting a bus to pick us up.

"When we got to Stalag 19, we saw the flashing head-lights. It was pretty obvious what we needed to do. We went and got the car..."

"That was the best," said Zoe.

"Whose plan was the hole we fell in?" asked Marcus.

"Ahh, that was a big surprise," said Orla.

"I sat looking out in that direction eating my lunch a few times," I said. "There was just a short stretch of road that I could see from the base. I was hoping that and the lights would be enough to pinpoint where we would be coming through. I was horrified that the lights weren't on that night."

"We'd seen the lights so far away from the main base. We knew something was going on there, but didn't realise it was you," said Connor.

"I had my heart in my mouth, watching you plough towards that electric fence," said Dad.

"Jenna had already broken it with her scary brain," said Orla.

THE HOUSE HAD a porch along the back with a swing seat. Later, I sat in silence with Marcus. He seemed out-of-sorts, but I put that down to him being dragged out of his comfort zone and having been worried about me.

"I wish I didn't know," he finally said. "I wish I was back at Hilltop and still one of the good guys."

I didn't know what to say.

He let go of my hand, stood up and walked to the edge of the porch, looking out into the darkness.

"But I guess I never was one of the good guys." He turned back to me with a lopsided grin, not big enough to form his cheeky dimples. "I'm just trying to get my head around all this, but I wouldn't want to be anywhere other than by your side."

I walked over to him and lifted my face to his for a kiss.

"I can see we're going to have to have "the talk"," said Dad.

"Oh my God, Dad, really?" I said, feeling myself blush as Marcus jumped back about three feet.

He laughed. "Sorry, I couldn't resist it."

"Good night, Bunny," said Marcus. He kissed the end of my nose and went in.

"Well, that was mortifying," I said.

Dad came out and hugged me. "He calls you "Bunny" and you think I'm mortifying? You've changed a lot."

"Well, I'm a freak of nature, have you heard?"

"I witnessed it, remember?" he said. "I meant you've grown up a lot. You remind me of your mum." He hugged me again. "You need to get some sleep. You're in the room at the back of the house next to mine. At the opposite end of the building to Marcus. And you're sharing with the girls."

"Dad! Okay."

. . .

WHEN I WOKE up the next morning, Orla was sitting on her bed, chewing her fingernail.

"Are you alright?" I asked.

"I wish I had my phone. I want to be sure that Jason's okay. They must know it was him. Jenna, what if he didn't get away?"

"I'm sure he must have. Don't worry. Have you asked Dad?"

"They haven't heard anything yet."

We'd been at the house for three days when we heard helicopters.

"Is that a helicopter? Do you think it's them looking for us?" I asked.

"Probably," said Marcus.

That was the only sign we had had that anyone was looking for us. The house was in an isolated area of scrubland leading to a rock-strewn wilderness heading up into the hills. We would wear hats, keep our heads down and stretch our legs a little, but none of us went too far.

Connor appeared at the door and said, "How about if you come and help me make pancakes?"

As it turned out, Connor didn't need help making pancakes. He was a pancake master, which was just as well because Dad usually bought them ready-made from the supermarket and I'd never made a pancake in my life.

Hannah pawed through all the cupboards and the freezer and brought out more potential fillings than I would have considered possible. Orla thought the apple pancakes were the best and Zoe raved about the peanut butter ones. My favourites were the crispy bacon and maple pancakes. I didn't even think maple was a thing. Marcus seemed to like all of them, which was no surprise. He appeared to be coming around and even helped with the washing up, making me squeal by flicking me with soap bubbles.

Marcus had been mostly keeping his distance from me while Dad was around, which was pretty much always, except for when Dad made phone calls in the study. Later, as Dad muttered quietly on the phone, I chose a DVD and sat down to watch it with Felix on my lap. Marcus came and sat next to me.

He put his arm around me, leaned in and whispered, "Jenna, I have a question. Don't go mad, just hear me out."

"Okay," I said.

"Does your dad seem like your dad?"

"I don't understand what you mean."

"I don't know. All these phone calls and secret meetings with Connor and...I don't know. He seems to be different from when he was working at the Academy."

"He doesn't look different to me. I mean, he seems more serious, but given the circumstances..."

I left it there. Marcus didn't look deterred.

"You know how you can do the scary mind thing and Connor can apparently fade himself and other people. I just wonder if there might be Faders who can, I don't know, look like other people when they take human form."

"Marcus, that's mental. It's my dad. And this is my cat." I pointed to Felix, curled up in my lap.

"Okay. I didn't want to upset you. Just keep it in mind and keep your eyes open."

THE NEXT MORNING, Dad walked in with an overnight bag and announced that he was taking a trip.

"I'm sorry, Little Duck, but we're less than a thousand miles from the base. I'd rather be much further away. We've been planning the move, but we don't have a lot of people around here to help us. I can move around relatively safely alone. I need to do my bit."

The idea of him being out of my sight just made me sick, but at 8 am, I was hugging him goodbye and watching as his car pulled away.

It was nearly October, and although the summer seemed to be reigning during the daylight hours, the early mornings and nights were getting cooler. I stood there shivering in my coat long after he'd left. Orla handed me a tissue and a little compact mirror, saying, "You look a proper fright. Wipe the mascara off your face before we start calling you Coco the Clown."

I did my best and shoved my hands into my pockets, remaining out there for another few minutes.

"I'm going back to bed," I said, and stomped into the house.

"I'll tuck you in," said Marcus.

"No funny business," called Orla as we walked upstairs.

It had been my intention to lie there and sulk for a while. Marcus, true to his word, tucked me into the covers up to my neck. He then lay down behind me on top of the covers and cuddled into me, taking my hand into his.

"It'll be okay, Bunny. I'm sure it will," he said.

We'd been running and hiding for days, and now Dad had gone again. A great weariness came over me and I fell into a deep sleep.

I woke up in the afternoon, wondering how I had managed to sleep for half the day. The house was quiet. Orla was asleep on the next bed, and there was no sign of Zoe or Hannah on the bunk beds. I slipped out of the room and went to Marcus's room. The door was open; he wasn't there. I went down the stairs, and when I couldn't find anyone, I started to get nervous.

I put my coat and trainers on and walked outside the house.

"Marcus? Connor?"

The garage was empty, and there was one car on the drive. I walked around to the back of the house and started up the path to the wilderness. After a few minutes" walk, I rounded a corner to find Connor crouched down. I was just about to step out and ask him what he was doing when I realised he was perched over two still bodies, Hannah and Zoe. There was a knife in his hand and blood on the ground.

He hadn't seen me, but the shock of it made me open my mouth to scream. A hand came across my mouth and I spun around. I looked into Marcus's face. His eyes seemed slightly unfocused. They were pleading with me to stay quiet as they also jerked all around us. I nodded once, and he led me quietly towards the rugged wilderness.

When we were far enough away, he whispered to me, "I knew there was something wrong with him. I just felt it."

I couldn't believe it. "Zoe! Zoe and Hannah." I started to cry.

"Jenna, I'm sorry. You need to pull yourself together. We don't have time for this. I heard others, I don't know how many there are."

"Orla! Dear God, we've got to warn her."

"I need to get you to safety first."

He put his hand up to the back of his head and it came away bloody.

"What happened?"

"He got the drop on me. I was checking the tyres on the

car and the next thing I know, I'm waking up with an egg-sized lump on my head."

"Let me take a look."

"It seems to have mostly clotted now. It can wait."

I was unhappy with this arrangement, but agreed and moved quickly out into the unfamiliar rocks.

We found an outcrop which seemed to provide good cover. Marcus looked conflicted about leaving me. From the distance came the unmistakable sound of Orla's scream, and just as suddenly, it was cut off.

I took hold of Marcus's sweater and pulled him towards me, weeping into his chest. My body shook with tears.

"Jenna, we have to get away from here. They could be out looking for us now."

We continued walking.

After nearly an hour, we stopped for a rest. I was sitting on the ground with my head on my knees, trying not to think about what had happened to my friends, when I heard it.

It was my dad's voice calling me.

I moved to stand and once more Marcus's hand came over my mouth.

"Don't. I'm sorry, I don't think it's him. We can't take the chance. I won't take the chance."

I could see now that Marcus was right. We got up and continued to move away from the voice; from my dad's voice. All I wanted to do was to run towards it, but I couldn't be sure what that voice belonged to.

28

W e were running from the Agency, the military and the Faders, including whatever was using my dad's face. Our chances seemed non-existent.

Marcus was curled around me protectively, and I snuggled into him.

"I don't know how you have the strength to keep going like this."

He lifted a hand and stroked my hair. "I want to be with you for ever. I hope for ever is longer than the next few hours," he said.

"Please don't talk like that. Don't give in. We've got a good chance of getting away."

I felt like I was lying. He stroked my neck, and somehow I relaxed a little. I even began to feel sleepy.

As we lay there, Marcus started to chuckle.

"I'm sensing a little hysteria back there," I said.

"We've got a walk ahead of us, but I think we might make it back out to the highway."

"How do you even know which way to go?"

"I checked Google Maps before we left."

"Why would you...?"

He laughed again.

"I still can't believe how easily I got you away. I don't need anyone but you. You're the one."

I was starting to feel like something was wrong. I tried to shake away my desire to sleep.

"Nate was strong," he continued. "It didn't take him too long to bounce back. But you – you're like a power pack. Your energy replenishes almost as fast as I absorb it. That's why I call you Bunny. It's my little joke."

The hairs on the back of my neck were prickling.

"What? I don't understand."

I tried to turn towards his face, but his arm pinned me down to the ground.

"I had to be so careful with the others, only taking a little at a time. A handshake here, a slap on the back there. Up to my little mistake with Tiffany."

"Marcus, what are you saying?"

"I've known all along. What we are, I mean. Ever since my awakening. My parents tried to explain it to me, about the monsters, but I could see the yellow mist around them. I told them what I could see and they realised what it meant. They tried to get me away. They called the Academy and told them I'd be starting a little late because we were having a family holiday. It was the Agency that killed my parents, not the Faders. Not an accident, either.

"When they died, I was in the car, but I wasn't unconscious at that point. I saw a yellow mist rise from their bodies as they died and I reached out towards them, and somehow absorbed it. It came into me like another awakening. Like religion," he twisted my hair around his fist and pulled my head back, closer to his ear, "like love, like ecstasy.

"Your new boyfriend isn't the only one with talents. I can see the yellow mist in Faders and Trackers alike, even the Agency people. I can see the energy around everyone to some degree. Obviously, it's stronger in Faders because they've awakened and they don't have the capsule holding it back. Once I have my hands on them, the energy just flows out of them and into me. They couldn't fight it: Nate, Zoe, little geeky Hannah. The beautiful mist just flows into me.

"Do you remember the Fader in the cinema? I caught it before it got through the wall. I just stepped into the middle of the mist and absorbed everything. There was nothing left – no body, nothing. I felt bad about Nate. He was a good mate, but it was Zoe's fault."

I was shaking with terror, but managed to spit out, "How can you blame her for that?"

"She was saying that what happened to Tiffany was my fault. I mean, it *was* my fault. We were arguing. I grabbed her arm and took so much energy, she had a fit. Poor Tiff was never the same again. But I didn't need Zoe making people think that way. I was on my way to get her. I was wound up, and I hadn't seen enough of you. You see, after I had started drawing on you, it was like a tap that wouldn't stop. I couldn't get enough."

All the memories of us together, touching, filled my mind and I wanted to vomit. Then I thought of the tiredness, the times when I'd felt my knees going weak. I'd believed it was love.

"Then, I bumped into Nate. I was mixed up, shaky and confused. So I just smashed his head against a wall. While he was out, I cut the capsule out of his neck. That makes it come quicker."

"So that's it? You're just going to kill me?"

"That depends on you," he said. "Personally, I want to get

out of here. The longer I keep you with me, the stronger I'll be and the longer we might be able to outrun them."

I tried to move again. I felt sick, weak. Of course I felt weak. Marcus was touching me. He was absorbing my energy.

"I won't be able to run anywhere if I'm this weak."

"Don't worry. I just needed you compliant while we had our little chat. You'll perk up again in no time, Bunny."

"So who bashed you on the head then?"

"No one. That's not my blood. It's Zoe's. I thought you might need a little more convincing to run away with me. Turns out, not so much.

He pulled me roughly up to my feet, and we began to walk again. He kept his hand around my wrist.

"Why did you kill Tiffany? Was she just there?"

"I didn't kill Tiffany. I'd bet that was the Agency taking advantage of what they thought was a Fader attack to get rid of a nuisance. I don't blame them."

As he talked, I shoved my hands into my pockets for something – anything – that might help me. There were only two things in my pocket, but I thought one of them might be what I needed. The idea of it nauseated me, but I had taken enough self-defence classes to have a chance that it might work.

I stumbled in the dark; he lost his grip on my wrist. I wheeled my arm out for balance. He caught my arm and pulled me to him, giving me the momentum to drive the plastic spork straight into his eye. He screamed and let go of me. I raced off into the darkness without a clue of where I was going. I hoped I could get away and any trace of my direction would disperse before he could pick up the trail.

For half a minute, there was only silence behind me, then

he howled like an injured animal. I didn't stop. I could have been heading towards the edge of a cliff, and I wouldn't have seen it coming. I knew I couldn't hide from him, so I just had to keep moving. My best chance was putting distance between us.

Finally, I reached the edge of a formation of rocks and began to make my way around it. I could tell as I clambered over the rocks that my path was leading me upward, but I struggled to find a path that led back down. I worried this might be making me a glowing target.

After a few minutes of climbing came the inevitable misstep. I had reached the crest of the hill when I stumbled. The ground was further away on the other side. I just continued down, hitting rocks as I went. My foot lodged into a crevice, wrenching my ankle and causing excruciating pain.

When I finally landed, I instantly knew that I had broken my ankle. The pain was immense. I buried my mouth into my arm to try to stop myself from making a noise. Immediately, I began to go into shock. I felt a cold sweat all over my body and nausea in the pit of my stomach. I tried to move and whimpered into my hand as I dragged my leg across the ground.

In the slight sliver of light from the moon, I could see that I was in front of a small cave. The apex of the entrance didn't look to be more than seven or eight feet high. I couldn't tell how far back it went or what might already be in there.

I was trying to listen for Marcus, but I couldn't hear anything other than the blood rushing in my ears. I moved as quietly as I could into the entrance of the cave.

"We seem to be in a bit of a jam," said a rough, angry voice very close to me in the dark.

I screamed with fright. I looked up to see the hulking silhouette of Marcus as the clouds shifted across the moon.

"Shut up! If you bring Daddy, I'll have to kill him. As it is, I don't like your chances of survival much."

I tried to slide away from him deeper into the cave. The pain from my foot shot through me, and I vomited on the ground.

"Oh dear, you are in quite a mess, aren't you, and I don't recommend going any further into that cave. You know there'll be snakes and probably scorpions, and God knows what else in there." He paused for a few moments. "Actually, that might be a blessing, given the state of you."

A shadow dropped down from above, knocking Marcus to the ground.

"Dude, you really like to hear yourself talk, don't you," said Connor.

From the ground, Marcus said, "The Fader scum's arrived. I didn't think you'd be going anywhere after the whack I gave you with the crowbar."

Marcus's leg swept out, knocking Connor off balance, and he fell to the ground.

"You think that's gonna stop me?" asked Connor.

I blinked in to see Connor starting to fade. I screamed, "Don't fade. Marcus absorbs energy. If you fade, he can absorb you completely."

Connor didn't fade. He kicked Marcus in the side of the leg and jumped up. Marcus stood up, and they began to wrestle. In the blackness, Connor would have been almost blind, but Marcus would have blinked in and been able to see Connor's energy, even in human form. Every blow Marcus landed took away Connor's energy, and every blow Connor landed transferred his energy to Marcus.

Connor was getting tired, but managed to deliver a punch to Marcus's face so hard that Marcus fell.

Marcus simply reached out and gripped my broken ankle, drawing energy from me. I screamed; I was so weak, I could barely lift my head.

The clouds were moving away now, and the fighting pair were clearly visible. Marcus's right eye was swollen shut and rivulets of blood had stained his face. In the eerie moon-light, it looked black, making Marcus's face demon-like. He had lifted Connor right off his feet and was smashing his head against the rock arch above them at the mouth of the cave. Blood was trickling down Connor's neck.

Connor thrust his elbow into Marcus's face, and I heard the sound of Marcus's nose break. He dropped Connor. While Marcus stood dazed and spitting blood, Connor grabbed him by the chest and throat and lifted him. Connor wasn't a physical match for Marcus, but it looked like he was going to attempt to hit Marcus's head on the cave roof as Marcus had just done to him.

Connor's arm faded, and so did Marcus's head, which Connor pushed into the rock. He quickly withdrew his arm, and Marcus was left hanging with his head totally immersed in the rock, his arms and legs thrashing. His hand gripped wildly on to Connor's hair and jerked him close. As Marcus grabbed his head, Connor began to sway. Marcus would not be able to save himself, but as he suffocated inside that rock, he was making damn sure he took Connor with him.

I could still hardly move my body. I cast my eyes about for a weapon of some kind and remembered the second object in my pocket. Pulling out Orla's compact mirror, I managed to find the strength to smash it against a rock.

I took a sliver of glass and sliced and jabbed it into the

skin at the back of my neck. The chip was deeper than I'd expected. I didn't know if I was going to paralyse or even kill myself, but I couldn't think about that. I scraped and dug the glass about at the back of my head until I could feel it hit the capsule shaped chip.

I dropped the glass shard and dug out the chip. Instantly, with the fear and pain and anger, I felt the energy building up. I concentrated my mind, focusing on the chip in Marcus's head. I imagined it getting brighter and hotter.

Marcus's grip on Connor began to loosen. He let go completely with one hand and clawed at the rock from the outside. With all of my being, I threw out the desire to burst that chip with a massive explosion. I didn't even know if it was capable of that. All I heard was a dampened thud from inside the rock.

As dust sifted down, Marcus's hands fell limply to his sides. Connor dropped to the ground. I didn't know if he was dead or alive as he lay there below the ghastly sight of Marcus's body hanging from the neck.

After a minute, Connor started to cough. He moved towards me on his hands and knees and crashed down beside me.

"Hey, are you dead?" he asked.

"Not yet," I managed. "Although I might be paralysed and bleeding to death."

"Aww! Suck it up, Snowflake."

I laughed and then passed out.

I AWOKE ON THE SOFA. As I tried to sit up, pain shot up my leg and I groaned. I looked down at my foot. My ankle was strapped up with what looked like several rolls of duct tape and two decoratively painted wooden spoons. I gazed around the room, feeling pain everywhere as I turned.

Connor was sitting in an armchair beside an older woman I didn't recognise. He looked at me and gave a sympathetic smile as he continued to speak to her.

"It should be okay for now," he said.

"Do you think he'll be found?" asked the woman.

"I went back and pushed him all the way into the rock," Connor said. "He might be found in about a thousand years by archaeologists, maybe. Have you ever heard of anything like him?"

She shook her head.

"He nearly killed the girls," Connor continued. "He just grabbed their arms and drained their energy until they collapsed. It looks like he was trying to dig the capsules out of them. I was out looking for everyone after being knocked out and heard Jenna calling his name. I think that interrupted him. I found them just after that. I thought the Agency had caught up with us. There was blood on the ground; they were both so still, they looked dead.

"A few minutes later, Orla came around the path, took one look at them and started to scream, but they were coming round by that point and told us it was Marcus. That's when we realised Jenna and Marcus were gone."

A vision of Marcus hanging from the rock appeared in my mind. I closed my eyes as though that would make it go away, but it just became clearer and my eyes snapped open again.

"We'll be heading out as soon as possible," said the woman. "If everything goes okay we'll be there in a few days."

I tried to sit up. "They're alive? I want to see them."

"We're here," said Zoe from the kitchen behind me. It

was the most welcome voice I'd ever heard. I twisted around to see my friends sitting at the breakfast bar. Orla was applying gauze to the back of Zoe's neck while Hannah, shaky and pale, held her hand. I burst into tears.

The woman came to me across the room.

"It's okay, Jenna," she said, taking my hand. "You're safe now. Everyone's safe."

I was about a second from telling the strange woman to back off when Dad walked in.

"Ah! You're awake," he said. "And I see you've already met your grandmother."

"My *what*?" I said, so loudly that my head hurt.

"We can talk on the way," she said, kindly.

"I was hoping to get you into the car before you woke up," said Dad. "I'm sorry, sweetheart, this might hurt."

To the others, he said, "I want to be on the road in fifteen minutes. Can we do that?"

"We might stick out on the road at this time of the night," said Connor.

"We need to get further away. We don't know when Jenna might start emitting," said the woman.

Ten minutes later, my body was on the outside of a couple of hospital grade painkillers. I hopped sleepily towards the door with Orla and Zoe propping me up. As Dad opened the door, I awkwardly turned to take a last look at the sofa where Marcus and I had snuggled and watched DVDs. I shuddered and walked through the door, knowing I wouldn't be leaving those memories behind.

EPILOGUE

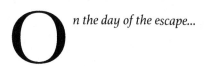

O*n the day of the escape...*

MAJOR TOMOWSKI BURST into the Comms Room.

"I want to know who's responsible for this. I want that person front and centre in sixty seconds."

He walked around the desk and sat down.

The Lead Agency Technician spluttered, "Responsible, sir?"

"Those kids must have planned this. Why didn't the alarm sound when the fence was breeched? How did they communicate with conspirators outside this facility?"

"Sir, we have Agents going through all video, audio and communication data on the base and during missions. The only communication off-base we've found was text messages between Orla McGinness and Jason Watts at Hilltop. In retrospect, it looks like they might have been worded to help them locate her on the base."

"In retrospect?" the Major repeated as he tapped his pen repeatedly on the desk before him.

"At the time, it looked like typical innocuous teenage drivel. As to the fence, we've been going through the feed from the satellite study lab. We think Miss Banks somehow disabled the cage and then disabled the fence. We opened the box and found half the boards melted."

"Get Dr Philipson in here," the Major barked. "Have there been any sightings? How long has it been?"

"No sightings yet, sir. It's been just over two hours since it was observed that they hadn't returned to their rooms. We went through the tapes and discovered they'd driven out to the mobile lab a couple of hours before that. We sent someone out there immediately. There was no sign of the kids. It took us another few minutes to find the fence had been breached."

"So they're gone?" Major Tom broke the pen in half and threw it across the desk. "We have the most technologically advanced military resources at our disposal and you're telling me they're gone?"

"Not completely," said Dr Philipson as he walked into the room. "We might still have ears on them."

"What?" asked the Major.

Everyone swivelled to face the Doctor.

"The inhibitor I placed in Marcus's head. It's got a listening device in it." He turned to the Tech. "Recording file PXMC01."

The Tech turned back to his screen and started clicking keys on his keyboard.

"Why didn't I know about this?" asked the Major.

"It was fully documented in the files, and it was also just something I was trying out. It hasn't been hugely successful.

The audio is somewhat muted because of the depth of the inhibitor, but you can just about work out what they're saying."

"Can their location be tracked?" asked the Major.

"I'm afraid not," said the Doc.

The screen opened with a directory of files by date and an executable file.

The Lead Tech pointed at two of his colleagues. "You and you, start going through these files."

They each positioned their headphones and went to work.

The Lead Tech clicked on the executable file and muffled sounds sprang from the speakers.

"*We need to go back for her,*" said Marcus's voice.

"*It's too dangerous. Connor will know what to do,*" said a voice familiar to Dr Philipson.

"That's Neil Banks, her father," he said.

"Well, at least we know where he is now," said the Major. "I want his picture circulated to local police."

"*She'll be okay, Marcus. You know how resilient she is,*" said Orla's voice.

"*I can't believe it. Everything you've told me,*" said Marcus. "*I feel sick.*"

The conversation lapsed into silence and all that could be heard was the sound of the engine.

"I want someone listening to that twenty-four seven. I want a report every hour. The moment they reveal their location, I want to hear about it, day or night. I want every reference to people or any location – a road, a building or a stone on the ground – documented and sent to me. Starting with this "Connor"."

· · ·

MAJOR TOMOWSKI SAT at his desk with the phone pressed to his ear.

"Professor Banks has told them everything. He's remarkably well informed. Of course, they'll all have to be dealt with."

"Not the Banks girl?" asked General Cavendish.

"No. We'll move her somewhere more secure and continue the experiments."

"Alive or dead?"

"That's up to her," said the Major. "Has there been any sign of your man, Jason?"

"He was on perimeter watch. It looks like he just walked off the base and wasn't seen again. We're assuming he was picked up so we've been checking local CCTV. It's unlikely we'll find anything now. He knows how we work."

The Major's door opened after a single knock.

"Sir?" said the Agent in the Major's outer office. "The Comms team."

"We're getting an update. If it's anything, I'll get back to you."

Major Tomowski disconnected the call.

"We might have something to go on, sir."

They played an audio file.

"*Whose place is this?*"

"*I can't tell you.*"

"*How are we supposed to trust you if you're going to keep secrets?*"

"*Marcus! It's Jenna's dad. It's Mr B. We already trust him, don't we?*"

"*Marcus, I literally can't tell you. Connor booked it through Airbnb.*"

"Right," said the Major, "I want you inside Airbnb's

server, searching every booking in the country. I want to know about bookings in the name of Connor anything, Mr C. Anyone. Bookings beginning tonight. Concentrate on secluded properties with several rooms."

"We're on it, sir," said the Lead Tech.

Within hours, they had discovered there were thousands of Airbnb bookings which needed to be investigated. It could take weeks.

SEVERAL DAYS LATER, the Major was back in the Comms Room listening to a recent recording.

"*Is that a helicopter? Do you think it's them looking for us?*"

"*Probably.*"

"How many choppers have we got out?" asked the Major.

"About a hundred and fifty, sir. Covering eight states. Also, that might not be ours."

"I want to know exactly where every bird was in the sky when that conversation took place. Then compare it with the data you're compiling from Airbnb."

After several hours, an Agency analyst was knocking at the Major's office door.

"Sir, there were no bookings in the name of Connor, and all the Mr C"s were a bust. There were seventy-eight birds in the air above accommodation locations at the time specified in Utah, Arizona, Colorado and Wyoming."

"Forget Colorado. They're won't be in Colorado any more. I want you to fly several birds over each location at thirty minute intervals, low and loud. We might pick them up through the audio or someone could mention them."

As plans were being made, one of the Techs picked up his head.

"Sir, the conversation's getting quite interesting."

"*Does your dad seem like your dad?*"

They continued to listen.

"If they're getting paranoid, this could work to our benefit," said Dr Philipson.

"Let me know how it works out," said the Major.

The next morning, the Major was called in again.

"*We're less than a thousand miles from the base. I'd rather be much further away. We've been planning the move, but we don't have a lot of people around here to help us. I can move around relatively safely alone. I need to do my bit.*"

"Get the maps up," said the Major.

"They're up, sir. A thousand mile radius has been drawn on the map. We're cross referencing the other data."

"And Neil Banks is on the road. When we get a location, I want roadblocks up."

Hours later, they were still trying to pin down the location.

"Sir, something's happening."

The Tech put the recording on to speaker so everyone could hear it.

"This is just a few minutes ago."

"*Oh, it's you, Marcus. You made me jump,*" said Hannah's voice.

"*Creeping around, Mr Headley?*" said Zoe with a giggle.

"*You girls shouldn't be so far from the house. Let's get back, shall we?*"

"*It's okay, Marcus, you don't need the hands-on approach. We'll come quietly.*"

"*I don't feel...What's happ...*"

"*Marcus...what are you doing? You can't...*"

"What is going on there?" said the Major.

No one replied.

The sound of running and no speaking for some time had the listeners perplexed.

"I knew there was something wrong with him. I just felt it."

"Zoe! Zoe and Hannah!"

"Has the Fader done something?" asked Major Tom.

As they listened over the next few hours, they were astounded by Marcus's revelation.

"Your new boyfriend isn't the only one with talents. I can see the yellow mist in Faders and Trackers alike, even the Agency people. I can see the energy around everyone to some degree."

"Make sure he's not killed. I want him alive," said Dr Philipson.

The Agency people in the room were looking around at themselves and each other.

"Focus!" said the Major, but he was as shocked as everyone else.

Dr Philipson was looking speculatively at the people in the room, realising for the first time that he had a whole planet of subjects to experiment on. His gaze rested on the Major, who was looking speculatively back. Philipson looked away. The Major could only have been wondering who he might have to kill to keep a lid on this. That wasn't a list the Doc wanted to be on.

They continued to listen as Marcus admitted to killing Nathan. Then they all jumped when they heard him scream and the sound of Jenna running away.

"Oh dear, you are in quite a mess, aren't you, and I don't recommend going any further into that cave."

"Caves!" shouted the Major as the Techs went to the maps again.

They heard a struggle, and then the sound was almost totally muted. They heard muffled screams and the sound was lost.

"Sir, I think we have it. Colossal Caves in Arizona. An Airbnb booking by a Mr C. Caldwell. We were looking for recent bookings, but this one has been active for weeks. It must be where the father's been staying. Our choppers have made several runs over the area."

"Okay, I want a team there – yesterday! Go in quietly, we don't want to spook them." Major Tom grinned. "Until we're ready to spook them."

THE AGENTS CREPT around the house, waiting for orders. The Commanding Officer made signals with his hands and the men moved into position.

"We're waiting for the Go, sir. Wait, someone's opening the door."

Two of the men ducked behind the car on the driveway as the door opened.

DAD OPENED the back door of the dark red eight seater SUV for me as I hobbled out with Hannah and Zoe. A shuffling sound came from the other side of the car. Dad turned quickly as a figure rose up.

"Connor! You made me jump."

"This tyre needs air," said Connor, wiping dust from his jeans. "It should be okay until we get to the first stop."

Dad sat in the back seat next to me.

"Where are we heading to?" asked Orla.

"We've used most of the safe houses already," said Connor, "but there's a few more dotted around. We've got an Airbnb house near Colossal Caves. That's the closest, only a few hundred miles away."

"No more caves," I shouted from the back.

"Wasn't this an Airbnb place?" asked Dad.

"No, it was just empty," said Connor.

"I'm pretty sure you said it was booked and paid for," said Dad.

"Yeah, that sounds like something I might have said. Colossal Caves are in the wrong direction anyway. I think we should just keep heading west."

"West it is," said Dad.

The car pulled away from the house and I didn't look back again.

MARIA HAD BEEN CLEANING rental homes for twenty-five years. This one was the last on her schedule for the day, and she was just coming to the conclusion that it might be time to retire. Standing on the porch of the house with her hands in the air, she stared from the black-clad men before her to the red dots dancing on her coat. She dropped her mop and bucket as the men moved silently towards her.

"I got Green Card," she said as they rushed past her and into the empty house.

I RESTED my leg across the back seat, elevated on Dad next to me, as Vanessa, my grandmother, told us her story. When she talked about my mum, her face became haunted. We shared the same heartache. The aching loss for someone we'd never really known.

Throughout the journey, when I wasn't dozing, I was thinking of Marcus. Funny Marcus with the dimples. Happy Marcus, swinging me around, laughing. Killer Marcus. Monster Marcus. I couldn't understand my own feelings. My heart ached. I hated him. I feared him. I loved him. I mourned him. I had to come to terms with the fact that I'd killed him.

Felix meowed inside his cage. I dangled a finger to stroke him. He scratched me. I dozed again.

After two and a half hours, we arrived at a ranch on the outskirts of Phoenix. The owner of the ranch, who doubled as the local livestock vet, looked at our injuries. He redressed my ankle and Zoe's neck.

After a week, we were on the road again. I couldn't believe that so many people were helping us. They loaned vehicles to transport us and bedrooms for us to sleep in. We zigzagged our way across to California, circumvented Los Angeles, and finally arrived at a vineyard south of a town called Santa Maria.

We drove through the gated entrance and past row upon row of vines up to the house at the centre of the vineyard. Connor and Orla were helping me out of the car when the door to the house opened and I heard a familiar voice.

"Have you had breakfast? You know it's the most important meal of the day."

Orla screamed, "Jason!" and pretty much dropped me, leaving Connor to stop me from falling over. Jason ran out to catch Orla and kiss her. Something about it reminded me of Marcus and my eyes stung, but I was so happy for Orla.

"Aww!" said Zoe and Hannah at the same time.

Dad came around the car and put his arm under my other shoulder. He and Connor half lifted me as I attempted to hop up the steps. They helped me through the door and on to the nearest sofa.

LATER THAT EVENING, after dinner, we gathered in a seating area before a large fireplace.

"I can't stop thinking about that girl on the cosmetics counter." I shuddered.

"You couldn't have known, dear," said Vanessa.

"I won't let this continue," I said.

"How do we stop it?" asked Hannah. "They are everywhere. They hear everything. We can't even contact our own families. We don't know if they're safe. The moment we tell other Trackers, we risk another slaughter."

Hannah was echoing my own thoughts.

"They won't touch your families," said Vanessa. "They're more useful alive. The Agency will be leaving them as bait, hoping you'll try to contact them."

There were a few people milling around the huge house who had helped us to get settled. As they moved closer to the seating area, I looked at them. There were men and women and a few kids. They weren't monsters, they were just regular people. I felt ashamed.

I thought again about the woman from the cosmetics store. I thought about Cheyenne Mountain. How many Faders were up there, unconscious? What was the Agency doing to them? I shivered at the thought.

"Faders are already being slaughtered," I said. "This has to change. I'm going to change it, even if I have to do it alone."

"You won't have to do it alone," said Jason.

"Are you sure you want to do this?" asked Dad.

"Absolutely," I said.

"Yes," said Zoe.

Orla and Hannah were nodding their heads in agreement.

Vanessa stood, walked to the side of the fireplace, and looked at Connor and Dad. They both nodded.

As the group of Faders joined us, she looked at each of us.

"Then welcome to The Network."

READ the next book in the series. mybook.to/thefaders2

Or turn the page to read chapter one of THE NETWORK.

THE NETWORK - CHAPTER 1

We stood in a row, Orla, Zoe, Hannah and I, all facing the wall. Behind us, Dad and Jason sat at a long, ancient-looking wooden table, while Connor leaned against a bookcase in the corner of the room.

"So, this is it?" asked Zoe.

"Yes," said Dad.

We continued to stare at the wall.

"It's a map with lines drawn all over it," said Orla.

"Correct," said Dad.

"Okay, Dad, you've had your fun. Show us the Network," I said.

"You're looking at it. Look closer!"

"Do these lines represent secret tunnels?"

"No, they're not secret tunnels."

Dad wasn't giving much away. It was like he wanted me to get it without his help.

"But…"

"It doesn't matter how many times you ask, this is it," said Connor.

"It's a grand map," said Orla, nodding her head as though she understood it.

"It looks sort of familiar. I've seen a map like this somewhere before." I continued to look at it, squinting and turning my head this way and that.

"Here it comes," said Dad.

"Are they... are they ley lines?" I asked.

"There it is!" Connor grinned.

"I told you she'd get it."

"So, the Network is a network of ley lines," I said.

"You got it," said Connor.

"And not a network of heavily armed, technologically advanced cyborg faders?" asked Orla.

"Nope," said Jason.

"Not a network of secret underground lairs?" I asked.

"Sorry, Beautiful, but we're not Ninja Turtles."

I flicked an annoyed look at Connor. He kept calling me that.

I turned to my dad. "But, in Glastonbury, you said ley lines were nonsense. I thought you were going to thump that strange-smelling hippy who was 'Feeling the ley line energy, Man.' You called him a doped-up imbecile."

"I was wrong about the ley lines, but in my defense, he was a doped-up imbecile. The last time I saw him, he was standing in a water fountain, trying to flush himself into the Ministry of Magic."

I turned away from the map on the wall, dropped into a chair at the table and rested my head on my arms on its surface.

"We're all going to die, aren't we? My new granny is a crackpot, and we're going to die."

Dad rolled his eyes. "I need coffee," he said. Scratching his beard, he stood.

"Hey, do you want to fade over there?" asked Connor.

"I thought you'd never ask," said Dad, shaking himself out like he was about to exercise.

Connor put his hand on Dad's back, and the two of them disappeared.

"Oh my God, that's so funny," said Orla. "Your dad gets such a kick out of fading. That's the third time this morning Connor's faded him from one room to another."

"Yay! Comfort break," said Hannah, grabbing Zoe by the hand and walking quickly through the double doors out onto the deck.

Orla dropped into the stout wooden chair next to mine. "How are you?" she asked.

"Oh, I'm grand, so I am," I replied in a rubbish attempt at an Irish accent.

"That was a rubbish attempt at an Irish accent," she said.

I smiled.

"Let's have a wander-slash-hobble onto the deck. I can't look at that liney map anymore," said Orla.

I looked over to where Connor and Dad had faded, blinking in to see a yellow mist trailing off through the wall. I was relieved Connor had left the room. Ever since the night Marcus had died, he had been following me around, either trying to talk to me or just watching me. It was getting on my nerves.

We got up and went out. I glanced over at Zoe and Hannah, who were holding hands down at the corner of the deck, looking out at the rows of grape vines which seemed to stretch for miles. Orla looked at them too and tutted.

"What's wrong?" I asked.

"Zoe's emitting again," Orla said, shaking her head.

"I don't think it ever stops now," I said.

I blinked in and saw Zoe was lit up like a Christmas tree. I looked down at myself, but there was no yellow mist.

"Is it my imagination or has the radius of that yellow mist actually grown?" asked Orla.

"And it looks brighter than usual," I said.

My inhibitor had been switched on and off so many times by Doctor Philipson during his tests, it was odd that Zoe had started emitting within a few days of having had the capsule cut out of her. It made me realize I could have begun emitting at any time. They'd have killed me at the academy the second that happened. I shuddered.

I thought back to a couple of weeks before when Marcus had attacked Zoe and Hannah. He'd got as far as removing Zoe's capsule when he'd been disturbed by Connor. Otherwise, he'd have killed them—just as he had killed his best friend, Nate—to syphon their energy.

I touched the back of my neck where my injury was healing. I was lucky not to be horribly scarred. The memory came to me of hacking at myself with the edges of a broken mirror, gouging out my own inhibitor to free my ability and use it to end Marcus's life as he tried to murder Connor. Immediately, the thought of Marcus hanging from the roof of the cave invaded my mind. I reached out for a glib comment to push it away.

"Maybe we could put baubles on her," I said.

"I see it in your eyes, you know," Orla said. "Right before you make some silly joke."

"I guess there's no hiding it from you."

"There's no hiding it from anyone. We can all see you're hurting, but *you're* trying to hide from *it*. Also, the screamy nightmares are a bit of a giveaway, but well done for not exploding things anymore."

"Sorry. I asked if I could sleep in the basement, but Nanna said no."

"If she hears you calling her Nanna, she'll probably shoot you. And why would you want to sleep down in the gym? You'd be woken at some ungodly hour every morning by a bunch of grunting blokes."

A little girl came squealing around the corner of the building with an older girl of roughly twelve years. They were chasing a cat as it jumped at a small plastic ball.

"Those kids have stolen my cat," I said.

On hearing my voice, Felix stopped and looked up at me. A light breeze caused the ball to move again, it became the cat's primary goal once more, and the little girl resumed her squeals.

I sighed and looked back to Orla. "I miss him. I keep having dreams where he's lifting me up and kissing me, and I'm so happy. Is that weird?" I asked.

"Who, Felix?"

I looked at her with an eyebrow raised and shook my head.

"Marcus was your boyfriend, and you loved him. How can that be weird?" Orla asked.

I counted the points off on my fingers. "He was an unhinged killer. He killed Nate. He would have killed all of you, and eventually me, I suppose. Every memory of him I have is tainted. When he hugged me and I felt giddy, it was because he'd been syphoning my energy. I thought that was how love felt." I shuddered. "Do you remember, he said he wanted to be a physiotherapist like his dad? I see now he just wanted an excuse to syphon people."

"Don't torture yourself with these thoughts," said Orla. "Anyway, that's not the worst part. Your dad told me that Marcus's father was a bloody milkman."

My jaw dropped. "Aren't you angry? You and Zoe knew him for five years. He fooled you both."

"Well, I always thought he was a bit tactile. I guess that makes sense now. But I don't think that's really what's bothering you."

"Of course that bothers me. But you're right. I killed him, Orla. I mean, he'd have died in minutes anyway with his head stuck in that rock. But that didn't kill him. I did, and I can't stop thinking about it. So yes, I make jokes. I'm trying to keep out those thoughts."

I turned around, leaning my back on the rail. Orla did the same.

"How's that working for you?" she asked.

"Not so well." I barked a bitter laugh.

"The only way around it is through it."

"Oh God, you sound like Helen." I rolled my eyes, thinking of the counselor from Hilltop tracker Academy back in England.

"Maybe you could call her for a consult. What could possibly go wrong?"

"Five hundred agents turning up at the door?"

I turned at the sound of footsteps approaching us along the deck.

"We're heading back in," said Hannah.

"Oh yes. The liney map. I can't wait," said Orla as we followed.

It had helped to talk to Orla. I decided I'd try to focus more on our current problems during meetings and deal with the past another time.

We assembled before the map again.

"So, how do these things figure into this mystery plan?" I said, pointing at the lines.

Dad stood beside me and smiled, indicating he could see my head was back in the game.

"You know the story. There are ley lines around the world which are supposedly pathways of energy between ancient sacred sites. It's mostly pseudo-science and has never been proven. But it appears that when you get a fader near a ley line, it does have an effect."

"What kind of effect?" asked Zoe.

"For most faders, not very much. You know that feeling when the hairs on the back of your neck stand up?"

"Yes," said Zoe.

"I think so," I said, feeling my eyebrow rocket to my hairline.

"Well, apparently most faders feel that quite strongly near a ley line, and they tend to emit more than usual."

"Are we, by any chance, on top of a ley line right now?" asked Zoe.

"I'm afraid not, Zoe," said Dad. "That's all you."

Zoe slumped. She'd started looking tired lately.

"Okay, so how are these ley lines going to help us?" asked Hannah.

"Good question," I added. "I get that strange feeling whenever a fader or tracker is looking at me while they're blinked-in. I always have."

"Really? I used to wonder how you knew you were being watched," said Dad. "I just assumed you were unusually observant. Although you never seemed to observe when your bedroom needed tidying."

"Dad! Really?"

"Sorry Litt... Jenna."

I took two steps and hugged him. I couldn't be mad at him—I'd spent months thinking he was dead, and I would never take him for granted again. I kissed his cheek. Actually, I kissed just under his eye because I struggled to find some face that wasn't covered in his new scratchy beard. Then I stood next to him, and he turned his attention to Hannah.

"As you know, some faders have other abilities. Those are usually amplified on a ley line."

Vanessa, my grandmother, entered the room. "We've already tried it with Connor. His ability to fade other people increased so he didn't need to be touching them. They only needed to be standing near him. We know you have an ability, Jenna. We need to see how it is affected near the ley lines."

"So what's next?" I asked.

"For you? Healing. Then we're planning a field trip," said Dad.

"There's a ley line which crosses a hundred or so miles from here. We're going to pay it a visit when you've recovered," added Vanessa.

"Don't you want to get started straight away? I can get around on crutches if I need to."

"It's okay, we hope to use the time to resolve another issue. In the meantime, we need to work on making you all less recognizable."

The meeting broke up, and I went to rest my leg on the sofa.

"Hey," said Connor, walking in.

"Hey," I replied with my face intently in a book. I hoped he'd get the message and keep walking. He stood around for about a minute, then tried again.

"How's your ankle?"

He wasn't going to leave me alone. I dropped the book down with a sigh and faced him.

"Broken and painful."

"You don't spend enough time keeping it elevated. You need to rest more."

"Thanks for the diagnosis," I said, picking up my book again, trying to signal an end to the conversation.

"The first one's free," he said.

I was opening my mouth to make some snippy reply when I heard a scream. It was Orla. I flew off the sofa, as well as I could, and hobbled through the vast house. As I went, my mind flooded with memories: Orla's scream at the place in Arizona; Marcus pulling me away into the night. I shook the thoughts away.

Connor had instantly faded and raced ahead of me. By the time I arrived up on the next floor and down the east side of the house, he, and pretty much everyone else, was already there. A woman I'd seen around but didn't know was standing outside the bathroom with a pair of scissors in her hand.

"Come on, you're being silly," she called through the door in a Spanish accent.

"Keep that crazy slasher woman away from me," shouted Orla from inside the room.

The woman raised her arms in exasperation and turned away from the door. She looked at Hannah and pointed at her with the scissors.

"You, come with me, now," she said.

She marched off down the stairs, and Hannah looked at me, shrugged her shoulders and trudged after the woman.

I had no idea what was happening. I looked at Connor, who had been leaning against the wall when I arrived. He shook his head and wandered off.

I knocked on the door.

"Orla? She's gone. Can I come in?"

I heard the click of the lock and entered the bathroom. Orla leaned against the sink and folded her arms.

"What on earth is going on?" I asked.

"Look, I know all this is very 'life and death' and everything." I had to hide a smile. Orla had actually drawn air quotes around the words life and death. "But that woman is not touching my hair with those scissors."

"Oh! I see. Well, don't worry. She's got Hannah for now."

"She can dye it, and she can straighten it, if she must," Orla continued. "But if she tries to come near me with a pair of scissors again, I'll smash her face in."

"Okay. Point taken. What color do you fancy—blond?"

"No bleach. I'll go brown, but no other color."

After a few seconds, she put her head in her hands and sighed.

"I suppose I'd better go find Sofia and apologize to her."

"Sofia?"

"The woman with the scissors. I shouldn't have been so melodramatic, I suppose. I think I could love it here, you know? I miss my family like crazy, but I know as long as I don't try to contact them, they're safe."

We'd only been here a day, but having Jason back had altered Orla. She had an optimistic outlook that I envied.

I sat down on the side of the tub.

"I hate it," I said.

She looked at me with her mouth hanging open.

"Okay, I don't hate it. It's just... Have you seen the way some of these people look at us? They know we were with the agency and they hate us. Some of them have lost family because of us. I don't blame them. I hate myself for it."

"Well, yes. Things might be a little difficult for a while, but they'll get to know us, and they'll see we're not bad people. Vanessa was a tracker..."

"A hell of a long time ago. And since then, she's given them all this." I waved my arm out to indicate the house, the vineyard, the safety—everything.

"Jason was a tracker, and they like him. They seem to get on well with your dad. Give it time, and don't forget, we're going to help them, aren't we?"

"I want to, more than anything."

"We've been on the inside of the base. We've got information that can help them. We know the faces of Agents and trackers. That kind of thing must be of help."

I nodded, and we went to sacrifice ourselves to Sofia Scissor-Hands.

AN HOUR LATER, I was sitting with my head in a plastic wrap. Sofia had calmed Orla enough that she was able to take a fraction of an inch off the ends of her hair. My hair loss was a little more dramatic: a good amount of it was on the floor. When Sofia had finished, gone was my long, fine dark-blond hair. Instead, I had a sharp, edgy graduated bob which grazed the back of my neck and came down into sharp points just past my jawline. Also, my hair was now black. I was confident that Dad was going to hit the roof.

I left Orla and Sofia arguing over colors and went to find my dad to horrify him with my hair. I found him on the deck with Vanessa. Dad looked up as I walked out and did a double-take.

"Well, that'll take some getting used to," he said. "Very pretty, though. You look like your mum." I tried to shake the feeling that I had somehow been cheated out of a girly scream of horror from Dad. "Take a seat, we were just talking about her."

Vanessa had begged Dad for every memory of Mum that he could think of.

"I'm sorry I can't show you any other pictures of her. Everything went up in the explosion. I've just got that one of her in my wallet."

"I took the pictures from your office, but I had to leave them in my room," I said. "It would have been noticed if I'd taken them with me on the night we escaped. Sorry."

"Would you mind waiting here a moment?" Vanessa asked, and walked into the house.

I sat next to Dad and hugged him. "You smell like the jumper," I said.

"The one from my office? Marcus said you kept it in a ziplock bag until the night you escaped."

I flinched at Marcus's name.

"Sorry, Little Duck," he said, kissing the top of my head. I could tell he wanted to talk about Marcus, but didn't know how to approach it. I was relieved.

Vanessa returned with a large black plastic box. Dad swept magazines from the table-top, and she placed the box down and took off the lid. Inside were thousands of pictures of Mum as a baby, a little girl, a teenager. There were wedding photographs of Mum and Dad, and more. Photos of our family, even pictures of my friends and me.

"Where did you get these?" I asked.

"A few of the baby photos were in my purse the day I met the faders," she said. "Later ones came from various criminal activities. Fading into the local pharmacy at night for photographs developed for her adoptive family, until she was taken to the UK. I had a local contact who would do the same at your local pharmacy before everything went digital. Later, hacking Jenna's social media accounts."

I looked at her in shock.

"What is it you kids say these days, dear? Sorry, not sorry."

I barked a laugh. Diving into the box of photos, I couldn't believe I had all these pictures of Mum, Dad, Gill and me, and other friends; I had accepted that I would never be able to access my social media accounts again. Dad was already lost in a wedding picture.

I looked up from the photos to see a girl standing at the balcony on the deck, looking out towards the vines. I hadn't heard her come up. She had straight white-blond hair all the way down to her waist. Most people here were strangers to me; it made me a little nervous.

I looked down to see she was wearing boots. She was wearing Orla's Ugg boots.

"Orla?" I said, shocked. She turned around with a massive smile across her face. "Holy smoke! I didn't recognize you."

"I know, right?" she squealed. "I couldn't believe the length when she straightened out the curls. It's ridiculous! What do you think, Mr B?" She swished her hair about.

"Well, it was very nice before, but it's lovely. It does the job—you look like a different person."

"Do you think Jason will like it?" Orla asked me.

As though he'd been summoned up, Jason appeared around the corner of the deck, walking towards us.

"Have you seen...?" He glanced at Orla, and then looked back at her again. "Mother of..." he was silent for two seconds, then recovered "...dragons." He took two steps to her, lifted her up and kissed her. "My Khaleesi," he boomed.

Orla squealed again as he marched away with her in his arms.

"Oookay then," I said.

Dad and Vanessa returned to the photos.

"I'm going to get some water. Want anything?" I asked.

"No thank you, dear," said Vanessa, and Dad just shook his head while he gazed at the pictures.

In the kitchen, I found Zoe and Hannah. Zoe's hair hadn't been touched, but Hannah's hair was candy-floss pink.

"You look like Selena Gomez in her pink hair phase," I said.

"That's what I said," said Zoe.

"I didn't say that, because I'm too self-deprecating, but I thought it," said Hannah.

'Erm... what's going on with your makeover?"

Zoe shrugged. "She says I have to wait."

"Apparently, Sofia has other plans for Zoe," said Hannah.

"I don't mind waiting. I don't have the energy for it anyway. I'm going to lie down."

Zoe's eyes looked heavy. As she walked towards the sofa, Hannah and I exchanged looks of concern.

I hobbled my way up the staircase to our room, stopping to look at my new hairstyle in a mirror on the landing. Loving it, I smiled until I noticed the reflection of a man watching me from a doorway across the wide staircase. He sneered, stepped back into his bedroom and closed the door.

CLICK   to   download   The   Network   now! mybook.to/thefaders2

ACKNOWLEDGMENTS

Thank you to the people who gave valuable insights and offered support to help me do a better job of relaunching this book the second time around. Jon Evans, Remy Flagg, Chris Patterson, Nicole Grotepas, Annabel Chase, Amanda Lee, Erika Everest, Jamie Davis, Sarah Noffke, Erika James, Lasairiona McMaster, Natale Roberts, Merri Maywether, John Kang, Sine Màiri Ni Ailpin, Kate Ruth Johnson, Jamie Davis, Trish Heinrich, Patricia Carr, and all the EFB team.

THANK YOU FOR READING FADE

Join my VIP reader list and grab THE FUGITIVE LEGACY.
The free prequel of Legacy of the Shadow's Blood.

https://dl.bookfunnel.com/olndiiuzje

Hi, I hope you enjoyed this book. As an indie author, reviews mean the absolute world to me. It would make this author very happy if you would head over to wherever you like to leave reviews, and let me and other readers know what you thought.

facebook.com/egbatemanwrites

twitter.com/egbateman

instagram.com/egbatemanwrites

ALSO BY E. G. BATEMAN

The Faders Series

Fade

The Network

Portal

Legacy of the Shadow's Blood

(With Michael Anderle)

The Flawed Legacy

The Bound Legacy

The Rising Legacy

Dawn of the Shadow

Order of the Shadow

Heart of the Shadow (August '21)